Thresher

Winter Grip

To Helen with best wishes –

Joel Allng (Author).

1/11/2016

THE BATTLE INTENSIFIES AS SNOW, SMALLPOX
AND SHEEPSTEALING TAKE THEIR TOLL...

Thresher

WINTER GRIP

NOEL ALLSUP

Matador
9 Priory Business Park,
Wistow Road, Kibworth Beauchamp,
Leicestershire. LE8 0RX
Tel: 0116 279 2299
Email: books@troubador.co.uk
Web: www.troubador.co.uk/matador
Twitter: @matadorbooks

ISBN 978 1785899 423

British Library Cataloguing in Publication Data.
A catalogue record for this book is available from the British Library.

Printed and bound in the UK by TJ International, Padstow, Cornwall
Typeset in 11pt Aldine401 BT by Troubador Publishing Ltd, Leicester, UK

Matador is an imprint of Troubador Publishing Ltd

To Benjamin Jesty (1736 – 1816)
The pioneer of human smallpox vaccination,
for his discernment, inspiration and courage
in the face of ignorance, superstition and prejudice.

Acknowledgements

I wish to acknowledge with grateful thanks the help of Liz Munslow for her essential and first-class help in copy editing, Richard Nicholls of Enrich Design Limited for graphics and cover illustrations, Mr. and Mrs. Jesty, Waddock Cross, Dorchester for historical information regarding Benjamin Jesty, the pioneer of smallpox vaccination and the kind encouragement of shepherd and author Larry Skeats, Stourton Caundle, Dorset.

Prequel

Crippled at the Battle of Waterloo, Lieutenant Richard Gomer returns to his family's West Dorset estate; during Richard's absence, his father Ronald dies after losing a fortune at cards and half the estate comprising Home Farm is seized by his creditor Ezra Jones, neighbouring owner of Destro Farm, to repay the debt. Money that Ronald Gomer withdrew to repay his gambling losses is secretly embezzled by the Gomers' agent Bowen Dranley in league with Ezra's son Hugo Jones, doubly impoverishing the Gomer family. Dranley was later found drowned in the sea off Golden Cap. Richard's engagement to Lady Katherine Goodboys, daughter of Sir Absalom and Lady Eleanor of Copley Estate and sister to Edmond Lesden, the Goodboys' adopted son, has been broken off based on a false rumour that Richard had died in battle; Katherine is now married to Hugo Jones. Left with Wychcombe Farm's dilapidated buildings, a rump of land of mixed fertility and acres of unforgiving gley swamp, Richard, brother Giles and their mother, the Honourable Susannah Gomer are also faced with a mysterious and implacable enemy committed to destroying their livelihood and lives.

Katherine falls in love with Giles Gomer and her affair with him coincides with her pregnancy and marriage to Hugo, who hires four Irish labourers, Seamus, Patrick, Shaun and Dermot, to harm Giles. Farmhand Joshua

Wicks, formerly working for the Gomers on Home Farm until taken over by the Joneses, and fellow-poacher Walling, who kills a gamekeeper, become fugitives. Walling dies and Joshua hides on Wychcombe Farm. This first volume of the Thresher trilogy *Thresher – Autumn Fall*★ concludes with the discovery of the identity of the Gomers' enemy as William Lesden, alias Reverend Lessop-Dene and brother to Edmond Lesden aka Goodboys. William Lesden is killed and his body submerged in the gley swamp on Wychcombe Farm. With the stolen money unrecovered, the Gomers now face winter impoverished and struggling to survive in spite of hostile and unresolved relationships.

★   Thresher – Autumn Fall (2012) © Noel Allsup
    www.thethreshertrilogy.co.uk
    ISBN 978-0-9557706-1-6

The battle intensifies as
snow, smallpox and sheep-stealing take their toll …

CHAPTER ONE

The Gley

Four pregnant ewes were missing. Thomas the cowman trod along the frozen ridges of Wychcombe Farm's cornfield, blew on his chilled chapped hands, crossed his arms and thumped the sides of his chest to generate heat. His steel-heeled boots crushed the lumpy frozen soil and flattened the brittle corn stubble, as his sharp eyes searched for any sign of the strays in other fields. He moved downhill into the foxmould pasture, unfastened and retightened the string tied through the shawl of sacking covering his thin coat closer to protect himself from the piercing wind, then wiped his dripping nose on a ragged sleeve. The sky darkened and snowflakes gained force in the strengthening wind; a blizzard was on its way.

December 12th 1815, West Dorset

How Thomas longed to be at home resting in front of a blazing wood fire in his tied cottage or even checking the cows in the warm byre. Give me cattle every time, he thought. The sheep hardly glanced his way, as if familiarity

1

bred contempt, their breath exhaled in milky clouds as they clawed with sharp hooves at the petrified vegetation. Thomas sighed; Asa, Wychcombe's shepherd, believed in half-starving the flock to break their dependence on stored hay and corn, encouraging them to forage on frosted grass. Luckily the September lambs were housed for the December market, he mused.

Asa was in the foxmoulds counting the sheep for the second time when Thomas joined him. Asa scratched his head.

"Foive of 'em missin' now, Thomas. Where can they be?"

"Ye mean, where could they go, Asa?"

They viewed the gates; all were closed and secured. They surveyed the hedges for any breaks; none were evident. They continued their search, walking westwards through a gate into the northern border of the gley swamp meadow and walked southwards. A barn loomed into sight. They trod through fast-settling snow, their boots cumbersome with snow-packed soles heavier at each step, bending their heads in the howling blizzard. They kicked the barn walls to clear their boot soles. Asa pulled open the rickety wooden door; the pair entered into darkness.

"Are ye there, Joshua Wicks?" he shouted, but no answer came.

He repeated his call; still no answer.

"Have ye got tinder, Thomas?" Asa asked.

"Aye," Thomas answered.

He removed the lantern from under his sackcloth cloak, opened the glass cover, lit the lantern's wick and replaced the glass, bathing the barn in yellow light. It was empty.

"No sign of ewes 'ere, dead or alive, Thomas; let's check 'round the gley."

Thomas nodded, covered the lamp and followed Asa into the howling blizzard.

They gazed south-westward towards the swamp.

"Oi hopes they aren't too far down yonder, Thomas. Oi feel certin we've lost ewes in that bog before."

The pair trod south down the gley meadow, avoiding crusty frozen cowpat covers, crushing rime-sprinkled grass and dodging islands of sharp reeds until they reached the edge of the swamp. The mire was covered with ice through which the bog's blue-grey mucous was visible. No sheep carcasses were seen but Asa's eyes located a point in the swamp itself.

"Uncover your lamp, Thomas!" shouted Asa above the storm, pointing to an area about ten feet from the bank. Though snow swirled over the ice, Thomas's lamplight exposed a lighter area resembling a recumbent window pane through which a bloodless face with sightless eyes peered. It was the bloated face of William Lesden alias the Reverend William Lessop-Dene, vicar of St. Bartholomew's. The labourers stood transfixed, then:

"The vicar!" Asa gasped, "so that's where he finished up!" The gley bog had given up its gory secret.

"Get back to yon farmhouse, Thomas, and tell the maisters, then get Jamie t' hitch up one o' the drays to a cart, fetch some ropes an' a tarpaulin sheet, get more help and hurry back 'ere sharpish!"

At Destro Farm, Hugo Jones heard from Abel his chargehand that the vicar's body had been dragged from the gley swamp at Wychcombe Farm. Hugo reasoned that there could have been foul play. Could the vicar have been alive on Gomer land before he was killed rather than have been carried there? Surely, he was not there by accident, because he knew his parish like the back of his hand. How did he finish up in the gleys unless he had been overpowered and killed and his body thrown into the bog?

Did the vicar's body show any telltale marks of violence? This presented an opportunity to incriminate the Gomers if the vicar had been murdered. Hadn't Richard Gomer been hurt in some kind of a fight, according to gossip? Hugo resolved to find out how the vicar had died.

Lesden's body was carried to St. Bartholomew's vicarage where a crowd of curious villagers gathered in response to the rapid spread of the news. One sympathetic, if misguided person tolled the church bells as the vicar's remains were carried into the kitchen and laid on the bare table, releasing the repulsive gley stench as the body thawed.

The verger of St. Bartholomew's threw half a bucket of hot water over the corpse. The local butcher cut open the dripping clothes and stripped the cadaver bare; he threw the clothes on the floor, exposing the vicar's naked body. The verger, somehow overcoming his desire to vomit, threw more hot water on the body. Doctor Needman, with rolled-up shirt sleeves and wearing an oilskin apron retrieved the articles of clothing, and examined each one; ragged, circular holes were exposed in the coat, shirt and vest. Dr. Needman pressed his finger into the flesh over the chest and penetrated a ragged hole. At his signal, the butcher turned the body over. High up on the back was a neater hole.

"What d'ye make of it, doctor?" queried Ezra Jones.

The doctor stopped his post-mortem examination and turned to the onlookers.

"Apart from Mr. Jones, the verger, the butcher, the constable and myself, the rest of you leave!" he ordered, and the crowd shuffled out, muttering.

That night at Destro Farm, Ezra and his son supped on cold pheasant and mulled wine.

"So he were shot, father" Hugo observed. "Was a ball found in his clothes?"

"No, Hugo, just two holes and some blood in his vestments. I reckon that a pistol ball hit him in the back, went clean through his body an' out at the other side."

Hugo mused.

"Perhaps a few well-placed rumours could stir up his parishioners. The vicar were found in the gleys at Wychcombe Farm. It could spark a riot among the religious peasants to wreck the farm and perchance harm the Gomer brothers."

Then: "Father, Giles Gomer knows that we've got the debt moneys as well as Home Farm."

Ezra Jones gave a start.

"How did he find out?"

"Harvey told that scoundrel Wicks, who escaped fro' the barn at Home an' fled to the Gomers' farm."

"An' how did Harvey know?"

"Walling told 'im."

"How d'ye know all this?"

"Wi' a bit o' persuasion, I wrung it out o' Harvey, one of the poachers with Walling and Wicks. Walling saw me takin' money from Bowen Dranley at Wychcombe estate office the night Dranley wus drowned."

"Walling an' Harvey are dead, so that leaves Wicks, the Gomers, you an' me?"

"Aye, father, but the Gomers can't prove anything and Wicks is finished, a fugitive from justice and accessory to a gamekeeper's murder. Nobody will ever trust his testimony an' when he's caught, he'll go to the gallows."

"That could still be bad fer us! What d'ye intend t' do, then?"

A moment of silence.

"I doubt that Wicks'll come back fer his missus an' litter while they're still at Home Farm but I've a plan to force his hand and catch him. So I'm kickin' his family out – they'll have t' go to Wychcombe workhus. And if we forced the Gomers out, father?"

Ezra paced the living room.

"You tell me, since you've all the bright ideas."

"If we could take Wychcombe over, lock, stock and barrel, they would ha' no chance t' reclaim the debt money, get their farms back and pay off the debt. A few rumours about the vicar's death would help."

"We musn't be seen to have anything to do with starting up any rumours. People know that there's bad blood between us an' the Gomers. So, how d'ye think we can light such a forest fire?"

Chapter Two

Riot!

The following evening Richard and Giles were seated in the kitchen of Wychcombe Farm when they heard loud cries mingled with the crackle of tramping feet over frozen stubble. Both brothers ran to the door; lantern lights approached the farmhouse.

"Hang 'em! String the lot up, the murtherers!

They must 'ave killed ower vicar! 'ang 'em an' we'll 'ave done God's work an' avenged ower holy shepherd!" the mob cried.

"Quick, Richard! I'll rouse Jamie to saddle the horses."

"No, Giles, let's wait 'til they reach the yard, then I'll go out to talk to them. We have nothing to fear, for we didn't kill Les … the vicar."

"Tell that to this bloodthirsty mob! They'll not listen …"

Giles turned to Richard,

"What happened out there? What d'ye know about the vicar's death?"

To Giles, Richard's silence was expressive.

"Then you do know something of what happened to him. How did it happen?"

"I cannot say now, but trust me, Giles."

"Wake up, brother! We must do something now or risk a riot and … bloodshed at the hands of this mob."

Richard shook his head.

"I'm going out to speak to these people. It's possible some of our workers are among them."

"No, Richard! They'll give no quarter; they want blood. I'm getting Jamie to saddle up Hal and Sally."

Giles exited the kitchen and reappeared minutes later dressed in an overcoat and boots, then ran to the stables, shouting for Jamie the ostler. Moments later, with the help of Berkeley, the Gomer family's retainer, Richard donned a greatcoat and stepped out into the chill air, treading snow, narrowly avoided by Jamie on horseback.

"Richard, at least meet the mob on Hal and avoid being trampled to death!" shouted Giles, riding his mare Sally and leading Hal, Richard's saddled gelding.

Richard turned and gazed at the approaching lantern lights, grasped the pommel on Hal's far side with his right hand, pushed his right foot into the stirrup, swung himself up and into the saddle and retrieved the reins from Giles.

About fifty men, brandishing clubs and pitchforks and carrying torches and lanterns, broke into a run towards the farmhouse, from behind which Richard, Giles and Jamie holding a lantern appeared.

"There they be, the murtherers!", someone cried, then a roar of angry voices.

Suddenly, a horseman rode from the darkness and joined the brothers and Jamie facing the crowd.

"Stop!" cried Edmond Lesden, aka Goodboys, Sir Absalom's stepson, "you've no right to trespass on this land".

"Vicar were found on Gomer land," a man shouted, "so they must know somethin'!"

"You've no right to be on this land and unless you leave peacefully and return to your homes, you'll bring the law down on your heads!"

Richard and Giles were amazed at Edmond's boldness and assurance. The crowd halted, uncertain, a leaderless disorderly rabble facing a closed line of four determined horsemen.

"There be on'y four of 'em! They can't stop all of us," came a voice from behind the mob, to a chorus of cries and threats.

"If any man takes one step further, I'll put a ball in his head!" Giles threatened, drawing a flintlock pistol from his belt.

Meanwhile, Hugo Jones, taking advantage of the tumult, rode from Home Farm past Wychcombe Farm along the connecting track to the southern Bridport to Dorchester road. He knew that the gley bog did not extend the full length of its enclosing meadow. He reined in his mare and walked her towards Copley until he found a low enough hedge to jump her over. He checked the field in the dim light, to ascertain they were avoiding the swamp, turned the mare onto scrubland, faced her towards the gley meadow and spurred her at speed towards the hedge.

Mount and rider cleared the thornbushes but the mare's forelegs sank into soft mucoid slime, her sudden halt throwing Hugo with a thump onto hard reedy ground.

He had miscalculated the full span of the gley swamp. Hugo peered through the growing dusk. Fearing that his voice would carry, he tugged vainly on the struggling mare's reins, gave up the tug-o'-war and fled through a break in the western hedge onto the connecting track.

The mob and defenders had reached a stalemate; neither group moved.

"Charge 'em, there's more of us!" shouted someone conveniently rear of the mob, but no-one seemed prepared to be the first to be shot. The raw cold, snow cover and icy wind were beginning to cool their tempers also.

"Go to your homes, men, and do nothing you'll regret!" Edmond shouted, but none of the disorganised band moved. Then a clear and recognised voice of authority rang out:

"Stop this nonsense at once!"

Fifty pairs of eyes turned to look behind them at the commanding figure of Sir Absalom Goodboys in greatcoat, muffler and hat, seated on a massive charger flanked by a dozen mounted men, all carrying muskets attached to their saddles. The would-be rioters were now trapped between the mounted defenders and Sir Absalom and his men.

"Them Gomers killed ower vicar an' we're here t' get justice! An' there's still more'un twice as many of us than them. Oi say rush 'em!"

"Who said that?" Sir Absalom demanded, looking around, then…

"There he is", pointing to a man at the rear of the mob.

The man broke away, running towards the eastern boundary of the farm. Sir Absalom signalled to one of his party, pointing to the fleeing man.

"Bring him to me!" he ordered.

A horseman galloped through the mob, overtook and grabbed the fleeing heckler by his coat collar, then carried and dropped him at Sir Absalom's mount's feet.

"Who are you, and who do you work for?"

The man rose and stood in sullen silence.

"Answer me! I'll have you horsewhipped if you refuse to answer!"

Silence.

"He be one o' the Joneses' werkers," a man shouted.

Giles turned to face Richard, smiling, but Richard's expression did not change.

"Who put you up to this, you damned rabble-rouser?" Sir Absalom demanded of the cowering man. "Out with it, man, or I'll have you arrested for starting this affray!"

Then turning to the rest of the crowd:

"Now, disperse and return peacefully to your homes or you will all answer for trespassing on my neighbours' land! Otherwise …"

On cue, his retinue presented their muskets. Pitchforks and mattocks were no match for such weaponry; the mob backed off, turned and fled, leaving the wretched heckler at the mercy of Sir Absalom and the Wychcombe Farm defenders.

CHAPTER THREE

Hugo meets the Irishmen

Hugo ran up the track connecting the two parallel Dorchester to Bridport roads. It was almost pitch-dark, so he hugged Wychcombe Farm's snow-covered hedge for guidance. He gasped for breath, his heartbeat drum-drumming with the effort. He slipped, cursed and stumbled on the icy track, but managed to keep his balance until he was knocked face forward into the snow by a blow to his back.

He rolled over in spite of the pain, to view the shadowy figure of a man whose hand held something upraised. Hugo raised a trembling arm, but no blow came.

"Well, if it ain't the squire of Home Farm unhorsed an' runnin' the devil knows where," spoke his attacker with an Irish lilt, lowering a club. "It be good luck that oi recornised ye, master Jones."

Hugo staggered to his feet, rubbing his wounded back and facing Seamus with club, Shaun and Patrick, his three hired Irish labourers.

"It would ha' gone worse fer ye if ye'd harmed me more than you have. As it is, I could ha' turned in the lot o' ye as fugitives; the Gomers are lookin' fer ye and they won't rest until they get their hands on the lot o' ye," Hugo blustered.

"Mebbe, zur, but you'll be worse off if we decide t' spill the beans on yer neat little plot t' harm young Gomer," countered Seamus.

"Seamus be right, master Jones," Shaun added.

"Ye made such a poor job on't and who's going to believe a bunch o' thievin' Irish tinkers?" Hugo argued, now more certain of his ground before the three Irishmen

"We can still rob an' kill ye wi'out a thought, master Jones, an' nobody would know who did it. We'd be well away wi' no proof t' connec' us," snarled Patrick.

"But ye won't, fer I can still make it worth yer while t' finish off the job proper after makin' such a pickle of it last time," Hugo affirmed.

Seamus scowled and spat on the ground.

"Alright, le's make an agreement twixt thee an' us, master Hugo; we work fer ye regular like in exchange fer dealin' with master Gomer."

"Aye, I'll think on it, providing ye finish the job an' leave no trace of anything that'll return to our doorstep."

"Make it worth ower while an' we'll oblige ye," Seamus replied, "so in the meantime, le's shake on it."

Hugo hesitated, reluctantly pressed flesh with Seamus, then wrenched his hand free as if he had just made a pact with the devil.

"Where's yer horse?" Shaun queried, observing Hugo's crop and muddy riding boots.

"Probably at the bottom of the gley swamp by now," Hugo answered. "We fell in an' I left her there."

The Irishmen's faces expressed horror.

"What sort o' man are ye, t' leave yer poor nag t' drown in yon bog?" snarled Patrick.

Hugo's face reddened.

"There were nuthin' I could do t' pull her out" growled Hugo...

"But why did ye not get help?" Patrick demanded.

"I didn't want the Gomers to know I was there; I was lookin' fer Wicks, one o' yon poachers," Hugo replied.

The three Irishmen viewed Hugo with disgust.

"Ye'd better git back to yer farm, master Hugo. Perhaps we could meet ye somewhere there this night t' find shelter on yer farm," Seamus ordered.

"Meet me at the haybarn just afore midnight the day after tomorrow an' I'll see 'bout putting up the three of ye. Dermot your other partner-in-crime's at Home Farm an' crippled. Ye'd better stay in the haybarn fer now. Wicks's wife an' litter are bedded down in one of our cottages but I'll have 'em out by the morrow. Now begone to where'er ye're hiding until the day after that, afore one o' the Gomers comes ariding an' sees thee."

The three thugs shambled off south, muttering.

Hugo tramped to Home Farm; he was unhappy. He'd compromised himself fleeing from the gleys and meeting the Irish gang. Somehow he must get the upper hand. He would hire them to harm Giles Gomer, deny all knowledge of the plot then cast the blame on them in some way.

"Where's your mare, Hugo? Are you injured?" Katherine asked, as Hugo staggered into the farmyard.

"She tripped an' fell over a tree root on the lower road

below Wychcombe Farm, threw me and galloped off," lied Hugo.

"When did this happen, dear?" Katherine pursued.

"I can't remember, woman, perhaps a half hour ago and I've just a sore back, nothing to worry about."

What was Hugo doing below Wychcombe? Katherine wondered. And why was he there when she'd heard from Abel Hands, their chargehand, that Wychcombe was under siege? And Hugo's surefooted mare should have returned to the farm if he'd unhorsed Hugo half an hour ago.

"Why don't you get the ostler to take your mare's stablemate to help find him? She might be lying hurt somewhere, since she's not returned after all this time."

"Nonsense! She'll find her way back in good time."

Katherine kept her peace, suspicious that Hugo was concealing something. Was he involved in the riot or just innocently out for a ride? She mentally dismissed the latter.

The same night, in the copse below the ruins of St. Stephen's church, Seamus sank his teeth into a piece of mutton roasted on a wood fire.

"Foine meat, this, from one o' the Gomer's ewes," he grunted between chews.

"Aye, Seamus, but oi'd be glad when we get some beef at Jones's farm instead o' sheepstealin' an' lightin' fires in this 'ere wood," replied Patrick.

"Day after t'morrow, lads, soon as master Hugo gets rid o' the poacher Wicks's wife an' litter", Seamus added.

15

"Oi don' care fer this setup one jot," muttered Shaun, "nor do oi trus' master fancy airs Hugo Jones."

"Mebbe ye're right 'bout 'im, but, bejabers, we 'ave 'im by the short hairs. If 'e tries t' shop us, we'll side wi' the Gomers and turn King's evidence that Jones hired us to kill the younger one ..."

"But we'd still be sentenced fer attempted murder," interrupted Shaun.

December 14ᵗʰ 1815

Two days later, just as Wychcombe village's church clock struck a quarter to midnight, the three Irishmen shuffled through the snow into the haybarn at Home Farm. Fifteen minutes later, Hugo appeared at the barn door, his congested face resembling an illuminated gargoyle in his lantern's light. He stepped inside, followed by a flurry of snow.

"Get ye down t' yon cornbarn at cockcrow this morning. There be plenty o' work hand threshin', since a body smashed up our machine!" he grated.

"Gi' us time t' wake up, zur," groaned Seamus, pulling hay from his hair and beard, aware that Hugo was not in a conciliatory mood, "an' we'll need some vittles".

"Here's a cold joint o' beef and some cider t' be goin' on wi' and there'll be bread an' cheese in yon threshing barn an' a flagon o' cider t' swill it all down. Look sharp t'morrow, I need to sell the corn ye thresh to pay yer wages," Hugo growled. He placed a basket and flagon on the barn floor and disappeared.

"This'll be better fare than wot them threshers be gettin'," Seamus announced, biting off a lump of beef, chewing and swallowing it between mouthfuls of bread.

"But we're goin' to miss this grub fer a while until we're settled in other parts," added Patrick.

Patrick and Shaun eyed each other with broad smiles.

"Shush yer gob, Patrick! There be ears in these barn walls and a word out o' turn will land us in trouble. Now finish them vittles off," warned Seamus.

"What are ye doin', Patrick?" Seamus growled, as Patrick parted hay to expose earth.

"Jus' burying this mug I filched from the Penny Farthin'," he replied, extracting a pewter tankard from inside his grimy shirt. "It'll come in handy fer fetching a groat or two. Gimme that pitchfork to break up the ground."

Ezra and Hugo were seated in Home Farm kitchen at half past midnight.

"Where have ye hidden yon Irishmen, Hugo? We don't want the Gomers to know that they're here."

"They're in the haybarn, father," Hugo replied.

Ezra's face paled; mouth opened, he bared his teeth, eyes flashing.

"Do ye realise what ye've done, ye half-baked fool?"

Hugo looked blank.

"Wha … wha … I've done, father?"

"Ye brainless idiot, ye've let them bed down over where ye've buried the Gomers' money!"

Hugo's mouth opened wide but remained soundless.

17

"Ye'll have to dig it up early today while they're threshin' wot morsel o' corn we've rescued from the fire that's not scorched nor got black spot from the storm. So get the worthless tinkers out sharpish!"

"Ye … yes, father," Hugo tremored.

"I'm off to Magistrate's Court at the crack o' dawn this morning an' I'll be back tomorrow, and I'll expect ye to hand over all thirty thousand pounds when I return."

December 15ᵗʰ 1815

At six o'clock the same morning, Hugo hurried to the threshing barn where men were already hand-threshing the corn. Abel the chargehand approached Hugo and touched his forelock.

"The Irishmen ain't turned up yet, Maister Hugo. Oi'll send a man t' rouse 'em," he said.

"No, no, I'll go an' sort 'em out," Hugo cried and exited the barn.

He crossed the icy path to the haybarn; the barn door was open. He stepped over the threshold, shouting,

"Get up, ye lazy tinkers, get up! Men have done a day's work while ye were dozing!"

Nothing stirred.

"Get up, I say, or ye'll have no vittles for breakfast!"

No reply. He tightened the grip on his riding crop, thrashing at the hay. No sign of the Irishmen. Desperate, Hugo ran under the central crossbeam and located the apex of the pitched roof supported by the crossbeam then visually drew an imaginary line from the apex through the crossbeam to the ground. He bent down, swept aside loose hay and found an area where soil had recently been disturbed. Panic-stricken, he scrabbled, dug and threw the earth aside with trembling hands. He winced as his hand hit a harder object and swept aside the earth around it, exposing the lid of a metal box. He dug again, uncovering its sides, then lifted the box out easily, too easily, and opened it. Empty. Crying with rage, he hurled the box at the barn wall, sobbed and pounded the earth with his fists.

Hugo wiped away his tears. I must recover the money before father gets back, he mused. He dreaded to think what his father would do to him if he met Ezra empty-handed. A horsewhipping would be merciful! If he didn't recover the thirty thousand pounds, where could he get hold of it and how? Would Katherine help? He dismissed the idea since she'd question why he required so much. If he told her, she'd be reluctant to part with any money her parents had placed in trust for any issue from their marriage, whatever deceit he used to hide the truth. Who else could help him? He needed to pursue and apprehend the thieves or mortgage Home Farm, but it wasn't his – yet! His only option was to hunt them down himself and somehow wrest the money off them. The thieves were on foot, and on horseback he had the advantage of speed. How much advantage had they if they'd fled shortly after discovering the money?

CHAPTER FOUR

The Hunt

Earlier the same morning, before Hugo discovered that the money had disappeared with the Irishmen, Richard was still awake when the hall clock struck two o'clock at Wychcombe Farm. He rose and left his bedroom. As he was about to pass the landing's oriole window, he saw a distant light moving southward. Richard retrieved his spyglasss and focussed on the light, which silhouetted three moving figures. Giles appeared at Richard's side.

"What is it, Richard?"

"Look!" Richard exclaimed, handing his brother the spyglass and pointing eastward.

Giles followed the pointing finger.

"What d'ye make of it, brother?" Richard asked.

"Three men, and I have a healthy suspicion who it is. Should we go after them?"

"What would we gain if they are who we suspect and catch up with them?"

"We could find out if Hugo Jones put them up to attacking you."

The brothers dressed, Richard with Berkeley's help, and woke up Jamie sleeping in the stables; he saddled Hal and Sally and the brothers rode south through falling snow, The moving light was close to Wychcombe village hamlets. The brothers rode through a gap in the foxmould meadow's hedge, trotted Hal and Sally south onto the southern Bridport-Dorchester road, quickened their speed east and entered the village. Their movements had been heard; cottage windows lit up with lantern-light as faces appeared.

"What be goin' on there?" shouted a villager.

Richard and Giles reined in.

"We're after three vagabonds!" shouted Richard.

"What meks ye think they're 'ere?" came back the query.

"Follow the lantern light," shouted Giles, pointing.

The light disappeared. Richard and Giles spurred their mounts on, anxious not to lose the fugitives in the darkness.

"Who be ye, then?" a villager demanded, but the brothers had passed out of earshot.

The brothers guided Hal and Sally to the far end of the village; they reined up, surveyed then turned around. Where had the hunted men gone? Villagers with lanterns approached. The moon appeared, exposing the village dwellings, the workhouse, the Penny Farthing Inn and St. Bartholomew's church. The brothers rode slowly, tracking the snow for prints …

"Wait, Richard, we saw no footprints beyond the church; let's return to St. Bart's and check the entrance."

Richard nodded. The brothers turned their mounts, passed the darkened Penny Farthing and the square in front of the workhouse until they reached the church, connected to the road by a lychgate and a snow-covered pathway.

From the lychgate to the church, two clear sets of hobnailed boot prints were visible in the snow. The prints continued to the church then disappeared round the side of the building. The brothers exchanged glances. Only two sets of prints. By the side of one set of prints was a deeper impression in the snow, indicating something dragged. The brothers dismounted and led Hal and Sally along the grass verge of the path to track the two pairs of prints. They passed around the side of the building. The prints stopped outside a rear door. Giles tried the heavy metal handle and turned it; assisted by the wind, the door swung open. A single lit candle stood at the head of a coffin on which a brass plate marked the remains of Reverend William Lessop-Dene.

They checked the room; wet bootprints tracked from the door into the church; they entered. Candlelight illuminated the sacristy. Giles walked along a fading track of melting snow down one aisle, along the rear of the church and up the next aisle, past the font facing the altar and down a third aisle. Suddenly, two figures appeared from behind the rood screen and disappeared, slamming the church door behind them. Pandemonium broke out beyond the church with the clatter of hooves and high-pitched neighing. Giles blew out the candle and placed it on the church floor. The brothers raced outside, caught and calmed their horses, glimpsing two men disappearing into the graveyard.

"The cunning thugs! We can't ride the horses in there!"

Giles exclaimed, pointing to ice-covered, half-toppled and fallen headstones and crosses.

The brothers stood at the cemetery entrance. Richard turned and held a finger to his lips. Silence. The moon disappeared behind a massive grey cloud and the snowfall began to thin. Then they heard a muffled cry followed by a thud. The brothers tied their horses to the iron cemetery fence and entered the graveyard. Giles led the way, tracking visible bootprints in the snow. Suddenly two figures leapt from adjacent tombstones brandishing clubs. Richard withdrew his sword, struck at and opened Seamus's cheek. The Irishman's club fell into the snow as Giles ducked a flailing blow from Patrick and wrestled him to the ground. The four men fought violently; Richard, blinded by spurting blood from Seamus's wound, tried to free his swordhand from Seamus's grip as the Irishman repeatedly punched Richard's face with his free hand. Giles knocked Patrick's club arm against a tombstone, floored the Irishman then threw the club into the dark. Turning, he saw Seamus battering Richard.

"Richard!"

For a distracting moment, Seamus loosened his grip on Richard's swordarm, which Richard wrenched free, reversed the sword and smashed the haft into the unharmed side of Seamus's face. Seamus, howling, raised an arm which never descended, his fist held in Giles's iron grip, who then flung the Irishman off Richard, punching him in the face in transit. Giles then sat Richard up, wiping his brother's bleeding face with his own neckerchief.

"Can ye stand, dear brother?"

"Aye, Giles."

Richard rolled over onto his knees and, with effort, raised himself, using his sword as a support.

"Look out Giles!" he cried, tugging at his sword as Seamus felled Giles with a clubbing blow followed by a kick to Richard's groin.

Giles fell, but Seamus saw Richard standing with raised sword, and disappeared through the curtain of snow. Giles turned to look for Patrick McAlerty; he too had fled.

"Let's call it a night, Giles," Richard sighed, "Did ye notice that there were only two of the rogues?"

"Aye, brother, and what happened to whatever one of them was dragging?"

"Heavy eno' to be dragged, but not through the graveyard. They've hidden it somewhere.

CHAPTER FIVE

Death in the Copse

Home Farm, 7 a.m. the same morning

When Hugo discovered the money had been stolen, he ordered the ostler to saddle a strong hunter gelding. Ezra was away attending Magistrates' Court; Hugo had a little over twenty-four hours to overtake the robbers and return the money to his father. He strapped a musket to the saddle, stuffed a flintlock pistol and powder case into a jacket pocket then put bread and cheese wrapped in muslin, a corked bottle of claret and a spyglass into the saddlebag. He mounted and sat in the saddle. Which way? Had they split the money and separated? They might feel safer together. Had they cut and run inland or to the coast? Dorset had a long coastline; Lyme Regis, Bridport and Weymouth to the West and Poole and Swanage to the East.

They had six hours' start on him, but were disadvantaged, travelling on foot in snow. He spurred the gelding onto the road connecting the north and south Dorchester to Bridport roads. A watery yellow sun glowed weakly over the land, exposing field upon snow-covered field squared off by half-concealed hedges. He reached the southern Dorchester to Bridport route west of Wychcombe, slowing the gelding to a walk. Light snowfall and mingled hoof and foot prints hindered his search.

Hugo walked the gelding slowly east into Wychcombe. Villagers had risen; lights shone through windows and smoke curled through chimneys. Eyes peered through dusty panes above snow-caked sills. Hugo saw hoofprints moving eastwards until he reached the western end of St. Bartholomew's church, then darkened spots tracking from the churchyard entrance. He stopped, dismounted and dipped his finger in a spot, and examined it – blood-red. Hugo remounted and turned the gelding westwards, eyeing the snow with great care. He peered from left to right, slowing down because the sun had risen, painting the snow a dazzling silver. Someone shedding blood had fled towards the copse near St. Stephen's ruin, Hugo suspected. He turned the gelding round, dismounted and walked him through the church gate towards the church portico. Red smudges mixed with foot and hoof prints tracked around the building until they reached the lychgate. The sunlight exposed more blood, footprints and a club.

At seven a.m. also at Wychcombe Farm someone battered on the door; dogs started baying, then Berkeley appeared, climbing the rickety stairs holding a lantern as the brothers stepped onto the bare wooden landing.

"Sirs, Asa's here and wants a word with you."

Giles hurried downstairs. An icy draught penetrated his nightshirt.

"Brrr! Come in and shut the door, Asa!"

The shepherd shuffled over the threshold, snow and ice on his sackcloth covering melting rapidly in the comparative warmth, his ice-covered beard glistening in the light of Berkeley's lantern, head and beard covered by frosted hair. A pool of melted ice began to collect on the hall floor. He spoke through chattering teeth:

"Maister Giles, zur, oi've found who be stealin' our ewes. Oi wager it be yon Oirish rogues. There be a trail of torn fleece from our grazings over to the copse. Oi were feeding the flock in St. Stephen's field an' oi heard voices and smelt burning flesh in the copse, then one o' the scoundrels …"

Giles, with Richard, waited while Asa gathered himself.

"… so oi takes me lanthern and treads careful like into the copse. The brutes had slit a ewe's throat, torn off its limbs, dragged it inside and built a fire to roast the flesh".

The brothers eyed each other, faces hardened.

"Poor ewe had had twins," Asa cried, tears mingling with thawing ice on his bearded cheeks, "I felt like killing them scoundrels wiv me bare hands!"

"Did ye go further into the copse, Asa?"

"Nay, maister Giles, I was afeared they'd slit me throat too. That's why I'm here," Asa replied.

"Richard, I suggest we get some breakfast first, then we'll ride to the copse in St. Stephen's field. Asa, check that the other ewes are safe."

"Aye, maister Giles," Asa replied, touching his cap and exiting the farmhouse.

27

Hugo followed the trail of blood spots until they mingled with bootprints. He suspected that the the Irishmen had fled from Home Farm to Wychcombe with his money, had entered the churchyard cemetery and, after an altercation, had retraced their path westward towards the copse near St. Stephen's ruin.

Seamus's cheeks were swollen and congealed with blood. He touched them, winced and cursed the one-armed perpetrator. He squatted close to a blazing woodpile in the copse roasting ewe meat impaled on a makeshift spit. A rustling noise? Nobody would be about at this time of day or know they were here. He thrust the stick into the heart of the bonfire.

Hugo knocked Seamus to the ground with the Irishman's discarded club.

"You're a fool t' light a fire here. Did ye think ye could get away with my money? Well, scum, what hast ye done with it?"

"I dunno wot yer talkin …" Seamus screamed as a third blow cracked a rib. He tried to rise; Hugo pushed him back into the snow.

"Ye know that for once ye're helpless an' I could brain you if I wanted to, but all I want is my money back, let ye go and think no more on it. Otherwise …"

Hugo lifted the club menacingly.

"Well, what's it to be, the money or this?"

Seamus opened his mouth:

"Wot's that noise?" pointing beyond Hugo.

28

"Don't try to fool me, idiot!"

Then he too heard the muffled beat of distant hooves. He ran to the edge of the copse. About two hundred yards away, two horsemen were approaching St. Stephen's ruin. Hugo dodged back into the copse.

Richard and Giles rode steadily, turning towards the copse.

"Let's leave Sally and Hal here and go inside, Giles," Richard said.

"We must take care, there could be danger. Have ye anything besides your sword?"

"No, Giles, but you've a flintlock."

The brothers reined their mounts in, dismounted and tied the reins to a low-hanging tree branch, then entered.

"Stop!" Richard whispered, pointing. Four fresh hoofprints and a single pair of human bootprints appeared to have tracked from Wychcombe into the copse.

Giles eyed Richard.

"Ready, brother?"

As Richard and Giles entered the copse, Hugo exited from the far end, passing through the village, and galloped up a hill northwest towards Home Farm.

Winter sunlight filtered through the copse between trees and space. The brothers almost tripped over two bodies – the eviscerated remains of a sheep and a recumbent human by a dying woodfire. Giles pushed the man's body over to expose Seamus O'Brien's bloodied head and face.

"Poor wretch! He's met his just merits, I'll wager," murmured Giles.

Richard knelt down, unspeaking, pressing Seamus's bloodstained neck, then put his face close to the Irishman's mouth.

"He's not dead, Giles, but almost gone. Quick, get a handful of snow and rub his face with it."

Giles made a snowball, rubbed Seamus's face and lips with it, forced open Seamus's mouth and shoved a piece of ice inside. Seamus gasped, shook his head and retched. Giles grabbed the Irishman by his coat collar and shook him violently.

"Stop, Giles! The man's dying; treat him with respect, however undeserving he is."

Richard knelt over the dying man. Seamus mumbled something to him, each word accompanied by a gush of dark red blood from his lips. Unconcerned by blood staining his face and greatcoat, Richard applied his ear close to the man's mouth, listening carefully.

"What's he saying?" Giles demanded, but Richard did not answer.

Seconds later, Seamus's breath came out in spasmodic grunts followed by a dreadful rattling noise. He half rose, shouted a single word, his face turned purple, and with eyes cast upwards, the poor wretch expired. The brothers stood over the still form, struggling to take in Seamus's horrific end.

"Seamus dead and Dermot a cripple on Home Farm

and at Hugo Jones's mercy; that leaves Shaun and Patrick the other two Irish vagabonds to find."

"We can't leave his body to the foxes, Giles. He was a rogue but he should be given a decent burial."

"But we've nothing to dig with and this ground'll be rock-hard; and if ye decide to bury him at the farm, I don't relish carrying his corpse there, Richard. Let's cover the body with something and get Asa to bury him in the gley field."

Hugo had extracted little information from Seamus, but reasoned that St. Bartholomew's cemetery held a clue to the whereabouts of the stolen money. Dermot, crippled and confined to servitude at Home Farm, and Seamus, now deceased, were accounted for; Patrick and Shaun were still at large. If he could find either of the two survivors, one might be all he needed to find where the money had gone. He reined in the gelding north of Wychcombe, took out the flagon from his pannier, uncorked it and took a generous swig, the spirit burning inside his chest and warming his body from the freezing cold. The thieves had found the money he'd buried under the haybarn, fled after midnight, entered Wychcombe graveyard, were involved in a fight and had fled, Seamus returning to the copse, he reasoned. Hoofprints other than those of Hugo's gelding indicated that someone on horseback had been following the Irishmen to the church then had given up the chase. Clearly, others were searching, possibly even the Gomers. He must find the surviving Irishmen and the money before others did.

Richard and Giles returned to Wychcombe Farm and ordered Asa and Thomas to bury Seamus in the gley meadow. Giles was keen to know what Richard had gleaned from Seamus's dying words; there was no reason why Richard should not tell him. To Giles's surprise and at Richard's signal, they rode into Wychcombe village, through St. Bartholomew's open church gate, around the building and up to the lychgate. Richard dismounted, Giles followed suit and, following his brother's example, tied his horse to the gate and entered the cemetery. Without hesitation, Richard carefully threaded his way between the snow-covered tombstones and stopped by a recently excavated empty grave; turfs were neatly stacked at the side. Strange, thought Giles, why had his brother brought them here?

Giles broke the silence:

"I feel certain that the Irishmen who attacked me are connected with Jones. I wasn't fooled by his lies when I confronted him with Dermot, who'd already confessed to me."

"I'd go further, Giles. If it was Jones who bludgeoned Seamus, he wasn't bothered about killing him, so long as he got the information he wanted."

At Wychcombe Farm, Richard and Giles lunched on cuts of salted beef with chunks of bread washed down with ale.

"We must return to Wychcombe village as soon as possible before the Irishmen escape, Richard."

"Yes, Giles, and extract the truth from them about what they were carrying that was so heavy. Remember, two of them had injured arms, leaving Seamus the ringleader the only one capable of carrying whatever it was. It may have been too heavy even for him to lift and had to be dragged then hidden," added Richard. "But tomorrow's the vicar's funeral, so we must postpone our hunt until the day after tomorrow."

CHAPTER SIX

The Vicar's Funeral

December 16ᵗʰ, St. Bartholomew's, Wychcombe

Two people experienced restless nights before the day of the vicar's funeral. Neither wished to attend but they knew that their absence would be noted and excite suspicion, seeing that their families paid patronage to the parish. Worse still, villagers participating in the abortive riot would be present.

Richard Gomer and Edmond Goodboys resolved to maintain their secret for as long as they could, or forever, but it was probably a burden on their consciences.

The day dawned overcast over the snow and ice-bound land, a chill wind setting the scene for the vicar's funeral. Inside the church, a single candle in a bronze candlestick before the coffin had kept a vigil through the night. The coffin had been sealed after the Dean and churchwarden had decided that the vicar's remains were unfit for viewing. The attenders, villagers and workmen filed in, dressed in rough-hewn clothes, dispersing manure-tainted smells, hobnailed boots echoing on St. Bartholomew's stone floor. The coffin had been moved from vestry to nave and, there being no next-of-kin present, the front row of pews remained empty. The organist, intermittently blowing on cold mitten-clad fingers between hymn and liturgy, sat amply clothed under cassock and surplice.

After hymns and a requiem for the deceased vicar, the Very Reverend David Carshall, Rural Dean of the parish, began his sermon with a biblical text that some parishioners would have deemed appropriate: Cain and Abel (Genesis 4 v.1–8). Closing his address, he expanded on his subject:

"The death of Cain was the first human murder in the history of humanity. Why did Cain slay his brother? Because his offering to God was not approved of by his Maker, whereas Abel's was. So Cain in his jealous fury murdered his brother. Since then, many murders have been committed, for many reasons. Jealousy, and yes, crimes of passion, greed, for gain, revenge.

"Why was your beloved vicar killed? His parishioners would vouch that he had no enemies. Yet, he could be very forceful in his condemnation of evil. My suspicion is that he knew something about someone in this parish which could have resulted in his untimely death. Perhaps people will suspect that the owners of the property on which his body was discovered were involved, but there is no proof that they were. But remember this; Cain became a fugitive with a curse on his head. And that curse still applies. Someone, somewhere, is harbouring a secret that will trouble his conscience until the day of his death unless he confesses. As the scriptures say in the book of Galatians, chapter 6, verse 7: *'God is not mocked for whatsoever a man soweth that he shall also reap'*. Unless the perpetrator confesses, he will have no rest. Let us pray that he will surrender or be arrested and confess his crime. And let us pray for the soul of our dear, departed brother, that he will rest in peace. In the name of the Father, the Son and the Holy Ghost". The Very Reverend David Carshall closed the massive bible on the lectern as the congregation bowed their heads.

The funeral cortege moved slowly from the church, out through the front door, the coffin carried by pallbearers preceded by the undertaker dressed in black top hat, full-length black cloak and shiny boots, grasping a silver-headed stick in his hands covered by black leather gloves. A distance of four paces behind the coffin bearers the Dean walked, head bowed, followed by the verger, then members of the parish church council – Ezra and Martha Jones, Sir Absalom and Lady Goodboys, Katherine and Hugo Jones, then Richard Gomer and Edmond Goodboys, side by side and lastly villagers from Wychcombe. Giles's absence provoked little surprise for he made no secret of his aversion to any form of religious observance.

The procession turned left outside the church building and went slowly, to the fading sounds of organ music. Hugo Jones walked side by side with Katherine, a glint in his bloodshot eyes. The Dean's reference to Cain and Abel connected with suspicions concerning the vicar's death. Edmond Goodboys walked grim-faced side-by-side with Richard Gomer. Villagers watched silently as the cortege progressed down the side and back of the church, then through the lychgate into the cemetery. As the group stopped at the entrance, a man dressed in a homespun jacket, woollen trousers and hobnailed boots lurched towards the funeral party clutching a half-empty bottle of furmity and pointed a finger at Edmond and Richard, shouting:

"Murtherers! One o' ye killed our vicar! Oi knows! God'll 'ave 'is vengeance!"

Edmond and Richard stood still, outwardly unmoved by the labourer's ravings.

"You're drunk man! Begone! You're defiling this holy occasion and showing no respect for the dead!" cried the Dean.

"Bu … bu … bu … but oi knows who did it! One o' these genilmen, oi swear!" the worker persisted, pointing to Richard and Edmond, "becos the vicar knew somethin' about 'em."

Before he could continue, two burly villagers seized the man and dragged him away, shouting. The funeral proceeded without further event and after a commital at the grave, the invited guests congregated in the manse, situated by the church. Covert glances were cast on Edmond and Richard, who miraculously showed no embarrassment. Hugo had excused himself and Katherine joined her parents at the buffet.

"Why do you think that man appeared to be accusing Edmond and Richard Gomer, dear?" Lady Goodboys whispered to her husband.

"I have no idea," Sir Absalom replied.

The Dean approached Richard. "Mr. Gomer?"

Richard nodded.

"Could I have a word with you, sir?"

"By all means," Richard replied.

"I am, as you may have been informed, the Rural Dean

of the parish. Shall we go into this room?" said the Dean, pointing to a door.

Richard nodded. The two went into the room.

"Mr. … er … Gomer, I'm sorry that that labourer marred the sanctity of this occasion, but he was voicing the suspicions of other villagers. A number of us are concerned that to the plain man, the circumstances surrounding the Reverend William Lesden's … er … Lessop-Dene's death and the discovery of his body in the bog on your land cast suspicion on your family's involvement."

"Are you accusing us of his death?" Richard replied, slightly taken aback by David Carshall's slip of the tongue exposing knowledge of William Lesden's double identity.

"Was it true that your family destroyed any hope of his family pursuing their inheritance in working land of their own, resulting in William's father drinking himself to death and leaving William seeking justice?" queried the Dean, confirming his knowledge of the vicar's identity.

Would he call killing sheep and hamstringing cattle justice? And attempting to murder me and somehow dispose of my mother and brother, Richard thought. The Dean obviously knew more than Richard would have credited him with. Richard felt that he must be careful not to betray his and Edmond's secret.

"That was a most unfortunate thing to happen."

"Yes, and why should the vicar be killed unless he knew something incriminating about someone?"

"Possibly, but any proof of that will probably go with him to the grave."

Surely the Gomers must have some inkling of what happened? the Dean thought.

"It would be a travesty if the perpetrator got away scot-free, especially as the victim was St. Bartholomew's esteemed vicar. What do you think, sir?"

To Richard, the question posed to him put him in a difficult position. His knowledge and concealment of the facts were wounding his conscience.

"I have nothing to add to what is already known," he said, choosing his words carefully.

"But isn't it strange that the vicar's body should be found on your land?"

"It is, but it does not prove our family's involvement," Richard replied.

The Reverend David Carshall changed tack.

"Did you ever find out who let your sheep into the clover field and hamstrung your cows?"

A piercing question; he knows more than he's letting on, thought Richard.

"We had our suspicions," he replied, instantly regretting his slip of the tongue.

"Who did you suspect, sir?" the Dean ventured, seizing Richard's reply.

"Alas, they are only suspicions with no proof," Richard replied.

The Dean smiled.

"Is it true that the 'accidents' on your farm stopped about the time the vicar died?"

"Now that's an interesting observation, Dean."

He's probing me, Richard thought, perhaps hoping to breach my defence and expose the secret Edmond and I are concealing.

"And shot in the back with no opportunity to defend

himself? What a brutal and cowardly act, don't you think?"

How much more does this Dean know? Richard mused.

"Did the vicar confide in you about his own circumstances and true identity while he was incumbent of this parish before he died?" Richard asked.

From the look on Mr. Carshall's face, Richard knew he had hit the jugular.

"Wha ... what do you mean?" blurted the Dean.

"What I said. If you knew about the vicar's background and his relationship to the Lesden family, you must know more. You must have known how he felt over his father's demise."

"What are you getting at, sir? Are you inferring that the vicar could have been involved in the acts of cruelty to your animals in revenge for some reason? Surely there's no proof and it shows no respect for his memory, now he's dead."

"Was that personal information your predecessor had confided to you? Surely those facts weren't common knowledge until after his death, especially when his surname as vicar apparently bore little if any connection to his family name? Is that the route you're taking with your questions?"

Once more the clergyman's face expressed shock.

"No sir, I'm concerned, like others, to get to the bottom of the vicar's mur ... death ..."

"I would recommend that you leave the relevant authorities to do that, unless you have further information that would help to solve the mystery of the vicar's demise."

The Dean did not answer.

Richard bade him good-day and joined Edmond. They waited until Mr. Carshall was out of earshot, then Richard disclosed his conversation with the Dean. Edmond bowed his head.

"I cannot keep on hiding the fact that I killed the vicar; my conscience will not allow me to conceal it any longer. Nor, I suspect, does yours," spoke Edmond.

"But you saved me from being murdered; the vicar was a madman. There's no telling what he would have done to satisfy his evil lust for vengeance on our family."

"Nevertheless, I willingly shot him and you need not be implicated. I can testify that we quarrelled and I shot him in self-defence. After all, he was powerful enough to overpower either you or me."

"But, Edmond, you will be charged with murdering the vicar, not saving my life from a madman! No-one will believe you did it in defence of me. The law will not be on your side."

"I'll take my chance. There's no reason why you should have any link with Lesden's death, Richard."

"Except that his body was found in the gley bog on our land. How are you going to explain both without quite rightly incriminating me?"

"I can testify that we were not at Wychcombe Farm when we quarrelled and that I decided to hide his body in the gley. It was much easier than to bury him in frozen ground."

Richard shook his head.

"It's all too far-fetched. And how can you explain the presence of both of us on our farm? If you must give yourself up, I must join you. The testimony of both of us will stand better in court."

"But, Richard, I did the killing. Why should you pay the same penalty as me?"

"You saved my life, Edmond, I owe you my life."

Tears coursed down Edmond's cheeks; his chest heaved with great, racking sobs. Richard put his arm around Edmond's shoulders and began to weep with him.

CHAPTER SEVEN

The Graverobber

December 17th, St. Bartholomew's graveyard.

The graveyard was shrouded in uncertain darkness; dark clouds allowed momentary glimpses of moonlight. A solitary figure holding a spade crept across the cemetery, stopped by the new headstone marking the vicar's grave, looked around, then removed the recently placed turfs from over the grave and dug into the loose earth, tossing spadefuls of soil to one side. This action was repeated until there was a dull, resounding sound of the spade striking something more solid. The digger knelt down and brushed soil from the coffin. After removing the soil, the man felt for the join between lid and coffin, then jammed the shovel blade between the two and prised it with all his strength. The lid moved slightly but didn't give way. The gravedigger moved to the head of the coffin and repeated the operation. This time the lid moved upward to expose the head of the corpse followed by an awful stench. Ignoring the overpowering smell, the man prised up the lid until the nails securing the rest of the coffin lid gave way.

The yellow, decomposed face of William Lesden, aka the Reverend William Lessop-Dene, peered sightlessly from the shroud. The man, disdaining any traditional respect for the dead, grabbed the front of the shroud, raised the corpse and lugged it to the side of the grave, to expose the base of the coffin. The man swept his hands around the base until he felt a sack, still intact. The man let out a gasp of relief, opened the sack, removed a bundle of notes and quickly counted them. He removed three more bundles, stuffed them into his breeches' pocket, closed and returned the sack, pushed the corpse back into its resting place and jammed the lid back on the coffin. He rapidly shovelled soil and placed the turfs over the coffin, fleeing from the cemetery as fast as his burden allowed him. He climbed over the hedge bordering the graveyard and field and disappeared.

Shaun the Irishman, now hidden above Wychcombe Farm, licked his lips and emptied his pockets onto the damp earth. He felt that he'd be safer on Gomer land. By now young Jones would have discovered the money gone, put two and two together and decided to hunt them down. He shivered to think of the consequences if any of them were caught. The banknotes were tied in bundles of twenties. He counted a bundle, then each twenty-pound note in one bundle – fifty, a total of one thousand pounds! He could hardly believe his eyes. He counted the other bundles – four in all, making a total of four thousand pounds! He was rich beyond his wildest dreams! He stuffed each bundle into his breeches' pockets and the pockets of his jacket he'd 'removed' from St. Bartholomew's until there was no more room.

He stumbled south through the snow until he could see the lights of the Gomers' farmhouse, made a wide detour east then south to one of the haybarns. He staggered into the darkened building and moved well into its interior until his eyes became accustomed to the dimness. He bumped into a hard object and felt it – a cornsack! He opened the neck, grabbed a handful of grain and held it tightly. Finding the ladder to the loft, he climbed it and then moved well away from the ladder. He must lie low until night-time, then where to go? Although he felt safer here, the Gomers would be looking for them to avenge their attack on young Giles.

Where were Seamus and Patrick? He was ignorant of Dermot's fate, then he remembered that the Gomers had caught up with him. The last recollection of Dermot was of him crying with pain after one of the Gomers' men clubbed his knees to cripple him. Perhaps the other two were looking out for him, they'd talked about meeting at the Three Sailors Inn at Bridport, splitting the money and paying for a ship's passage well away from England. Gathering loose hay around himself, he lay down, contemplated his course of action then drifted off to sleep.

The cock crow awoke him. It was still dark, but if he left the barn now, he might run the risk of rousing the farm dogs, who were now in the farmhouse, and be caught. In spite of chewing and swallowing the handfuls of corn, he was still hungry and thirsty. Oh, for a noggin of Dorset ale and a hunk o' pigeon pie! There was a grocer's shop in Wychcombe and the Penny Farthing pub should soon be open to quench his thirst. He rose. In spite of his hunger and thirst, he thought better of venturing to the village, climbed down to the barn floor, opened the door and slaked the dryness of his throat and mouth with handfuls of snow, plucked a massive icicle hanging from the barn's eaves and returned to his improvised bed in the loft.

At nightfall Shaun left the haybarn after assuring himself that the coast was clear. He made his way onto the north-south track until he reached the southern Dorchester–Bridport road, turned west and walked along, hoping to reach Bridport before morning. Fortunately, the hedges on either side sheltered the road from drifting snow and exposed the direction he had to take. The moon illuminated the white landscape with a glowing sheen to light his way. He stopped, cupped his ears but heard only the subdued whistling of the wind over the snow-drifted hedges. Satisfied that he was not being pursued, he forged on, careful where he placed his feet. He had no sense of time except by the moon's trajectory and changes in the sky's light.

December 19th

The next morning the brothers walked to the haybarn and checked the cornstores. All but one sack was tied at the neck, the cord lay on the floor amidst remnants of scattered corn and husks.

"A clever rat might have untied it, but I suspect a human rat did this," Giles observed.

"If it was someone, they must have been desperately hungry to eat raw grain," Richard observed.

"If they've got fire, they could roast it," Giles replied.

The pair moved around the barn and beyond the cornsacks to the massive stack of hay. The smell grew stronger as they approached a clearing in the pile.

Giles knelt down and retrieved an object from the floor – a crumpled, wet £20 note.

"Someone with possession of money has spent the night here."

Hugo needed to discover not only where the remaining Irishmen were, but where they may have planned to be heading. Perhaps, he mused, with some persuasion Dermot might reveal a secret or two as to what the gang had planned. Hugo exited the house and strode over to the haybarn, where Dermot would be grinding corn for the kitchen maid to bake bread from. The barn was unoccupied. The crippled wretch can't be far away, Hugo mused, after all, he could hardly crawl, let alone walk.

"Dermot!" he bellowed, "Where are ye?"

The chargehand and ostler came running to the barn. Hugo shouted Dermot's name again, cursing under his breath.

"Search the buildings for the cripple!" he commanded the two workmen, "he can't be far away!"

The two men ran off in different directions; five minutes later, they joined Hugo.

"No sign of him, zur," the chargehand claimed.

"Oi checked the stables, maister Hugo, and Duke yer gelding's missing," the ostler added.

47

"Has the tack gone as well?" Hugo demanded.

"No zur, it's still hung up in his stable."

"Then he won't have got far without bit, saddle or stirrups. Without them, he'll soon be unhorsed. Duke's never happy with any other rider. The Irishman's a cripple – he couldn't swat a fly. He won't get far with those useless legs of his. Obadiah, saddle up the mare for me," Hugo ordered.

A few minutes later Obadiah led the saddled mare out, Hugo mounted her, dug his heels into her flanks and rode out of the yard. The ostler stood scratching his head. But how crippled was the Irishman? According to Jamie, the Gomers' ostler, both Dermot's kneecaps had been damaged and Giles Gomer had dragged him from Wychcombe to Home Farm on foot, roped to his horse. But were all the injuries to Dermot enough to prevent him fleeing the farm? Dermot could have pretended they were worse than they appeared. Obadiah remembered that he had left a halter on Duke the last time he'd fed, watered and bedded the gelding down. To him, the inference was clear – if Dermot had managed to mount Duke, he could use the halter's two side ropes to guide and control the gelding. If he wasn't thrown, that was.

Obadiah was right. On the night before Hugo decided to question him, Dermot limped furtively to Destro Farm's stables, entered Duke's stable and fell on the gelding, who had been sitting in the straw bedding, before it could rise. He dug his heels into Duke's sides and pulled sharply on the halter ropes. No saddle or stirrups, but he could still ride a horse, a fact he'd concealed. Gripping the gelding's chest firmly in spite of broken knees, he again pulled Duke's head back to discourage the mount from throwing him, kicked the gelding's flanks hard and rode out of the yard, snow muffling Duke's hoofbeats.

He hoped to find the other Irishmen where they'd planned to meet and divide the spoils. He was taking a big risk of dying of cold before he'd met his cronies, but the thought of Hugo Jones catching him spurred him on.

Late that afternoon, Dermot reached the outskirts of Bridport. Snow had not settled there and he trotted Duke along the potholed track past old fishermen's candlelit stone cottages, their fronts littered with lobsterpots and nets. Dermot remembered their planned meeting place and was certain that Shaun had most of the stolen money. Seamus and Patrick were dead and buried on Gomer land according to gossip at Destro, which meant that he and Shaun were the sole survivors. The cobbled harbour and ships loomed into sight and the greystone Three Sailors Inn, its board depicting the faded faces of three sailors, swinging in the wind. On the edge of the cobbled road lay a pile of clothes. He approached the edge of the water – a body appeared, bereft of garments, bobbing on the huge tidal waves smashing against the harbour wall. The body rotated to expose the blood-covered face and chest as those of Shaun. Dermot viewed the clothes, the floating body and the banknotes.

"Shaun!" Dermot gasped, recognising the clothes and body.

He watched, weeping, as the tide dragged under Shaun's body and the floating notes. As he wiped his eyes, an object blew past; Dermot grabbed at it, examined it and snatched at others as they floated past him. He dismounted, holding Duke's halter with one hand, using the other to pick up any littering the quayside, shoving them in a pocket of his trousers. Pocketing the last bank note, he remounted Duke and turned towards the Inn. Shaun had reached their meeting place, but was no longer; he himself was the last survivor of the four Irishmen.. He needed lodgings for the night, but he must be careful not to end up like Shaun. He dismounted, led Duke to a hitching rail, tied the horse to it and limped through the inn door.

Inside the poorly-lit inn sat two men dressed in seamen's sweaters, oilskin trousers and leather boots drinking ale at a rickety wooden bench and smoking clay pipes. The inn smelt of stale ale and pipe smoke; the floor was strewn with sawdust into which the men periodically spat. Dermot limped to a long, chipped and stained bar behind which stood a man pouring ale into a jug. He was of medium height, dressed in a collarless shirt over which was draped a dirty stained apron. His head and face were bare apart from black sideburns flowing down bloated purple cheeks into a thin moustache and untidy whiskers. He was cross-eyed, the pupils flicking nervously above a purple nose, thick purple lips and a sagging chin, adding to his ugliness and lending an air of slyness to his demeanour.

"Have ye got a night's lodging fer a weary traveller?" Dermot asked.

"Oi might 'ave, if the money's good," the barman

replied. "A night's lodging'll cost ye a florin. There's a spare bed up yonder, if ye can pay," he said, pointing to a flight of uneven, cracked wooden steps.

"O'im crippled, zur. Have ye a room down 'ere?" Dermot responded.

"There's only the kitchen an' scullery through there, with no bed. Ye could rest in the chair by the hearth. The fire's dying, but ye'll be warm fer the night. A bottle o' furmity 'll help ye sleep," the barman said, laughing, to which the two men joined in.

"How much fer the be ... chair fer the night, the furmity and my horse stabled with hay and water?" Dermot asked, pointing to the door.

"Two florins," growled the barman, holding out an open palm. "Bring yer nag round the back to the stable and leave him there. Ye can get back through the kitchen door."

Dermot put his hand in his pocket to take out a note, then produced two florins, money Hugo Jones had used to bribe each of the four Irishmen to injure Giles Gomer. Dermot was now fearful for his safety. The two men were watching him closely, the barman was distinctly unfriendly, and the discovery of Shaun's bloody, naked body and scattered notes near to the Three Sailors Inn made him wary of revealing any of the stolen money he carried. The barman held out his hand, but Dermot closed his fist on the coins.

"The money's yours if ye throw in half a pint of ale an' some o' that pigeon pie on the bar as well," said Dermot. "O'im short o' money," he lied.

"There be no profit fer me if I agree," the barman grumbled.

Dermot stood his ground without replying.

"Alright then, an' nuffing more. Now gi' me the florins," the barman growled, extending his grimy hand again.

Dermot handed over the two florins and took a seat and table by a window overlooking the harbour. Muttering, the barman poured a half pint measure of ale into a mug and cut off a slice of pie, placed it on a tin plate, brought them over and slapped them on the table. At this point the seamen left. Dermot slowly quaffed the ale and munched on the pie, watched the barman but kept the harbour in view. About an hour later, the sky had darkened and men were climbing ladders from the quayside carrying loads from horsedrawn carts to a sailing ship bobbing on the tide. Others were standing on the ratlines of the masts unfurling the sails. Dermot trembled from excitement; the ship was preparing to sail while the tide was in! He had no time to waste if he was to get a passage and get clear of Dorset. He finished off the ale and pie, and rose.

"I'll bring Duke round to the stable," he addressed the barman.

The barman nodded.

Dermot limped outside, loosened Duke and led him to the stable. Leaving him in the stable, he closed the stable door, circuited the inn on the side obscured from the inn windows and limped along the darkened quay. He stopped at the ladder and spoke to a sailor carrying a load:

"Where be ye sailing to?"

"Americky," replied the sailor.

"Oi want t' see the cap'n," Dermot said.

"What for? Are ye wanting passage?" queried the sailor, with a sly grin.

"Oi wants to speak to the captain," Dermot persisted.

"He's busy. Where's yer baggage?"

"That be none o' your business. Oi want t' see yer captain," Dermot insisted.

"Ye don' look as if ye've got one groat t' rub agin another, an' ye're not fit t' work ship," the sailor laughed.

"WHERE'S THE CAPTAIN!" Dermot shouted, attracting the attention of other sailors.

A man wearing the peaked cap of an officer appeared at the ship's rail.

"What d'ye want?" the officer demanded.

"To speak with the man in charge of this ship!" Dermot declared.

The officer descended the ladder.

"We don't carry wastrels or cripples on the Dawn Explorer," he said matter-of-factly.

"Oi'm no wastrel an' oi can pay for my passage," Dermot replied.

The officer's eyes narrowed.

"Ye've no baggage; are ye a wanted criminal running away from justice?" he demanded.

"Wanted criminals are chained and shackled, an' ye won't find any marks on me. What oi've got oi've earned," lied Dermot, "and oi can make it worth yer while t' take me t' Americky".

"Let me see the colour of yer money, then."

Dermot took out a twenty-pound note.

"There's more where that came from," he said.

"How do ye know that we won't rob ye of yer money an' throw ye overboard once we set sail?"

"Oi don't, but oi would be trusting ye as an officer an' a gentleman not to harm a paying passenger. Are ye the captain?"

"I am," the man replied, "but what will you do when we disembark? Ye're just a cripple."

"Oi'm stronger than ye think."

For a moment Captain Frobisher was silent.

"We're a cargo ship, not a pleasure boat. If I took you on board, ye'd have to rough it in a bunk wi' the sailors. We'd feed ye well an' fit ye out wi' waterproofs … fer a guinea or two," he quickly added.

"How much fer the trip?" asked Dermot.

"Twenty guineas. Have ye ever sailed afore?"

"Aye, captain," Dermot replied. "From Oireland t' England."

"This'll be different, now winter's on us. If ye can pay, a daily ration o' rum an' ship's biscuit will help keep things down when the gales hit us."

"Oi'm ready fer any o' that, captain. If ye're willin' t' take me, let's shake of it. My name's Dermot Doherty."

The captain held Dermot's hand in a strong grip, which Dermot returned.

"We're ready, cap'n!" someone shouted.

"All hands on board!" roared Captain Frobisher. And to Dermot:

"Can ye climb up, Mr. Doherty, or will ye need to be lifted?"

"Oi can climb wi'out help, captain," Dermot replied and proceeded to ascend.

Once Dermot reached the deck he was taken below and after the captain had given the order to cast off, harbourmen released the ship's ropes. The harbour pilot took the ship's capstan; with sails unfurled and filled with the sea breeze, the Dawn Explorer moved slowly out of the harbour and into the English Channel.

CHAPTER EIGHT

Katherine

As he took her pulse, Doctor Needman observed bruises above Katherine's wrists, but made no comment.

"You are well, Lady Katherine?"

"Of course, doctor."

Doctor Needman saw no change of expression on Katherine's face. Apart from the bruising, she showed no deterioration in health, rather, it seemed to dispel any effect the wounds might have had on her wellbeing and outward composure.

"That's good, Lady Katherine. Your natural functions are in order?"

"Yes, Doctor Needman."

"I will prescribe a tonic for you to take. One of your servants will be able to purchase it for you from the apothecary. And be careful, my dear."

After Katherine's departure, Abraham Needman sat in his lounge musing. From the pattern of the bruises, she'd tried to release herself from a strong grip or ward off heavy blows. He knew the perpetrator, but as the Jones' family physician and now Katherine's he had to keep his knowledge to himself. Such attacks could put at risk her unborn child. The Hippocratic Oath he'd taken to save life was a disquieting thorn in the sensitive core of his mind. What could he do? His vow to preserve confidentiality warned against disclosure, but his heart questioned the rightness of such a decision.

At Home Farm, Harriet, Katherine's maid, gently smoothed ointment on her mistress's arms, weeping. She had been sworn to secrecy with a steely firmness by her mistress. The maid had heard the shouts and stifled cries, running feet, a slammed door and the click of key in lock. Another drunken assault, Harriet knew, and wept silently. Yet Katherine never complained nor showed self-pity and maintained an air of detachment and independence which never wavered.

Hugo's drunken assaults on Katherine ended in pitiful sobbing and a grovelling plea for forgiveness after he sobered up. Katherine's response and lack of enmity disturbed him all the more. He could not shake her composure. She was not imprisoned at Home; she had the opportunity during her early pregnancy to flee to her parents at Copley, when Hugo was drinking in the Prince of Wales in Dorchester or visiting Destro. But she stayed at Home Farm.

But Katherine knew that she had to avoid further beatings for the sake of the child she was carrying. Now four months pregnant, she had a strong feeling that she was with child to Giles. She and the unborn child would always be in danger at Home Farm and after its birth. If she left the farm, where could she go? Destro, her father-in-law's farm, would be out of the question, even though Martha her mother-in-law might be sympathetic. If she appealed to her parents, they would urge her to return to her legal husband. And society would not favour her deserting her husband and breaking her marriage vows, even if she had the means to live elsewhere. The Church, in its firm stand on the sanctity of marriage, would frown on her separation from Hugo and might withhold whatever umbrella of blessing and ministry it might provide. The local church, so dependent on the patronage of the Jones family, would hardly take her side and, like society, would turn a blind eye to her plight, in favour of Hugo.

She would be treated as a pariah, particularly by her own sex, even though many of her gender felt compelled to endure philandering spouses in a loveless marriage themselves. How many wives could be existing in the state she was in? She fingered the bruises under the sleeves of her blouse. What about the Gomers? Was Susannah Gomer someone who could help her? Alas, that poor woman was close to death with smallpox. Even if the Gomer family would be prepared to take her in, there could be some danger to both her and the Gomers. If the Honourable Susannah Gomer recovered or died, Katherine's presence at Wychcombe would cause conflict between the brothers and ignite bloodshed between the Joneses and the Gomers. Richard and Giles would become scapegoats of Hugo's hatred.

Longing for the freedom of being outdoors for a while, she confided in Harriet that she would enjoy a short spell on horseback.

"But, in your condition, milady, an' more so in this weather, ye cannot travel wi'out something bad 'appening," Harriet replied. "Should you not take advice from Dr. Needman?"

"No further questions, Harriet," Katherine ordered.

Dismissing Harriet, she sat, contemplating her situation. All avenues seemed to lead to a cul-de-sac. There was no way out of her dilemma. She must pray. She gave a start. What made her consider such a thing? Although she had been brought up to regularly attend church, the absence of any spiritual experience had not led her to believe a God existed or loved His creation. To Katherine, no such God existed, or if he did, he was indifferent to mankind and the staggering inequality around her. She loathed the hypocrisy of her contemporaries who professed to be followers of God and called themselves Christians yet showed no evidence. Yet just now she had felt like praying!

Harriet's parents lived in Wychcombe, a fair distance from Home Farm to travel on foot, and Harriet's duties took in the daylight hours, especially as Katherine's confinement was progressing and she needed to protect her mistress when Hugo was at Home Farm. How could she, in some way, spread information about the domestic goings-on, or at the very least, get these events to the ears of … she concentrated her thoughts. Who should I tell? She knew that there would be terrible trouble if Master Hugo got to know. Who to send a note with? Or to? Too dangerous. Could she go to see someone herself? At night, it would be a perilous journey. She could be waylaid by footpads, and robbed then assaulted, or, she shuddered, killed to silence her tongue.

CHAPTER NINE

The Dean is Summoned

December 19th, evening

The Very Reverend David Carshall, Dean of Dorchester within the Bishopric of Salisbury Cathedral and, since the death of William Lesden, alias Reverend William Lessop-Dene, acting incumbent of the parish of St. Bartholomew's until the appointment of a vicar, rode into the yard at Home Farm forty minutes following evensong at St. Bartholomew's, Wychcombe. He was unsure why he had been requested by written note delivered at matins by Harriet Anscomb, the maid, to visit Katherine, 'if convenient', after evensong that night. The fact that he had been asked to meet Katherine at such an unsocial hour in the grip of winter underlined its importance, tinged with a degree of mystery. Under normal circumstances, a newly appointed vicar would have been the incumbent of the church following the recent vicar's death or even a curate if a new vicar had been non-resident and the living of the parish fell vacant. The Dean had recalled that the Act of 1813 had established stipends for curates of not less than £60 which elevated the curate's status. As it was, since the sudden death of the vicar, Lessop-Dene, the living of the parish of St. Bartholomew had fallen vacant and no vicar or curate had yet been appointed. A lady of Katherine's position demanded a visit from a cleric of a higher level than a lowly curate, unless the next incumbency could only be filled at such a clerical level. Moreover, she had requested a personal visit from the Dean. Though he came unprepared for the meeting, he'd heard rumours that all was not well between Lady Katherine and Hugo Jones, but he dismissed thoughts of pre-judging the reason for her request.

The ostler took the Dean's horse. The clergyman trod through hardening snow to the front door, which was opened, before he knocked, by Harriet holding a lantern. She must have been looking out for me, he thought. She shut the door after him, took his hat and cloak, hung them on a hook in the hall and preceded him through the hall through which the lantern cast flickering shadows and light, up a staircase and onto a landing. Further along, Harriet tapped on the door of a room, followed by a gentle "Come in" and maid and minister entered the room where Katherine sat facing the door. The Dean bowed.

He was a tall man, his height enhanced by a full-length cloak half-concealing a dark tunic over breeches and buckled black shoes, all of which fitted his ample form well. His soft blue eyes set in an unblemished face of ruddy complexion conveyed a kindly disposition and there was a firm, intelligent appearance in them that belied any weakness of character. His hair was profuse and dark in colour, almost hiding traces of baldness on the crown, the hair extending down his ample cheeks in short sideburns. His hands and wrists were large and strong.

"Good evening, Lady Katherine," he greeted her.

"Good evening, Dean, so good of you to come at such an unsocial time after evensong and on such a wintry night," spoke Katherine, rising and offering her hand. "My husband is away and I wished to speak to you privately. Do sit down," she said, waving him to a nearby chair. "You must be tired and famished after such a long day. Could I get Harriet to provide you with some refreshment, a glass of mulled wine or some more substantial fare?"

Where was Hugo Jones and why did she desire this private meeting? He was brought back from his reverie by the ensuing silence and expectant expressions on the two women's faces.

"Oh, … er… a glass of mulled wine will be sufficient, milady."

Harriet curtsied and left, closing the door behind her. The Dean let his eyes wander. A single place was set at a small table holding the remnants of a meal, with a glass containing the dregs of what he surmised was wine. A single bed stood at the far end of the room. He glanced around until his eyes rested on the door; a key was in the lock. Harriet returned carrying an amply filled glass of mulled wine, and departed. David Carshall looked at Katherine, who was watching him closely. She seemed relaxed yet he detected something in her demeanour, her eyes indicating a vulnerability. Seizing the initiative, he spoke first:

"How are you keeping, Lady Katherine? And your husband?"

"We are both well and in good spirits, Dean," Katherine replied.

"I must congratulate both you and your husband on a likely addition to your family, milady."

"Thank you, Dean."

"How can I be of … service, Lady Katherine?"

"Do you believe that there is a God, Dean?"

In a sense the question was not an unfamiliar one, as a Low Churchman was frequently faced with the same question posed by others. Yet he was unprepared for such a question so early in the meeting. It was unusual in his experience for a lady, especially one titled, to open the discussion without a conventional exchange of courtesies.

"Of course I do, milady. But why ask me of all people?"

"Because you are the spiritual shepherd of the parish."

Well put, he thought, but surely she hasn't sent for me to ask me such a fundamental question, unless there's a problem between her and God. He nodded, waiting.

"Although I may be counted among your parishioners, I do not disbelieve that a God could exist, who could be, if he exists, a God of love. My parents, as you know, attend St. Bartholomew's regularly and I have followed their example, in conformity with their wishes. However, since my marriage, I have experienced an intangible feeling, though some would put it down to some kind of female intuition or an overactive imagination, that there could be a God who *exists* and if so may be interested in us."

The words "since my marriage" resonated in his ears. How had her attitude to and feelings about God coincided with her marriage? Perhaps the connection would soon be revealed, something to do with her relationship that had motivated her to search for what many yearned for? He suspected that Katherine's change of heart had some connection with her marriage to Hugo Jones. He put aside his curiosity for the time being.

"People have longed for a personal encounter with Him, whate'er their motives…"

Katherine's cheeks flushed. The Dean pressed on:

"May I ask you, in confidence, milady, what has prompted you to seek after God?"

The Dean realised immediately that the question was blatantly out of order and he had unwittingly stepped beyond the bounds of social convention.

"You and I know that there are certain matters both private and personal within a marriage. If such a God exists, it would give me great peace of mind and even a desire to get to know him."

Katherine's last words touched a chord of empathy and understanding of why she had sent for him. She wanted help beyond human availability – from God Himself!

"Yes, Lady Katherine, I can vouch that He reveals Himself to those who earnestly seek Him. If I told you that God is more than willing to meet your need, it is true, but it has to be on His terms. After all, He made us in His image, but we've sinned and fallen below His standards. However, He has made a way back to Himself by sending His Son to pay the full price for our sin. Without the help of Christ, we cannot receive anything from God in exchange for what we have, what we do or what we are.

The Dean paused. Katherine was listening intently and made no comment.

"We all must acknowledge our unworthiness as created but fallen beings before a perfect Creator, and accept His forgiveness as a free gift…"

"Are there any circumstances in the eyes of God which bar a person from receiving God's forgiveness and love?"

David Carshall was taken aback, yet there could, he thought, be a connection between her question and her marital relationship with Hugo Jones.

"The Christ referred to one unforgiveable sin, but otherwise, forgiveness is always available to the repentant in this age of grace."

The Dean probed.

"Have you any particular sin in mind?"

"Would forgiveness, then, be available to one who has been unfaithful to their spouse?"

"If the offending partner is desirous of forgiveness and seeks to make restitution for such a sin and in so doing seeks reconciliation with the other party and God." Then,

"Can I help you in this matter, milady?"

Again the Dean felt that he might have appeared to lack sensitivity and have breached social etiquette, but if he was to be able to offer spiritual help, then he needed to know what hindered the lady's desire to receive God's forgiveness and love. He waited for her to answer. An intangible look in her eyes signalled 'no further'.

"I believe that you have answered my question adequately, Dean," she said, closing any further discussion on that subject.

David Carshall prepared to rise.

"But I have a further question to put to you – are there *any* justifiable grounds for one party in a marriage to leave the other?"

Now he strongly suspected why Lady Katherine had sent for him. He'd heard with half an ear the rumours that all was not well at Home Farm; Hugo Jones's heavy drinking and violent temper, and gossip of the two living separate lives in the farmhouse. Perhaps her search for God and her desire to leave Hugo were connected; on the one hand, a hunger for love, on the other, a desire for the same ill-afforded by her marriage.

"There are two recognised phases in a breakdown of marriage – one is separation and the other divorce. But the Word of God only speaks of one justifiable reason for the latter and that is the adultery of one or both parties."

"Is that the only ground?"

"That's what the Son of God told His disciples."

Katherine did not respond.

"I'm sure that you appreciate the prevailing attitude of today's society towards a wife's infidelity (not a husband's! thought Katherine). Even to leave one's husband on the grounds of his adultery would be frowned upon by a wife's contemporaries, Lady Katherine…"

"So a marriage made in heaven in the eyes of the Church becomes a marriage made in hell for one partner because adultery is the only ground to release that innocent party from such an existence? Surely there must be other grounds for separation or divorce, Dean?"

Lady Katherine had a clear grasp of the issues involved and a perception he had never discerned in a member of the opposite sex. The Dean was aware of the inadequate answer he'd given; he'd no solution in mind. Even though unmarried, he was aware of the blessing that God could bestow on a couple, but he knew with sorrow the curse of an unhappy marriage. As a man who had taken Holy Orders, he must uphold the sanctity of marriage and discourage break-ups, but he knew in his heart that separation or divorce even in the extreme case might free the weaker partner from a life of escalating misery and tyranny. He loathed the pretentiousness of a society that turned a blind eye to a husband's philandering and ill-treatment of his spouse. He was at a loss to offer any counsel which would resolve her dilemma. Perhaps, though, he could help her in her search for God.

"God is not far from any of us, for in Him we live and move and have our being, Lady Katherine," said the Dean.

"If he is so near, then why don't I know him, Mr. Carshall?"

"It is a matter of commitment, milady."

"What do you mean by commitment?"

"Firstly, you need to acknowledge your need for forgiveness, Lady Katherine."

"Why, Mr. Carshall?"

"Because His Word tells us that all of us have sinned against Him and fallen short of His standards. And secondly, that Jesus Christ His Son died on a cross to pay the price for our sins in order to be forgiven."

Katherine did not immediately respond. Perhaps I've moved too quickly for her, pondered the Dean.

"How can I know that this is true, Dean?"

"Only you can know by committing yourself to it in faith," David Carshall replied.

Again, there was a moment of silence.

"Will you help me?"

At the Dean's leading, Katherine opened her heart and prayed to the God she now believed in.

CHAPTER TEN

Wychcombe Workhouse

December 20th

"I think that Wicks 'aint coming back, so I'm kicking his missus and litter out – they'll have t' walk to the workhouse and we can get Mistress Scragwell to watch out fer Wicks going round, father," announced Hugo.

Winter had gathered strength, with heavy snowfall and frosts taking an icy grip on the countryside. Hugo sent two of his retainers to the tied cottage with the instruction that they must find other shelter the following day, taking only what sparse belongings they had. Hugo had already sent a warning to the labourers in other tied cottages that on no account must the Wicks be given food or shelter.

Two burly men broke into the cottage without knocking.

"Ye've got 'til dark today to get out wiv yer belongings," one said, "and don't expect charity from any of yer friends, cos they'll be kicked out if they give ye any food or shelter. Master Hugo has warned us ... so ye'd better be on yer way."

"Bu ... but me childer'll get consumption if they have to go out in this weather. And little Hezekiah is very poorly as it is. Have pity on us," Bess begged.

At this, the children began to weep.

At this heartbreaking scene, the two men were silent for a moment. Then the eldest gathered himself.

"We've our orders to see ye off the farm, but we'll see if we can gather a few tatties and some bread for ye to eat on the morrow. Ye can stay here tonight but ye'll have to leave before nightfall tomorrow."

That night Bess tossed and turned, though her children slept deeply. They were all awakened at dawn by a tap on the cottage door. Mrs. Walling entered and closed the door quietly behind her.

"Shhh!" she hissed as the children woke. "Here's some vittles for ye to keep your stomachs filled today, and a bottle o' cider fer ye, Bess," she added, placing a small sack of provisions on the earth floor.

Next day Bess and her three children were forced out of the tied cottage with little more than the clothes they wore, the children weeping as they clung onto their mother. Bess had wondered why, for weeks after Josh's disappearance, the Joneses had not evicted her and the children but now she realised their cruel intentions had been to let them live in hope that they could have shelter (and whatever food they gathered through the winter). The family departed in the afternoon; wind howled around mother and children. Bess shivered and pulled her shawl tighter around her. Hezekiah coughed again, his sunken eyes projecting the suffering of a sick child without respite– no medicine, little food and threadbare

70

clothes. His two siblings slipped their arms around him every time the coughing commenced.

"Can't we get some 'elp, mum?" Abigail piped. "We're goin' to lose Hezekiah afore we gets to the workhouse."

Bess wiped her eyes.

"Let's thank God he 'aint dead, Abi, and that Mrs. Walling be helping us wiv taters and jugged hare."

"But where's Dad, muvver? We need him to help us."

Bess struggled to control her emotions. Joshua was still free but hunted by the Joneses, unable to reach them. They were being watched the by Joneses' men in the hope that they would catch Joshua sneaking back to see his wife and children.

Bess picked up and carried Hezekiah's wasted body down the track from Home Farm towards the southern connecting road between Dorset and Bridport. His tiny body heaved with racking coughs. She tightened her threadbare shawl around him, shielding him as much as the shawl sheltered them from the icy blast. Abigail and Thomas ran and stumbled behind her, holding hands, with pinched faces, and red noses and ears accentuating their coldness.

Through watering eyes, Bess could see the grey huddled stone buildings of Wychcombe. They passed the broken gate to the gleys, almost slipping on the ice-covered black water that seeped where it thawed across the road and into the Bredey.

"Keep up, me loves!" shouted Bess over the howling wind, not looking back but assuming that her two other children were close. The sky had darkened, heavy with approaching snowclouds.

"Hurry!" Bess cried, breaking into an unsteady run, her tattered skirt swirling, twisting and hindering each step she took. Holding her ailing son to her with an arm and holding the sack of provisions with her hand , she grabbed the folds of her skirt with her other hand and lifted it to free her leg movement, stumbled and fell, protectively dropping her skirt and gripping Hezekiah with both arms to save him, but hitting her face on the frozen ground. Momentarily shaken, she rose.

"Oh mum, you're bleeding!" shrieked Abigail above the howling gale.

Bess touched the hot blood coursing then quickly congealing on her temple. She nearly swooned, then sat down, cradling Hezekiah. Her two children ran and put their arms about her, uncaring that her blood stained their faces too. The four lay together, as if frozen by the merciless gale, snowflakes gliding down their faces, melting on contact, leaving a glistening, quickly replaced by more flakes.

"Come on dears, we must get to the workhouse afore we fall asleep and die o' cold."

The pathetic little group stumbled past the village hamlets, lambent yellow lights flickering through windows transforming snowflakes like fading stars. The greystone bulk of St. Bartholomew's church loomed out of a curtain of whirling snowflakes. Heads down, the four travellers approached the workhouse, so close to the church that it appeared to be part of it, until Bess and Hezekiah,

Abigail and Thomas turned the corner of the road to face an uneven cobblestoned yard in front of a massive stone wall lit by a single lantern hanging from tall, rusted iron gates, making a prison-like vista. By the side of the gate in the wall was a recess, inside which resided a rusted iron handle.

Bess staggered to the gate, felt for the recess and pulled on the handle … the harsh ring woke up Hezekiah. They peered through the gates, waiting, the ice and snow forgotten. In the distance, a door opened and light flooded the cobblestoned workhouse yard, silhouetting a stooped, hunchbacked figure, her shoulders covered in a shawl, her face's dull eyes, beaklike nose, wrinkled face and thin, bloodless lips ending in a bewhiskered jaw.

"Heh! Heh!" gasped the crone, rattling a bunch of keys in a trembling hand as she tottered towards them, "Abandon hope all ye who enter here!" she mouthed, then gave a creaky laugh as she tried key after key in the rusty lock until it clicked open. She pulled on the gate which creaked open.

"Cum in! Cum in! Afore ye catches yer death o' cold!" she cackled, almost closing and locking the gate on Abigail and Thomas, then tottering ahead of them towards a distant building.

As the keyholder and Joshua's family approached the workhouse, a door swung open, its light partly obliterated by the ample form of a woman, her appearance from mob cap, shawl, gown and polished boots exuding a coarse authority. Suddenly, she raised her hand, with podgy fingers grasping a cane, an action which caused the children to shrink back.

"Stop!"

Small eyes in puffy lids, devoid of any glimmer of compassion, eyed Bess and the children for what seemed like an eternity to them. She saw Bess's bloodstained temple and cheeks but made no comment.

"Jus' as I thought. Wicks the murderer's brood! A murderin' coward who lets his family pay his debt to societee! Come in, me dears," the matron said, "an' I'll take whatever's in yer sack t'help yer wi' yer childer," the tone of her voice changing from threatening to wheedling. She stood aside to admit the family an entry, slapping the cane against her ample thigh.

Bess, in spite of the discomfort of her journey and fall, felt anger at the matron's reference to Joshua but thought better not to retort and was glad for the moment to get under shelter from the howling gale. The family waited as Mrs. Scragwell closed the door and propelled the gatekeeper along in front with a shove.

"Follow old Charlotte an' mind ye, I'm close behind!" she growled.

Charlotte tottered down the wet-stoned passageway, her unsteadiness causing the lantern light to swing, from one side to the other, enveloping the party in alternate darkness and light.

"Keep yon lantern steady, ye old faggot, or I'll give ye a taste of Sugar!" shouted Mrs. Scragwell, causing Charlotte to weave about all the more. It didn't take Bess long to conclude who or what 'Sugar' was!

Charlotte led the way down the stone tunnel towards the sound of a distant clatter and muted voices, then through a massive open door into a hall illumined by lanterns hanging from the ceiling at intervals of about a dozen feet above long benches at which were seated scores of women of all ages and sizes, their faces stamped with faded, weary expressions of resignation. Each sat scooping up and consuming the contents of a bowl, heads lowered as Charlotte, Bess, the children and Mrs. Scragwell carried on between the benches and through a door into a continuation of the stone passageway they'd left.

The sight, smell and sounds of the dining room made the children's tummies rumble, their heads turned back and eyes appealing.

"Tea's over, breakfast tomorrow for ye all, pity ye didn't make it in time," the matron barked.

Charlotte stopped, opened a faded wooden door and stood, lantern held aloft whilst Mrs. Hannah Scragwell roughly pushed the family into a cold room, bare but for two bedsteads covered by a single, stretched thin canvas sheet. In the corner was a privy.

"Ye'll sleep here and becos I'm kindhearted, yer kids can stay in this bedroom with ye. That scruffy snotty-nosed lad'll sleep with ye and the others in that other bed. Tomorrow I'll show ye, Mrs. Wicks, where everythin' is; you'll be working in the washroom whiles yer kids are at school. Oh, yes, the washroom fer ye all is down the corridor."

"Ye'll ha' t'sleep in yer clothes t'night. Charlotte'll find ye sheets t'morrow, if two of our inmates who're at death's door pass thro' to the other side afore then," she said matter-of-factly.

"Here's the kitchen, out of bounds fer all except the cooks and me and helpers. Come with me, Bess Wicks."

The matron led Bess along the passage. Condensed water dripped from wall to shiny cobbled floor made walking hazardous for Bess, trying to keep up with Mrs. Scragwell who was clearly used to hastening along.

"That's my room," the matron said, pointing to a large door, "and next door's my privy and bath, both completely out o' bounds."

They progressed through a dining room, beer house, dormitories, workrooms where scores of women sat sewing, a hospice for the terminally ill, a storeroom for clothes, sheets and blankets, tools and wood for the fires, then the washroom.

"This is where ye'll be, Madame Wicks."

The matron's sarcasm was not lost on Bess.

"Ye'll be fitted out wi' proper clothes an' we'll burn yer stinkin' rags. There'll be no sickness here."

The following morning, Bess and the children were taken to a washroom where they washed with soap and water in zinc tubs, dried on ragged towels and changed into workhouse uniform, then hurried to the dining room. Abigail and Thomas held frail Hezekiah's hand as they filed with other children to sit at the long tables and, after lengthy prayers, to await their turn to collect their bowls and receive watery gruel from the vat served by Mrs.

76

Scragwell herself. The children were dismissed to attend school. Bess had been conducted to the women's quarters for breakfast and to work in the washroom, boiling clothing in the vast coppers.

That night, after a tea of bread and cheese washed down with watery tea, the Wicks children joined their mother. The following days became routine, Bess and the children thankful that they had a roof over their heads and food supplied by the parish workhouse. But things were about to change.

Hugo thought that by bribing Mrs. Hannah Scragwell to ill-treat the Wicks family and let it leak out and reach the ears of the Gomers and their workers then if Wicks was in hiding there, he would surely appear.

"Mum, the gruel be so salty, it burns our mouths," cried little Abigail. Bess gazed at three pairs of watery eyes, felt their pain and searched for a way to stop what she suspected was an abuse of her children. They were separated from her at breakfast time until that evening and, to worsen matters, the other children did not appear distressed at breakfast. Bess determined to discover how the children were being poisoned and at the same time try to prevent it. It wouldn't be easy to doctor her children's gruel with salt without being seen if they were served separately.

"When ye go for breakfast, don't be served together. Go behind one of the other children and watch if the matron puts somethin' else on her ladle afore ladling the gruel and just have a little taste, Abigail. Make certain Mrs. Scragwell sees ye watchin her closely," she instructed her eldest child, "then just have a little taste. It may be that you watching her'll put her off poisoning yer food, if that's what she's doing."

The next morning, Abigail shuffled reluctantly towards the matron, who stood by the huge cauldron, complete with cane swinging in her left hand and a ladle in her right hand. When the child before her had been served and as Abigail approached, Mrs. Scragwell put down the cane, her left hand moving over the cauldron's rim. Abigail held out her tin plate for the gruel.

Mrs. Scragwell's gnarled, plump left hand moved out of sight and signalled with the ladle in her right hand for Abigail to extend her bowl, then advanced her left hand, took the bowl, poured in gruel and placed the plate by the cauldron. Abigail carefully watched Mrs. Scragwell hand it to her, wiping her left hand behind her skirt. Abigail looked at the gruel, then at Mrs. Scragwell, who in spite of her authoritarian stance, held the little girl's stare with difficulty. Mrs. Scragwell quickly ladled gruel into Hezekiah's bowl held in Abigail's other hand.

"Get on with ye! Don't stand staring at me, brat!" the matron spat at Abigail.

It was clear to Abigail that Mrs. Scragwell had not had time to add anything to Hezekiah's breakfast, so as she moved to a seat at the long, wooden table, she pretended to taste her serving, knowing that the matron's watchful eye was on her. Then she waited until her neighbour had wolfed his own portion down, then whispered to him, "Oi ain't hungry, can ye eat mine?"

The boy needed little encouragement, exchanged her tin bowl for his and began to gobble down its contents. Moments later he grimaced and spat out what remained of his fourth mouthful. "Groogh! Wot's in this? Oi've bin poisoned!"

Abigail pretended not to notice, dipping her spoon in the boy's bowl. Small, cropped heads turned to look at Abigail's neighbour as he groaned, holding his abdomen, vomited into Abigail's bowl and collapsed onto the hard stone floor.

"Get the brat out o' here!" the matron screamed to one of her helpers, as Abigail sat quietly, holding the sick boy's empty bowl with an air of innocence. Abigail and Mrs. Scragwell knew, nevertheless, what had been planned and failed. Were others likely to suspect what she was up to? Mrs. Scragwell wondered. She rushed to the table as one of the helpers carried the boy away, grabbed what had been Abigail's bowl and took it back to the serving table.

That night Hezekiah, Abigail and Thomas clung to their mother, the children clearly terrified at what Abigail told Bess had transpired. They were the intended victims of an evil plot to poison them. Bess Wicks knew that they were between a rock and a hard place. What could she do to protect her little ones? The workhouse was little different from a prison. Without keys, there was no way out and it seemed that they were completely at the mercy of Mrs. Scragwell, who was intent on harming them. Bess concentrated; strengthened by a powerful maternal instinct, she viewed their prospects: escape was, clearly, at present, an impossibility. If her children refused the food offered to them because it could make them ill, they would starve. If only she could steal and hide away food or save much of her own rations, they might be able to survive. She had to save her children. Could she trust anyone to help them? Old Charlotte? She fell into an uneasy slumber, her children clinging to her on the bed.

The village clock chimed midnight.

"Here's the keys, ye old witch. Now lock up, 'specially the kitchen, or else some thieving beggar'll 'ave their mucky fingers on the vittles. An' come back 'ere sharpish with they keys. Now be off wi' ye!"

Cackling to herself, the aged crone shambled along the dark dripping passage, first inspecting the dining room, then the dormitories. She opened the door of the single dormitory where the Wicks family slumbered on, a smile cracking her wizened features. She closed the door but did not lock it. She progressed to each part of the workhouse, then leaving dormitory and hospice doors unlocked, proceeded to the kitchen, entered and spent several minutes checking the contents of the scullery, the ovens, the dead embers in the fireplace, looked in the bread bins and inspected the primed mousetraps. For reasons known only to herself, Charlotte also left the scullery and kitchen doors unlocked, but locked up the stores, sewing room and washroom.

Apparently satisfied that all was well on her tour of duty, she approached the matron's room, jangling the heavy bunch of keys, which gave her a feeling of power.

"But the ol' dragon 'll 'ave me hide if she ever found out thet oi wuz moonlighting – it'd be the death o' me," she mused.

She shrugged her skinny shoulders and opened the door.

"Yer keys, ma'am…"

Mrs. Scragwell lay slouched in front of a chair by a blazing fire, her snores loud and long. Her left hand held a half-empty whisky bottle, with her cane in the other. The ancient retainer withdrew and gently closed the door, deciding to hold onto the keys as long as possible to prolong her sense of power. After all, she could explain to the tyrant that she held onto the keys to safeguard them until the matron was awake and fit to receive them. Cackling with glee, she hurried to her cubicle.

CHAPTER ELEVEN

The Grenadier

The guardsman felt fortunate to have gained employment when thousands of fellow soldiers had been demobilised and discharged with no prospect of employment now that the war had ended and the prosperity it had brought to the land was over. He desired to meet the man whose life he'd saved six months previously. But how? And, he mused, why was he interested in meeting a man who was superior to him in rank and clearly an aristocrat. An impassable social barrier existed between a private soldier and a lieutenant. Perhaps his desire to meet Richard Gomer was fuelled by what he'd heard of the further misfortune he and his family had experienced since Waterloo. Had family misfortunes started before Lieutenant Richard came back? And there were so many rumours flying about concerning the enmity between his employer Hugo Jones and the Gomers; and the local vicar was said to have been murdered and his body dumped in a swamp on the Gomer Farm. Really, he felt for the lieutenant, if all the rumours were true … an enormous gambling debt, Lieutenant Gomer's father's death, their loss of Home Farm and, if local talk was true, an unfortunate 'coincidence' of loss of livestock.

John Parker, the guardsman, had heard that ex-Lieutenant Richard Gomer was in dire straits. His mother was critically ill and the Gomers had lost half their estate. It was rumoured that a debt repayment owed by the lieutenant's father to Hugo Jones's father Ezra had disappeared with Bowen Dranley, the Gomers' estate agent, whose demise had revealed no whereabouts of the money. The land of Wychcombe Farm was little that the Gomers had of the estate to eke a living from outwith the unforgiving soil of the gley meadow and poisonous swamp. Moreover, the Gomers had been linked with the death of the local vicar, whose body had been retrieved from the gley bog on Wychcombe Farm, and Hugo Jones had made no bones of his enmity to the Gomer brothers, especially the youngest son Giles. John had not met Ezra Jones's son, but heard that he could be a violent-tempered man who suffered from bouts of anger and depression following periods of heavy drinking.

John sighed, then continued hand-threshing the sound corn in the barn.

"Ye're in the Wicks' place, aren't ye, and wi' yer wife?" Abel asked, more a statement than a question.

"Aye, Abel," John answered, copying Abel's smooth powerful strokes and wondering where the conversation was going.

"Did ye know who lived there before ye?"

John and Anne had just moved into the Wicks' former cottage, with no notion of who the previous tenants had been. All he knew was that there had been signs of family life – a minute ragged vest used as a dishcloth, a cracked and broken cup and saucer, a cot with mouldy sheets, a bed, table, chairs, a headless doll and a wooden rattle.

"Nay – who did?"

"The Wicks'. Joshua, who turned poacher on the run an' is somewhere out there hiding from master Hugo. An' a wife an' litter be in Wychcombe work'us."

Not our problem, John thought. "Why are ye telling me this?"

"Just t' warn you that if ye take a wrong step wi' young Jones, ye'll end up like them!"

Guardsman John felt a twinge of anger, but mentally let it pass and carried on threshing. He was prepared to endure much to keep his job and a home for his wife and himself. A job and lodging were precious gifts to treasure, especially when so many fellow soldiers had returned from the wars looking vainly for gainful employment. However, he was curious about the recent rumours circulating in relation to the man whose life he'd saved at Hougoumont.

"Let's part the grain fro' the chaff. Here's your tool, Parker, I'll show ye what to do," Abel instructed. He handed John a long-handled wide-bladed shovel.

"'Ere, gimme a hand t' heft the corn up," Abel commanded, "Up, up, up."

For a considerable time, chargehand and labourer tossed generous shovelfuls of corn and chaff high in the air until the corn was piled in a massive heap on the barn floor, whilst the chaff were blown to another part of the barn. John's arm muscles felt detached from their sockets.

"Hoi! Ye can stop heftin'! Le's get this bit o' corn into yon sacks!" He nodded. "Ye've done well fer a new lad."

John smiled. His first wage would happily complete the week.

Joshua was pining over the enforced separation from his beloved Bess and the children. He felt totally helpless – a wanted criminal on the run (and his wife and children driven to take shelter in Wychcombe workhouse) without knowledge of his wife and family's whereabouts. This was why he'd ventured, at risk of capture, to creep into Home Farm and to the tied cottage he assumed they were still living in. He quietly approached the building, guided by lantern-light shining through the snow-framed window. He ducked below the window and exposure to the light and peered through a space between the grain sacking curtains. Huddled around the inglenook fire were two figures – from their appearance, a man and a woman. Blood rushed into Joshua's face in spasms of anger at the thought that one of them might be Bess. One figure moved toward the window. Joshua ducked back just before a woman's face pressed against the pane – it was not the face of Bess! He felt relief in one sense, but a cold feeling of despair in another. Where were Bess and the children? As he pondered, the woman turned and said something, then a man's face appeared with her at the window. It was that of a stranger to Joshua, and lantern-light glinted from the buttons on his coat epaulette and jacket. The man was wearing the crimson tunic of a soldier. Joshua moved away from the window, devastated by his observations. He mentally wrestled with the desire to reveal himself and question the pair on the whereabouts of his family, with his reluctance to betray his presence and risk the couple raising the alarm. On foot, he would be no match for a horse. In despair, he sat down in the steadily freezing snow and wept. The village clock pealed the strokes of eleven.

The icy wind was drifting snow up against the cottages. He must do something, now that he'd determined that Bess and the children were no longer in their tied cottage. He'd come this far with no clear opportunity that he could return safely to this farm in the near future. Exhausted and cold, the balance of his intention tipped in favour of risking discovery and pursuit by the Joneses and their retainers. He crept around the cottage until he had reached the door and gently tried the latch – the door opened slightly. Without hesitation, he opened the door, entered and closed it behind him and, standing in front of it, put a finger to his lips. Startled, the man and woman turned, for a split second transfigured by the sight of the snow-covered, wild-eyed figure, ice caking his bedraggled beard. The man grabbed a poker from by the fire and positioned himself between his female companion and Joshua.

"Wha..a, who are you, forcing yoursel' into our cottage?" he cried, brandishing the poker.

Joshua held up his hands, a friendly gesture indicating he was unarmed.

"Oi mean ye no harm and beseech ye not to tell anybody of me whereabouts. Oi once lived 'ere with me beloved wife Bess an' me childer, but we've been separated from one another. Tha's why oi've come back t' mak' certin' that they be still 'ere. An' now oi kin see they're gone."

At this, he burst into tears, a pathetic figure, his body wracked with huge sobs, grimy fists knuckling his deep-set eyes.

The uniformed man found his voice.

"Ye must be Wicks, the poacher, wanted by master Jones for murder an' poaching!"

"Oi murdered no-one, tho' I was wi' the gang o' poachers. Oi gave mesel' up once, but escaped to warn master Jones's neighbour of evil intent 'gainst them."

"What d'ye mean?" the man asked, looking at his wife, who had touched his arm.

"Let the man set himself by the warmth of the fire, husband; can't ye see he's in need of care? If he'd meant to harm us, he would have taken us by surprise," she cried, overcome with pity for Joshua's state.

Her husband pointed the poker to the inglenook, still warily holding the weapon.

"Sit thee down on that seat an' warm yersel', and my wife will warm up a brew for ye," he said.

Joshua hobbled over to the fire.

"D'ye know where my family are, sir?" Joshua asked.

"We heard that the master thrust yer wife and family out of this cottage an' left them t' make their way to the workhouse in Wychcombe."

CHAPTER TWELVE

Fire!

December 22nd

The night after Joshua's visit to the cottage now occupied by the guardsman and his wife, fire took hold and swept through the workhouse while the inmates slept. The roar of the flames mingled with the high-pitched screams of women and children, terrified by their hopelessness to escape from this prison of impregnable walls, locked doors and bars. Bess's children clung to her, their only rock in the inmates' panic-stricken rush to flee from an unimaginable death from the choking smoke and flames. Mrs. Scragwell was nowhere to be seen or heard. They knew that she was the only keyholder to all the doors, the only route to safety. The smallest child could not wriggle to freedom between the window bars, even where the heat had shattered the windowpanes. Bess focussed on the furthest point from the flames.

"Quick, loves!" she shouted above the raging inferno, screams and shouts, "Come with me!"

She led them through the dining room, down a passage and through a double door into the workhouse kitchen.

"Shut the door, Abigail," she commanded her

daughter. Bess looked around the kitchen. The floor was littered with pots, pans and fragments of food, the latter being devoured by two enormous rats, from which the children shrank away, but the rodents took no notice of them. Bess picked up a pan, ran to a waterpump in the kitchen corner and levered the handle. A trickle appeared which strengthened to a gushing outpour.

"Abigail, hold this pan below the spout whiles oi work the lever."

The eldest child placed the pan on the floor under the spout, which quickly filled.

"Now, loves, you must do exac'ly as oi say."

"But, Mum, how's this goin' t' 'elp us? Cain't us get out? We don't want t' die 'ere," Abigail sobbed.

"Oi know, dear, but first we need t' 'ave a shower. Now bring anuvver pot over 'ere, there's a good lass."

"A shower, mum? We ain't that dirty, mum," the three chorused.

Wisps of smoke began to curl under the kitchen door, where the yellow of approaching flames was reflected on the shiny stone floor. Bess, with Abigail's help, filled another pan.

"Now, childer, put yer arms round one annuver by the pump and close your eyes," Bess ordered.

The children clung together in shivering anticipation as water arced its way above their heads and down.

"Brrh!" was followed by peals of laughter as Bess upended a huge pan of water over herself.

"Now, we must run t'gether to the big door an' pray that it be unlocked. Now, I'll carry Hezekiah an' follow me but don' look behind."

If it is unlocked, well and good, but if it's locked what then? Bess thought, and almost immediately dismissed the thought of dying in the workhouse from her mind; the thought of facing snow and ice soaked to the skin was infinitely preferable to being burned alive inside the workhouse. There was no time for such thoughts; they must get out.

The bedraggled little group stumbled through the door, water dripping from their clothes to become steam on the hot floor. They ran in crocodile file holding the clothes of the one in front, Bess leading with Hezekiah in her arms. The earlier screams had died out. Bess ran on, praying that Mrs. Scragwell had unlocked the main door. They ran through the Stygian darkness of the stone passageway to the huge main door. She tried the handle – locked. Her shoulders slumped; the way out barred and a distant roar signalled the inferno's approach. The fire had passed the kitchen. Bess pulled her children around her – if they had to die, they would go together. Bess closed her eyes and prayed soundlessly as the children sobbed with fear. Suddenly her prayers were interrupted by cries of fright from her children. Bess opened her eyes; a ghostly figure with a blackened face, wearing a ragged dress from which smoke emitted, approached coughing as she shook a huge bunch of keys. It was Charlotte, pursued by a crowd of inmates with children. She unlocked the door and pushed it open. A welcome icy draught swept over the hacking, smoke-blackened inmates.

"Quick! This way! 'urry afore the fire catches us or the work'us tumbles on us!" the crone screeched at the inmates as they scrambled to the door.

Bess sent up a prayer of thanks for their rescue. How Charlotte had the keys was irrelevant, as was the question of Mrs. Scragwell's whereabouts. They were safe for now.

On hearing the roar of the workhouse fire, the Dean of St. Bartholomew's hurried to the square fronting the blazing building, where a large crowd of workhouse residents and Wychcombe villagers mingled together. Women and children and a smaller number of old men from the workhouse huddled closely, many coughing and retching, smoke rising from their clothes and hair to form wispy clouds slowly floating and dispersing into the freezing air. Villagers and farmers, farm workers and a few farmers on horseback or driving horse-drawn wagons had already joined the crowd that extended beyond the square. No attempt was made to try to quell the blazing holocaust, the flames had too strong a grip on the building, now a shell containing the flames. If anyone else was still inside, they were as good as dead, and Mrs. Scragwell was nowhere to be seen.

The crowd suddenly parted to admit the tall cleric, a commanding figure dressed in a long black cloak over shiny black boots, raven hair blowing in the cold wind, who walked towards the burning building and then turned to address the crowd.

"All those of ye from the workhouse – women and

children," he shouted, and, as an afterthought, "ye men as well, ye cannot stay here to catch your death of cold. Ye must come inside the church for rest and shelter…"

He had hardly spoken these words when people began to run out of the square. The Dean held up his hands to quell the rush.

"Wait! Any of you parishioners from the village who are present, please supply whate'er food ye can and spare bedding for these poor folks, and be so kind as to let any who need to use your privies. We will use the pews as beds and the prayer cushions as pillows. Women and children first; make an orderly line and follow me."

The crowd cheered above the roar of the flames.

"Come on Bess, at least we've got a roof o'er our heads an' perchance some vittles too," a woman called.

Bess hesitated. Was this an opportunity to free themselves? But where could they go? Who would take them? And where was Josh, and would they all ever be together once again? Bess felt that they were little better off than if the fire had never happened. There was no refuge outside to go and hide, Josh on the run, Hezekiah frail and sickly and all this in freezing weather. Who could help them? Or would?

"Come on, Bess Wicks. What's keepin' ye?" the same woman cried, hastening towards the lights of the church with scores of women and children.

"Come on, Bess," an elderly woman advised her, "they'll want to move us to another work'us soon, oi reckon, but let's get inside the chapel 'til then."

Bess nodded, gathered her retinue together and followed the old lady into the church behind the Very

Reverend David Carshall. Candles and lanterns lit up the interior and two blazing braziers had been strategically placed at front and rear. A group of public-spirited villagers led workhouse inmates to their cottages. Some time later, the latter emerged with bedding, joining the ragtag, untidy crowd of all genders, and stumbled into St. Bartholomew's, already opened by a verger, who directed the people into the church, followed by villagers carrying bread and cheese and jugs of ale.

"It's loike feeding ye five thousand," the verger growled, as the villagers broke and apportioned the bread and cheese to outstretched hands and placed the jugs of ale on the communion table.

Supplied with old sheets, blankets and clean sacking, the workhouse women bedded their children down fully clothed on the pews, improvising the prayer cushions as mattresses and pillows, or on piles of straw taken from the nativity scene spread on the floor, then laid themselves between the pews. Bess placed Abigail and Thomas on a pew as near to one of the braziers as possible, sensibly avoiding the use of straw, covered Hezekiah and herself in a blanket and laid down by the pew.

The Dean surveyed the recumbent figures; in spite of the tragic outcome of the workhouse fire, he smiled at the sight of so many smoke-blackened faces peeping out from borrowed sheets, sacks and blankets. His thoughts turned to other issues: Did anyone perish in the fire? Would any records of inmates and staff have been rescued? He suspected that the answers would be yes and no respectively. Where could these people be properly accommodated? They couldn't stay in the church for long. They would need to be properly washed, fed and freshly clothed. Where could they go and how would they be transported?

A rough hand closed on Bess's mouth.

"Quiet, m'dear, m'love."

Bess turned and buried her face in his, her lips finding his for what seemed an eternity, their bodies merged willingly in spite of their soaked garments.

"How did ye find out we were 'ere, Josh?" she whispered.

"A hired hand livin' in ower old tied cottage tol' me ye were all 'ere in the work'us an' the fire were seen fer miles, so oi crept over from the Gomer farm an' waited until dark an' ye were bedded down."

Bess held on to Joshua, her body wracked with sobs, but shedding tears of joy.

"Whate'er we goin' t' do, Josh? You an outlaw an' us nowhere t' live, now that yon work'us 'as gone up in flames?"

"They beadles will send the lot o' ye to Stalebrook," Josh replied.

The two talked in whispers whilst the inmates slept on until the gathering dawn light sent rays through the stained glass.

"Oi mus' go now or else oi'll be arrested, but will find a way to get us all out o' the mess oi've got us into."

94

With one last lingering kiss and a quick look at the children, he was gone.

The next morning Bess and the children sat in the pew eating bowls of warm gruel supplied by the villagers. One of the poorhouse women sat next to Bess opposite to the children.

"Oi 'ere thet we could finish up at Stalebrook Poor'ouse 'cos Wychcombe will nary be fit fer usin' and Stalebrook be the nearest one from 'ere. 'ow we'll get from 'ere is in the lap o' the gods. An' Stalebrook be a pretty poor place t' live in, so oi hear. There be a lot o' poor livin' there in hovels at the back of yon workhus."

Bess shivered. Her companion continued:

"Worse than that, oi hear – three women and their childer all in one bed. Parish officers don' care. Sheep an' cattle be better looked after. Even dogs have clean dry sacking to sleep on. Pity Wychcombe burned down. At least we got a warm bed an' hot gruel. Miz Scragwell were the on'y problem. Anyways, she be probably dead."

Bess moved away. Come what may, she must survive to protect her offspring until Josh found a way to get them clear and in a safe place.

Bess viewed their future home at Stalebrook with foreboding for the future. The dark stone building towered above them, its dusty narrow windows dimming the candlelit rooms.

"Whoa!" cried the leading driver to his horses, and each cart drew to a halt; "we're here at Stalebrook, yer new home," he announced.

The weary passengers removed their sacking covers. The driver dismounted from his seat at the front of the cart, walked to the rear of the wagon, unfastened the tailboard ties and gently helped Bess and her three children onto the snow-covered cobblestones. The other wagons emptied, as tired, stiff and cold women and children were lifted from them and congregated together outside the massive open gates.

"This way!" the lead driver shouted, pointing to the building, then with the other drivers, led the stumbling, shivering crowd of women and children through a courtyard towards the waiting party of workhouse staff holding lanterns and standing outside the huge front door to receive them. The party passed through the doors into the workhouse, unaware that Joshua Wicks was concealed in the shadows, watching the arrival of Bess and the children. Anticipating the transfer of his family from the burnt-down workhouse at Wychcombe, he had preceded them to Stalebrook village and watched them with tears and a heavy heart, but he was determined not to abandon them. He was unaware, however, that he also was under scrutiny.

Joshua fought like a tiger, but three to one was too much even for a strong labourer, inured by years of toil and now used to living rough. He downed two men with his fists but a blow to the back of his head ended his struggles. Securely held and dragged to his feet, he faced his former employer. Assured that the worker could not fight back, Hugo dismounted, spat in Joshua's face and subjected him to a cowardly attack which continued until Hugo was exhausted. Joshua doubled up under the storm of blows and kicks, blood streaming from his nose and lips; searing pain knifed through his stomach. He slumped to his knees and was lowered to the ground. Hugo remounted.

Josh was helpless, pinned down by two burly henchmen.

"Ha! I knew where t' find ye once they carted yer missus to Stalebrook."

Hugo, looking down from his horse, stared meaningfully at one of Joshua's captors. Joshua cried out as a hobnailed boot cracked a lower rib.

Another glance from Hugo to one of the henchmen and a clenched fist sent reverberations through his head. At a signal, Joshua was hauled to his feet, then doubled up from a kick to his solar plexus.

"There's more to come afore ye be tried fer murder and hung, Wicks!" snarled Hugo, "then I'll deal wi' yer friends the Gomers!"

At an order from Hugo, the two thugs tied Joshua's legs, dragged him to a waiting flatbed wagon and driver and threw him onto its bare floor. Hugo spoke to the two henchmen, who boarded the wagon and sat on either side of Joshua. Hugo unhitched his horse from the wagon.

"Dorchester prison, driver!" Hugo shouted as he rode the gelding behind the wagon.

The jury at Dorchester Assizes had already found Joshua guilty of being an accessory to the murder by shooting of Stanford, the Jones's gamekeeper. Witnesses included the deceased man's fellow gamekeepers, who also testified to Joshua's help for Simeon the injured gamekeeper and Hugo Jones. The judge bent over his papers for a moment; the courtroom was deathly silent, waiting for the inevitable – death by hanging. Grim-faced, he looked up.

"Joshua Wicks, have you anything to say on behalf of yourself before I pass sentence?"

"Only, yer Honour, sir, that I played no part in the shooting."

"Has anyone anything to say on behalf of the prisoner before I pass sentence?"

He looked around the courtroom. Then, as he reached for his black cap, Richard stood up.

"Your honour, may I speak?"

"Who are you, I pray?"

"I am Richard Gomer of Wychcombe Farm and formerly Home Farm, about eight miles west of here."

"Well, sir, what's that to do with the prisoner?"

"He worked for us, then for our neighbours the Joneses when they took over Home Farm from us. I'm aware that he was part of a gang of poachers seeking to provide for his family, as he was unable to keep them on his meagre wages. He harmed no-one, and was an honest and industrious worker. As a chargehand, he could be trusted to pull his weight, your Honour."

"But if he was working for your family, why would he want to poach?"

"He was not poaching whilst employed by us, as I testified just now, your Honour, but for the Jones family."

At this emphasis, there was a stir in the courtroom and a buzz of conversation rippled through the assembly, at which the judge banged his gavel.

"Mr. Gomer, this man has been rightly convicted of being part of a gang of poachers who murdered one gamekeeper and seriously injured another, so what is the point you're making?"

"Your Honour, though Joshua Wicks was part of the gang, he sought to relieve the injury to the gamekeeper caught in his own gintrap and he carried no weapon. He is at heart a good man, trying to support his family to alleviate their poverty. I appeal to your Honour for mercy even if you decide to exercise justice for his part in the poaching."

"Mmm … thank you for pleading on his behalf, Mr. … er … Gomer, but the law must take its course. The evidence of his participation in this poaching venture cannot be challenged, even though he may have found himself the unwitting member of such a dangerous band. What you have testified on his behalf opens up mitigating circumstances, I grant you. I had in mind to have him executed as an accomplice to murder, but on yours and the testimony of the gamekeepers to the help he gave one of them, and your testimony to his previous good character, the alternative would be transportation. However, to send such an able-bodied man to Van Diemen's Land for the minimum term of seven years would constitute a waste when men are needed to do worthwhile work in our country, so I've decided to commute the original sentence I had decided upon, to seven years' hard labour in the Portland Bill quarries."

"Thank you, your Honour, it will offer hope to this man that he can return to his family, when he's paid his debt to our society," Richard replied.

"Yes, yes," the judge added impatiently, then:

"Officers, take the prisoner down!"

CHAPTER THIRTEEN

Patrick McAlerty

A shadowy figure approached Wychcombe farmhouse. All was silent indoors; the farm dogs Bruce and Sando were shut in the barn to guard the grainstores. The figure staggered to a window and tapped a tattoo on it. Bruce growled. The intruder continued to tap without response, then the air was rent with the dogs' bloodcurdling howls. Lantern light shone through a bedroom window, illuminating Berkeley's bleary-eyed face at the glass. The lantern light disappeared and moments later the front door was partly opened, the light exposing the intruder, who staggered to the door and fell over the threshold.

Christmas Eve 1816

"Ha' maircy on me, zur, I be asking fer yer maister's forgivenesss an 'oi've something' important t' tell 'em".

"Who are you to be awakening this household at this unholy hour?" demanded Berkeley.

"Oi'm Patrick McAlerty frae Ireland, hired with three

mates by Maister Jones o' Destro Farm. Afore oi clears off oi've something' to tell yer maisters".

Berkeley hesitated.

"Fer pity's sake, don' send me away," the pitiful ragged creature whined, coughing.

"What's afoot at this hour Berkeley, and who is this?" demanded Giles, appearing behind the old retainer.

"There's a vagrant asking to speak to both of you, sir," Berkeley replied.

"Let him in and take him to the kitchen, then we'll see what he's about."

Giles reappeared with Richard, grimly eyeing one of the four thugs who had attacked him. Berkeley escorted the Irish tinker to the scullery, then emerged with McAlerty holding a dish of bread and cheese. Berkeley pointed McAlerty to a wooden bench by the kitchen fire, placed his lantern on the chipped old oak table and stood by the kitchen door.

Patrick blurted out what he had told Berkeley, then burst into prolonged coughing.

"You can't stay here on our premises, even if we decided not to give you your just deserts for waylaying me," Giles grated.

"All I ask is that ye don' give me up, becos' maister Jones will kill us fer the money. Have maircy on me, zurs."

"I'll give ye some victuals and a noggin, but ye'll have to find your own way out of the mess ye seem to be in before Hugo Jones finds you," Giles replied.

"But oi don' ha' the money!"

Giles and Richard looked at each other.

"What money?" the brothers demanded in unison.

"Lots o' money! Shaun found a fortune buried in a tin in a haybarn at Home Farm when 'e wuz burying a mug 'e stole from the Penny Farthin'."

"Where is the money now?"

"When we were 'unted by you sirs, we hid it in the vicar's coffin t' pick up later an' split up. Oi went back later, but the money was gone. Oi don' know who has it, but oi suspect' yon man takin' the place of the dead vicar might know something, becos 'e were the last mortal to see vicar's body afore the lid were nailed down."

Patrick burst into another bout of coughing. Berkeley looked at Richard, who nodded; Berkeley motioned Patrick to sit down.

"Very well; fetch the man a drink," Richard ordered.

"Thank 'ee kindly, zur," whispered the Irishman.

He gulped down the ale with shaking hands, liquid spilling down his stubbly chin, neck and grimy neckerchief, drained the glass and wiped his mouth with a ragged coat cuff.

"Oi reckon, zurs, that someone else found the money in the vicar's coffin."

The two brothers realised that the money that the Irishman was talking about was more than likely their father's debt repayment which Hugo Jones and Bowen Dranley had stolen and that this Irishman had no knowledge of this.

"Why are you telling us all this?" demanded Giles.

"Becos' oi felt that you gentlemen would help me keep out of maister Jones's clutches."

"How?" questioned Richard.

"By givin' me shelter fer this night an' food fer me to

keep goin' until oi'm free of this land and get passage out of it."

"But how, when ye have no money?"

"Oi'll find a way, but first oi wanted to put the matter straight about the money. Oi knew where we left it, but it's gone an' it can't be me or me mates who's tekken it. Perhaps the churchwarden found the money in the sack under the vicar's remains. Oi, like Seamus and Shaun, knew where we hid the money, so oi opened the coffin an' found nuthin'!"

Richard was confused. The Irishman seemed sincere, but could he be trusted? Why had he bothered to come to the farm and risk not only a beating but arrest and imprisonment for theft? Of greater significance would be the implication of the Irishmen finding the money at Home Farm and an explanation would be required from the Joneses for its existence there.

"So the money had gone, but how can you know that a churchman had taken it?" queried Richard.

"Who else, zur?" They would be in charge of the vicar's funeral an' they would have overseen the vicar's remains put in the coffin and ha' seen later the body disturbed after we put the sack o' money under it and when the coffin were sealed. Then he would have heard about the fight in the graveyard ye know all about that, and have opened the coffin an' found the sack o' money."

"Other people were involved in the preparations and the committal; the verger, undertaker and his men, to name a few," Giles said.

"Aye, zur, whoever were closest to the vicar and would ha' been the last soul to see the vicar's remains into the box."

The brothers were aware of the validity of McAlerty's

reasoning. Could a church official have been the graverobber? If so, the money he was holding was surely their father's and now theirs.

"What about your companions in crime?" Giles demanded, "could any one of them have stolen the money for themselves?"

Patrick shook his head vigorously.

"Nay, zur. I heard that Dermot's a cripple on Home Farm at the mercy of master Hugo; Seamus be dead an' Shaun took off fer Bridport to wait fer Seamus and me to meet him there, split the cash and find a boat to Americky," Patrick replied.

The brothers were silent. If the Irishman was right and someone connected to the church held the money, how could they reclaim what they were convinced was theirs? But if he had not taken it, who had? How much could they rely on this vagabond?

Their thoughts were interrupted by another of Patrick's coughing bouts.

"Ye can stay the night, considering the hour. And count yourself fortunate that you have not been given a good thrashing for you and your companions-in-crime's attack on Giles. But be gone tomorrow and take yourself as far from here as possible. Say nothing to anyone of your visit here. We have no money to give you, but you can have some bread and cheese from the scullery and sleep here in front of the fire".

Patrick fell down at Richard's feet weeping, took Richard's hand and held it between trembling fingers.

"God bless ye, zurs. Oi will be ever thankful fer yer kindness, and if there's any favour oi can do…"

"That's enough, man," Richard interrupted, snatching his hand away, repelled by McAlerty's slobbering. "Berkeley will attend to your needs."

CHAPTER FOURTEEN

Christmas Day

Next morning, Giles rose, washed, dressed and entered the kitchen; the Irishman had gone and the scullery door was wide open. Giles peered inside. The cold roasted joint of beef destined for the day's lunch and a loaf of bread had disappeared. A flagon of ale from which McAlerty had been served the previous night was almost empty. Well, the ruffian's gone well-provisioned and without a good-bye, strange when he seemed panic-stricken at the threat of being put out last night, Giles thought.

Richard appeared.

"Our lodger's gone, Richard, taking some of our provisions with him."

"Good fortune to him if he hopes to get away from the Joneses. We have other business to occupy us. We need to make our in-lamb ewes safe. It's probably a bit too early to bring them in yet, but I'm tempted to get Asa to drive them into the haybarn, we have much empty space there."

"We could have had McAlerty arrested and tried for sheepstealing, Richard."

"We shouldn't be worried about sheepstealing, with the Irishmen scattered", Richard replied.

"That's the attitude we took when Asa found the sheep

carcass and we discovered its remains on finding Seamus the ringleader dying in the copse, Giles. McAlerty and his friends are still at large."

"They're probably no longer a danger to us. Who else is there who could harm us?"

Giles left Richard's question unanswered.

For a man who had appeared at the end of his tether, Patrick McAlerty seemed to have miraculously recovered. He ran steadily along Wychcombe village street and disappeared from view behind St. Bartholomew's church building, passed through the lychgate, stopped by the deceased vicar's grave and looked around. Apparently satisfied that he had not been noticed, he knelt down, removed the turfs, brushed away the loose soil, lifted the coffin lid and pushed it over to expose the corpse's decomposing face. Steeling himself from the sight and the overpowering smell of decay, he extended his hands under the shroud. With a curse he withdrew his hand as a rat scurried from the coffin. He sucked his hand, exposing two puncture wounds, then plunged his other hand into the coffin and lifted out the corpse, exposing the sack. He opened it and removed two bundles of notes, closed the sack, divided each bundle into two and stuffed the notes into the pockets of his jacket. He replaced the corpse in the coffin, closed it, placed handfuls of soil and the turfs on top of it and fled.

Christmas Day was a non-event on the four neighbouring farms. Under normal circumstances, the Joneses, Goodboys and other invited guests would have enjoyed West Country hospitality together over the season. The Gomers were mourning the loss of their mother, and the owners of Copley had quarantined themselves to avoid the smallpox epidemic. No-one at Destro, Home, Copley or Wychcombe Farms had the heart to be festive. Hugo and Ezra were not on speaking terms over the loss of the gambling debt money and Ezra had vented his fury on Hugo by refusing to transfer ownership of Home farm to his son. His father's anger persuaded Hugo not to visit Destro Farm over Christmas.

Before nine o' clock on Christmas morning, Hugo was slouched over the kitchen table, hunched over his second bottle of claret when Harriet entered, gave a start, curtsied and went to the scullery. Several minutes later, she emerged carrying a tray holding plates and cutlery, a half loaf of bread, a butter dish, the remnants of a pheasant and a glass of wine as she passed him. Hugo gazed at her through bleary eyes, but took in her buxom figure and graceful movement as she exited the kitchen, the sound of her footsteps fading as she climbed the stairs. If he could not have his present satisfaction with Katherine, he would have her maid instead. He took a generous swig from the flagon and slumped over the table.

Richard Gomer had laid off their meagre staff for Christmas Day, apart from Thomas and Asa, who had refused to leave the cattle unmilked, and had ensured the herd and flock were checked and tended to before returning to their tied cottages. Giles had travelled on horseback to the Penny Farthing to drink the seasonal health of the villagers. In Wychcombe Farm kitchen, Richard looked at the fat-layered offering representing a cut from half a cold leg of venison, which almost demolished his jaundiced appetite. He was suddenly aware of a cold rush of air and colder snowflakes showering his neck and turned round to see Giles shaking his cap and grinning.

"I've a fine morsel of news to give you, brother of mine. McAlerty spent the best part of Christmas Eve at the Penny Farthing drinking porter – not ale, but porter! 'Drinks on me all round,' he'd shouted, 'Oi've come into a tidy legacy!'"

"Tidy legacy?" echoed Richard.

"The landlord and his barman carried the villain up to bed, once the publican had made sure that McAlerty had eno' to pay for his lodging."

Silence. Richard poked the petrified meat with his fork. The gambling debt, the disappearance of father's repayment money, the Irishmen carrying a mysterious load and its contents into the church, the struggle they had in the church cemetery, the brutal beating and death of Seamus, and Patrick McAlerty's visit to the farm. And now the Irishman was in possession of money he had disclaimed. Was the rogue's previous visit to the farmhouse a ruse to put them off the scent and flee unpursued?

"I wager that the villain has had some of father's money. Let's hunt him down, Richard."

"Wait, Giles! We don't know that the money the

scoundrel had is rightly ours, even though stolen from father by Dranley and Hugo Jones. I suggest we wait for the weather to settle before we visit the Penny Farthing. He won't get far in this weather in his present state."

McAlerty had not risen from his bed at the Penny Farthing for three days. The publican scratched his head and addressed his wife:

"He's had a skinful o' grog, Hettie, so I'm not surprised that 'e's still in the land o' nod. Now look after our customers whiles I have a rest."

Their lodger lay supine in bed, his head and heart pounding. He'd had hangovers before, but not like this. His body ached and he felt sick; the thought of food made him want to vomit. He must get away before anybody came after him. He tried to rise but fell back. With a great effort he rose, threw back the bedclothes, turned, swung his legs round and collapsed onto the tattered carpet.

An hour later, the Irishman staggered through the snow from Wychcombe towards the southern extremity of Wychcombe Farm. His gait was no longer purposeful. He slipped and fell, lying face down in the snow for several minutes, then rose with difficulty. His memory was a blank. What had happened to him between the time he left Wychcombe Farm and now? His hands, concealed in the folds of his jacket limited his movements as he approached the snow-drifted southern Dorchester to Bridport road; he chose the middle of the road where the snow was thinner but was confronted by a snowdrift extending across his path. McAlerty tried to climb the drift, but slid down at each attempt. He turned and looked around. Behind him was a break in the snow exposing a hedge. He stumbled and fell through the opening in the drift, crashed through the bramble hedge, face bleeding from the thorns, and lay there, heart pounding. Gasping for breath, he clutched his body, hands club-like.

Giles decided to return to the Penny Farthing, buttonhole the tinker and wring the truth out of him about the money. He saddled and trotted Sally towards the village. At the Penny Farthing, the proprietor was washing the previous night's dreg-stained tankards. He nodded recognition and touched his forelock.

"Morning, zur. What can I do for ye?"

"Morning. Is your Irish guest still here?

"'fraid not master Giles. He left after breakfast," he replied.

"Did he say where he was going?"

"No, sir, but when 'e left, 'e went west towards St. Stephen's ruin."

Not a very specific answer, thought Giles.

"There be somethin' else, zur. He was acting right queer an' ate next to nothing – all that the missus prepared for 'im; ham slices, good ale, a generous slice of pigeon pie and her own baked bread. Unsteady on his legs, 'e was, an' it wasn't no 'angover."

"He could have had a chill."

The publican shook his head.

"This were different."

Puzzled, Giles let the innkeeper's observation pass without comment.

"What time did he leave, did ye say?"

"Oi reckons about 9 o'clock."

Asa, wading through the snow north of the gley, whistled Scruff his sheepdog to round up the pregnant ewes into a four-sided wicker hurdle in the north-eastern corner of the field. Scruff moved the sheep on towards the hurdle, then stopped, abandoned the sheep and ran south towards the hedge just beyond the swamp.

"Come 'ere dog, what are ye doing?" the shepherd shouted above the howling wind.

The sheepdog did not return immediately. Annoyed by Scruff's lack of response, Asa whistled him back, cuffed the dog's ears and sent him off to drive the flock into the hastily constructed paddock of wooden hurdles, tying the two open and adjacent end hurdles together once the ewes were penned. He then checked the straw bedding and rush-covered fencing of the shelter. Scruff was clearly distracted by something near the hedge, looking back every three or four steps as if drawn to the spot. Intrigued by the dog's behaviour, Asa made Scruff sit, fixed the dog with a look and pointed his finger in the direction beyond where Scruff had veered off.

"Find 'im!"

Scruff sped away, Asa following. Asa walked in the direction of Scruff's barks until he saw his dog sitting by a body. Asa turned the body over. Patrick Mc Alerty's face was as yellow as a newly minted guinea. A trickle of dark blood flowed from the corner of his mouth. His right hand was concealed under his jacket, his left clawlike. Patrick's breath exhaled a foetid odour overpowering the strong ovine smell on Asa's clothes and boots as the Irishman hissed and grunted between clenched teeth. Asa shrank away from the Irishman.

"This ain't the pock, it be like the Black Death!" he whispered to himself.

Patrick's hand moved under the jacket. Steeling himself, Asa pulled apart its folds; the man's right hand clutched a thick wad of paper. His hand was swollen and purple.

"Cor! Money!" Asa cried.

Patrick's hand held what looked to the shepherd like a fortune in banknotes, dripping wet but still recognisable in twenty pound denominations. Asa stretched out his mittened hand then withdrew it as if scalded. To Asa it had the smell of death.

Oi ain't touchin' anything' 'ere, the shepherd told himself. "Get back, Scruff!" he shouted at the sheepdog as it sniffed around the stricken man's body. Grabbing the dog's collar, he dragged him away and hurried through the southern meadow to Wychcombe farmhouse.

"Is he still alive, Asa?"

"On'y just, zur."

Richard rose from the kitchen chair.

"Then you must get him inside before he perishes. Get Jamie to hitch up one of the drays to a wagon and go with him to bring the poor wretch back. Hurry, man!"

"Aye, zur!"

Asa and Jamie rolled Patrick McAlerty's body onto the tarpaulin and lifted the load onto the wagon floor and climbed on, Jamie mounted the driver's seat and drove the horse through a space between towering drifts. They carried the Irishman into the farm kitchen, uncovered the tarpaulin and laid him on the floor. The warmth of the kitchen accentuated the stench from Patrick's clothes.

"I told ye, zur! An' look at 'is face!"

Bloodshot eyes rolled in shrunken sockets. McAlerty's facial colour was a gruesome mixture of purple and yellow. His breath was foetid. Richard shuddered, but moved nearer the Irishman. The Irishman's left hand was concealed under the Burberry; Richard reached towards its open flap.

"Nay, zur, there be death under that cloak, zur! Take care, maister Richard, there be death and 'e be dying. And he's grippin' some loot."

Richard walked to the fireplace, picked up a pair of firetongs, knelt down by McAlerty and opened the Irishman's coat with the tongs. McAlerty's left hand clutched a bundle of paper; with the tongs Richard gripped and gently pulled; a fraction was torn away from McAlerty's clawed fist. Richard dropped the torn piece onto the kitchen table and smoothed it out with the tongs. Richard deciphered '... Dev ... and ... Dor...Ban ...'

Could this be? Richard mused. Were the notes part of their father's debt repayment for his gambling losses, withdrawn from the Devon and Dorset Bank. Richard shuddered again – Asa was probably right; the money was probably beyond recovery, like their present possessor, a vector of disease and death. If the remainder of the fortune was infected, the repayment was lost forever. Coins could be cleansed, but not paper.

The man moved; his breathing gathered impetus, to a grunting, rumbling roar. Then, with one final expiring rattle of breath, Patrick McAlerty passed from this world. Richard covered the body with the tarpaulin and dismissed Asa.

"Well, Giles, this could well be part of father's debt repayment. If it wasn't to clear father's name and reclaim our rightful inheritance, I'd give up this hunt and get down to making a proper living from what's left of our estate."

"Surely, Richard, we could save some of father's fortune here, the smell and infection might die and who's to say that the rest isn't out there in someone's hands and clear of McAlerty's contagion. The rest would help us achieve something from Wychcombe and, with a little help from Lady Luck, the restoration of Home Farm?"

"No, brother, we musn't take the risk – you saw the state of McAlerty. Whatever killed him was in the notes too."

The brothers watched Asa and Thomas throw the last shovelfuls of soil onto Patrick McAlerty's grave in the gley field and covered the gravesite with the turfs they'd removed. Thomas hammered a crude wooden cross carrying the legend burnt into the wood:

Patrick McAlerty

Died of pestilence December 28th 1815

May the Good Lord Rest his Soul

Thomas took off his cap and waited. Then Asa laid his shovel down, approached Richard, took off his cap and touched his forelock.

"Beggin' yer pardon, zur, could ye say a few words out o' repec' fer the dead? Beggin' yer pardon, zur, would ye say ower Lord's Prayer t' mek it a Christian burial?"

Richard nodded and removed his hat and looked sharply at Giles, who gave a start and removed his.

"By all means, Asa. Let's say the Lord's Prayer together."

Four heads bowed.

"Our Father, who art in heaven …"

The four concluded with their "amens", replaced their hats and the two labourers left the brothers to gaze on the two graves.

Hugo Jones viewed Wychcombe Farm through his spyglass. The snow had not obscured the two mounds in the gley field. Deduction and a leap of imagination reasoned that the graves held the remains of two Irishmen. No local persons would have been buried in the grazings, they'd be in the local cemetery or in the village's common grave. Who were they, both without headstones but with two roughly tied wooden crosses? One was bound

117

to be Seamus, the ringleader, whom he'd left for dead, but who was the other? With Seamus dead, that left the other Irishmen Patrick, Shaun and Dermot. Dermot had somehow escaped on Duke the gelding; rumour had it that Patrick McAlerty had been throwing money about in the Penny Farthing and had left in a blizzard much the worse for wear. The innkeeper had vouched that the Irishman had not been drunk but ill. Hugo suspected that he had perished in the storm and his body was in the other mound. The only able-bodied Irishman left, then, would be Shaun. So, assuming that the two mounds on Wychcombe Farm held the remains of Seamus and Patrick, that left Shaun at large, the only key to the source of the money! If he could find Shaun, he'd deal with Dermot later.

"What did the fellow die from? And why burn the money?" Giles demanded.

"In answer to your first question, I have no idea, but I suspect some kind of plague; to your second, because of the possibility of infecting anyone who handled it." Richard replied.

"Bu … but what's all this about? Are you holding back something from me? What did the dying Irishman say to you in the copse? And why did you ride to the churchyard?"

"You know most of the answers to your questions already. When the thugs fled into the churchyard, the heavy load they'd carried had disappeared. Later, Lesden's grave had been ransacked, which pointed to there being something there that someone wanted apart from the body. This was not a bodysnatcher's way of doing things, so I suspected that the heavy load containing the debt money was hidden in the coffin. On Christmas Day McAlerty turned up at the Penny Farthing boasting that he had come into money and was throwing notes around. Then Asa found him dying in the snow near the gley field gripping the banknotes under his jacket. Seamus muttered something about 'vicar... grave ...'"

"And that's all?"

"No, Giles. I suspect that the banknotes McAlerty had on him were a small fraction of the money father withdrew to pay his debt of honour, so where's the rest?"

Silence.

"Richard, let's assume the three Irishmen fled from Home Farm with the stolen money. Two are dead – Seamus and McAlerty, and Dermot's a helpless cripple imprisoned on Home Farm unless Hugo's done away with him. That leaves ..."

"Shaun!" the brothers chorused.

"Where is he? If we can find the Irishman and the rest of the money, it will help us to build up our farm..."

"No, Giles! Even if the money is what father withdrew to repay the debt and assuming that the Irishman Shaun has the rest, that money's rightfully Ezra Jones's as a debt of honour and we must return it to him ..."

"No, Richard! Ezra then gets the money Dranley stole and will also have Home Farm by default as well."

"Giles, I agree that if Ezra is repaid, Home Farm rightfully becomes our possession, so I would hope that, once Ezra receives the money, he will be the man of honour I hope he is and return Home Farm to us."

"Man of honour, fiddlesticks!

"Your father's in the haybarn, Hugo," his mother informed him as he arrived at Destro, "and he's pretty choleric."

Hugo helped himself to a stiff dose of whisky from the sideboard, almost dropped the glass, replaced it and walked, inwardly trembling, to the haybarn. His father was browbeating the chargehand.

"Don' gimme any of yer lip, Hands! I've forgotten more about harvestin' than ye'll ever remember! Now begone afore I gi' yer job t' somebody who knows wot he's doin'!"

The chargehand disappeared through the haybarn door past Hugo. Ezra turned to face his son, waiting until the chargehand was well out of earshot. He glowered at Hugo, his face etched with anger.

"Well, have ye got it?"

"Not yet, father."

"Not yet? I gave ye long enough to recover my winnings."

"They've hid it somewhere's and it's goin to take…"

"How long, if ye ever find it? I can't trust ye with anything. I could find a dozen johnny-raws to better ye fer brains!"

"I'll get the money back if I have to kill somebody or it kills me, father; just gi' me more time".

"Fiddlesticks! What good's that now; I'll bet their trail's as cold as the grave and now they'll know how a fortune was hidden under the haybarn floor. The sly villains will've put two and two together an' come up with the right answers about the money!"

Hugo stood as if transfixed, open-mouthed, but no sound came out.

"What a pretty pickle ye've got us into. The Gomers now know the debt money wuz stolen by ye and Dranley an' if I know anythin' about them, they'll not rest until they find out where it's gone. I reckon that ye've not only lost us thousands, but knowledge of this will surely get out an' we could be in real jeopardy! What are ye going to do, son of mine?"

Hugo bit his lip.

"Well, I'll tell ye what *I'm* going to do! Unless ye find and return the money, I'm going to change my mind about letting ye have ownership of Home Farm. From now on, ye'll have responsibility o' running the farm, but until ye've repaid me the money through what the farm brings in or get it back fro' those villains ye hired, ye'll have no share in the profits from what ye harvest from it!"

That night, Hugo Jones returned from Destro to Home Farm, dismounted, stabled the gelding, dropped the saddle and halter on the bedding and took the saddlebags into the farmhouse. He entered the kitchen, threw the bags onto the table, took a half jeroboam of porter and a glass from the scullery, crept up the stairs in the darkness and gently tried the door of the bedroom he would normally share with Katherine; it was locked from the inside. Just as he thought. Furious, he lurched into a smaller bedroom and slammed the door shut.

Chapter Fifteen

Joshua Wicks

Joshua stumbled over the rocks in the limestone quarry, his leg irons moved relentlessly over bare legs, breaking the scarred skin until it bled once again. Wet lime from the rocks had burnt into and ulcerated the broken skin, adding to the pain and lack of healing. Wear and tear, supplemented by Dorset rain had reduced his prison trousers from below his ankles to just below the knees. His boots showed a split in the join between sole and upper, allowing water from the elements to keep his feet constantly wet and cold. He shivered; the winter frost and snow, then slush and pools of water when a thaw came, seemed endless. The unremitting rain, alternating with freezing snowfalls and dark sunless days had already left an unhealthy pallor to his face.

January 10th, 1816

He looked through the downpour at the waves crashing into the nearby cliffs, a symbol of freedom in spite of its savagery. Thwack! The warder's truncheon raised an immediate bruise on his back.

"Ye won't get any medals fer slackin', Wicks – the judge said 'ard labour, not a holiday, heh! heh! So get on wi' yer sentence."

Joshua bent his soaked, aching back, raised the sledgehammer and brought it down with force, splitting the rock. A second blow rendered it into small fragments. He turned to break the next rock and struck it; this time only a small piece fell off. He struck the boulder again – still it did not yield; his arms were aching from the impact of iron on rock, which sent shockwaves up his arm. He raised the hammer – his hand slipped from the handle and the hammerhead hit one of the links of his leg chain a few inches from the shackle. The impact sent a reverberating pain through his leg. He looked down; no bruise nor blood on his legs, but the connecting link to the shackle was slightly opened. A thought ignited his weary mind; carefully, he looked around to see if the warder was watching, and brought the hammer down on the link to close the gap opened by the hammerhead. Now, no gap was visible, but the metal had been weakened. He hammered at the link by the other shackle until it too was weakened, then closed it as before. Another day almost over, just like any other day for the last two months; there'd be many more days of agony before release, if he survived. He glanced at the warder out of the corner of his eye, a weary-eyed tyrant whose black uniform contrasted favourably with the dun-coloured rags the convicts wore.

The whistle pierced the quarry. Joshua slung the hammer over his shoulder, shuffled through the mud to the line of prisoners, dropped the hammer at the feet of the warders, moved in line, was counted and staggered off, the clanking chains sending a tuneless symphony which faded as the line of prisoners disappeared down the track into the prison. Inside, Joshua joined a line of prisoners escorted to the privies to relieve themselves, who were then given soap and rough towelling to wash themselves in a primitive washroom. After ablutions, they were escorted to the canteen, where they collected their supper, ate together at wooden tables, dropped the utensils into a tub of water and returned to their cells to be locked in for the night. A warder unlocked the shackles from Joshua's legs, hung them outside his cell and locked the cell door.

Joshua's determination to escape was now bolstered by the damage he'd unwittingly inflicted on the shackle. He would bide his time and further weaken the link attached to the other shackle. His chances of escape would be better when winter had passed and the weather was much improved, before planning to break out. Joshua removed his boots, laid back on the bunk, covered himself with the tattered blanket and almost immediately fell into the sleep of exhaustion in spite of the bitterly cold, damp cell.

CHAPTER SIXTEEN

The Angel of Death

Ezra and Hugo Jones stood drinking porter with their backs to the roaring wood fire in the lounge at Destro Farm. Despite Ezra's disappointment in his son, they were still on drinking terms, and Destro was still open to Hugo, but only when Ezra felt that Hugo had something worthwhile to share with him.

January 14th 1816

"I hear that the Gomers ha' the pox, father," Hugo remarked.

"Which d'ye mean, chancre or smallpox?"

It's a wonder young Gomer hasn't picked something up from some of the fancy ladies he's probably seeing, thought Hugo.

"Smallpox; it's rife among the riff-raff and some have died of it in Wychcombe. Now rumour has it Susannah Gomer's dying an' at least one o' their workers will soon be meetin' his Maker."

"That'll be another blow to the Gomers, I warrant,

if the mother dies. I reckon she's held things together at Wychcombe," added Ezra.

And if it's Giles, then good riddance; but if he doesn't die, his face'll be pitted like their bridle path and he won't be so attractive to Katherine, Hugo mused.

"Let's hope it don't hit this neck o' the woods," Ezra added.

At Wychcombe Farm, Rachel wiped her mistress's sweat-bathed face. The candlelit bedroom was filled with the choking stench of lysol. The door to Susannah Gomer's bedroom creaked half open. Richard peered around the door, holding a lantern, its yellow light casting shadows, though adding light to the semi-darkness. Burning wood hissed and crackled in a small corner fireplace.

"How is mother, Rachel?"

"She be sleeping, sir, not surprising the leechin' she's 'ad."

"And how are you?"

"Well, sir."

"I can see that you're tired. You may retire to your room; I'll stay with mother."

"Very well, thank you, sir," Rachel replied, curtseying.

Richard opened the door wider to let the maid pass, then entered, closing the door behind him. He approached the bed and sat in an armchair close to his mother's head. The room was silent apart from Susannah Gomer's rasping breath and the crackle of burning embers in the fireplace. With a hiss and a bang, red-hot sparks exploded from a burning log to land on the gnarled floorboards. Richard quickly stamped them out and regained his seat, suddenly aware that his mother was awake and watching him.

Richard rose rapidly.

"Richard, dear, don't ... too close ... she gasped, "but I've someth'... to tell you ..."

"Don't tire yourself, mother ..." interrupted Richard.

"The doctor has ... too late for me, but ... rest of our ... family ..."

She fell back in a bout of coughing. Richard rose, poured water from a jug into a glass on the bedside table and held it to his mother's lips. She sipped a little, gurgled, choked and pushed the glass away.

"Don't ... too close, my son ..." she croaked, "listen ..."

Richard stepped back and nodded.

"It's too late for ... but ... ye know Mallowfields?"

"The dairy farm?"

Susannah Gomer stiffly moved her head in affirmation.

"... saved his family ... "

"But it's here already, mother. It's ravaging Wychcombe, and Giles and I could already be affected by now."

"No, Richard, I ... sick ... for days and neither of you ... show signs ... farmer ... some of the matter ... cows and milkmaids' hands ... get for you and Giles."

"Rest, mother, and I will go after Rachel has returned from her rest", Richard replied, reclining in the bedside chair and closing his eyes. He had heard stories of a farmer who had injected material from cows into his sons and wife with no ill-effects nor signs of the pock which surrounded their farm.

An hour later, Rachel returned, followed by the Dean, who carried a packet under his arm.

Richard looked sharply at the Right Reverend David Carshall, who returned his gaze.

"I've come to administer Eucharist to your mother, who is a regular communicant, in view of her need to be renewed spiritually. Clearly, in her present state of health, she is unable to attend St. Bartholomew's, and …", raising a hand to be permitted to continue, the clergyman continued, "to pray with her for her recovery. I believe that God could if He so wished use the sacraments of bread and wine as a means of healing."

More like a Requiem Mass by this time, thought Richard.

"Aren't you risking your own health and running a grave risk of contracting the pock, since it's clear that mother is suffering from that condition?" Richard queried.

"I'm no more at risk than you, sir. It's too late for me to be concerned as to whether I am already infected or will contract the scourge, since I've visited several of the late vicar's parishioners in the same state as your mother, some of whom have already died. Having witnessed how well some of these people who share the same faith in God have gone to their Redeemer, I have no fear, since they, and sooner or later, I, will pass to a better place."

"Very well, sir, but I hope that you know what you're doing. As it is, I'm visiting a farmer who is reputed to have the answer to smallpox, so I'm hoping that he may be able to stop the spread within this family and among our few workers. Rachel will provide you with anything you need. Good night, Dean," replied Richard, moving toward the bedroom door.

"God speed, sir," replied the Dean.

In spite of their previous unfriendly encounter, Richard felt a grudging respect for this man of the cloth. Richard left the room and met Giles in the kitchen.

"Giles, on Mother's advice I intend to ride to Mallowfields to prevent us from getting the pock. Mother told me that Ephraim Jolly, the farmer who lives there, has found a way of stopping the pock from spreading."

"Then you must go to Mallowfields Farm alone, Richard. I'll stay to oversee the farmhands and help Rachel care for mother. Dr. Needman is to call tomorrow," Giles said.

Richard pondered. Both his brother and Rachel were at risk and unprotected, especially whilst they were in close proximity to their sick mother Susannah. But if his visit to Mallowfields proved successful, then lives would be saved. He went outside, called and instructed Jamie to saddle up Hal.

Richard spurred Hal on, hoping against hope that the farmer at Mallowfields could help them in some way. As horse and rider pounded down the road through windblown snow, Richard recalled with a smile John Gargery the corn factor's visit and his conversation with Giles and himself.

"I'm willin' to let bygones be bygones sin' our last meeting," the corn factor had said, "an' we can gi' ye a fair price and a ready market fer some of your corn. There should ha' been a glut this year but yon storm wiped out acres o' ripe grain in this part o' Dorset in spite of a measurably good summer an' left us wi' a small shortage o' corn to supply our regular customers," he said, putting undue emphasis on "small".

"How do ye know that we've got corn to spare to supply all your demands?" Giles had enquired with a twinkle in his eye.

John Gargery blushed.

"It be common knowledge that ye managed t' cut, thresh an' store the best o' your corn afore the storm, an' with a rusty old hand-thresher at that! And the Joneses an' Goodboys were hit afore most of their wheat wus ripe in the cob an' unready t' be gathered in. So now I'm here, cap in hand, to offer ye a good price per ton, providing o' course, that it's the best quality wi' no black spot whate'er."

Richard and Giles had exchanged glances but remained silent. Gargery continued:

"I'm trusting yer word that ye never sent that letter cancelling yer contract an' took it to be a forgery. Did ye ever find out who did it? My son James and me would like nuthin' better than t' resume our good relations and trade with ye, certainly fer this winter."

Richard smiled to himself, ignoring the question so cunningly inserted in Gargery's offer, and Giles did not respond either, perhaps not detecting anything deliberately hidden in the query or assuming that he and Richard had no answer to it.

"What are you offering, then, Gargery?" Richard had asked.

"If your grain's top grade, sixty guineas a ton, an' fer the next lower grade, forty guineas. An' I'll guarantee a reasonable price on anythin' poorer to match the quality. But no black spot, ye unnerstand?"

Richard and Giles had looked at each other.

"Oh, our corn is top grade alright; how much and when d'you need it?" Giles had asked.

John Gargery had almost exposed his need as he opened then shut his mouth in a split second.

"Fi … uh, subject to the, er, conditions I mentioned, about one or … two tons or more, perhaps?"

"When?"

Richard chuckled to himself at Gargery's discomfiture as he trotted Hal east beyond Dorchester along the old carriage road towards Mallowfields. A sale of some of their corn would help pay off the wages of their workmen and leave a little for them to live on after providing the cattle and sheep with hay and provender. Horse and rider passed a bleached fingerpost pointing crookedly to the village, the fading light from a rusty lantern swinging from the top of the post in a crooked, creaking windblown arc to faintly illuminate the distance – ten miles. The icy wind scattered a thick curtain of snowflakes in his path, rendering the way difficult along a track slowly obliterated behind him by gathering snowdrifts. Richard felt the wind's bitter cold through his greatcoat, diminished somewhat by Hal's warmth emanating around the saddle and his own legs and he pressed his gelding into a canter in spite of the settling snow, risking a fall to avoid being marooned in a snowdrift.

An hour later, Richard steadied Hal down a long winding slope towards Mallowfields, peering through the snow to where he guessed an opening into the farmyard entrance would be. Horse and rider had almost passed the entrance when Richard saw a light out of the corner of his eye and heard the distant sound of barking. He turned Hal and walked his mount over the thick carpet of snow towards a farmhouse light shining through a kitchen window bathing the yard. Richard dismounted in the yard and walked his horse to the lighted building. Aware of the threatening baying of the dogs, yet resolute, he kicked on the door, Hal's wet muzzle rubbing his equally wet shoulder. Light that flooded the yard, dazzling Richard, was suddenly dimmed by a large man's silhouette.

"Gud eve t' ye. What 're ye about this hour o' night?"

"Is this Mallowfields?" and, as the figure nodded, "Sorry to trouble ye sir, but I've come from Wychcombe on a matter of grave urgency. My mother is dying of the pock and she believes that you have the means to save me and my brother from this scourge."

"Whear's yer brother, sir?"

"I've had to leave him in charge of our farm. I'm Richard Gomer, heir to Wychcombe Farm, west of Dorchester", extending his sound arm.

"Come in, come in, Mister Gomer, afore ye freezes t' death", the man replied, enveloping Richard's hand in an enormous fist, then:

"Jack! Tek the gen'lman's horse an' stable it wi' fodder an' water."

A young man passed between the two men, took hold of Hal's reins from Richard and led the horse away.

The farmer and Richard went into the kitchen, the latter savouring the warmth generated by a blazing inglenook fire.

"Tek yer wet jacket off, zur, and sit ye down. Now, what can oi do fer ye?"

The farmer was a tall, weather-beaten man of ample size and advanced age. His lined, rubicund face surrounding soft, expressive eyes belied years of outdoor toil and he had a kindliness tinged with sadness reflecting, to an observant eye, some past suffering yet an excellent quality of character. He was dressed as if contemplating retirement to bed, in a thick open-necked collarless shirt exposing the top of a vast hairy chest above thick woollen trousers ending in stockinged feet.

"Wud ye loike a noggin o' mulled wine? Jack an' me were jus' partakin'. Ye mus' be half-frozen ridin' all this way out in this weather from west o' Dorchester. It must ha' been a chillin' ride fer ye. Ye're welcome to stay the night, it'd be foolhardy t' return home at this hour".

Richard gratefully received the draught and, in spite of its heat, drank generously.

"Thank you, sir, but my visit is of the utmost urgency and I must return to Wychcombe at the earliest opportunity. My mother is probably dying, but if ye could do something at this late stage for my brother and I ..."

The farmer raised his beefy hand, stopping Richard in full flow.

"As ye may have heard, oi'm Ephraim Jolly an' ye may have heard that becos o' what oi've been up to, many folks don't mek much o' me. They reckon that among the good folks who come t' me oi'm spreading the pock among they poor higgorant folks who I vaccinated wi' cowpox matter to stop they gettin' it. Perchance they be right, but nobody pricked with me needle 'as died yet, ner shown signs of the blisters, an' that includes me, the wife, sons and daughters n' mesel' sin' we were done some time ago."

"I'm willing to take a chance rather than perish; smallpox is rife in Wychcombe and thereabouts and we've heard that you're the man who discovered that your dairymaids with blisters from milking kine with the cowpox blisters don't get smallpox," Richard replied.

The farmer's face expanded into a huge smile.

"Aye, zur, it's somethin' like that. But oi won't tek all or most o' the credit fer it; we believe that there's a God who in his kindness guides simple men like me t' be used in a small way to save lives. Now, oi asked ye about yer brother, cos he would have needed t' be here like thee t' be treated wi' the cowpox matter while it be fresh fro' the cows."

"My brother had to stay to take care of our holding while I came here for help. Could ye vaccinate me to show me how it's done and give me some of the matter for me to take back with me, perchance it works on him?"

"Oi could gi' ye some o' the matter, but now that yer mother's so bad, oi can't gi' ye much hopes for her, but if ye've cowpox in yer herd, it might save yer brother. Oi'll gi' ye no guarantee that this'll work, o'ive never tried using anything but fresh stuff but oi can gi' ye some pus from my cows' teats t' tek back to yer farm at Wychcombe, but if ye can harvest some fresh stuff from yer own stock, better still. But be careful t' clean any dung an' dirt from their teats an' udder. My missus was sick after oi treated her an' oi fancy thet the cowpox 'ad dung mixed with it. Even so, I'll gi' ye some pus in a bottle to tek wi' ye back t' yer farm at Wychcombe. Oi don't know whether it would be fresh enough by the time ye reach yer farm, even if ye rode back tonight in this weather an' ye so tired. Ye're a plucky man t' ride from Wychcombe in this weather."

The farmer looked sharply at Richard, his gaze focussing on Richard's stump.

"But, as oi said, if ye can harvest some fresh stuff from yer own cows' teats, even better. An' clean the kine's teats well first."

"Come t' think on it, Thomas our herdsman was hale an' hearty when I left the farm and he lives in the village right in the middle of the outbreak. I wonder if he's been infected and protected by cowpox? And Rachel, our parlourmaid? She lodges at Thomas's cottage and has insisted on nursing my mother since she became sick and has shown no signs of having caught it."

The kitchen door opened, admitting a flurry of snow followed by the farmer's son.

"Jack, slip off yer jacket an' roll up yer left sleeve," the farmer ordered.

Jack removed his snow-covered jacket and rolled up his shirt sleeve, exposing a brawny arm covered in deep scratches decorated with lines of angry pus-filled blisters. Richard's face paled at the sight, inured though he was to seeing gory battle wounds.

Ephraim Jolly looked sharply at Richard then glanced meaningfully at his shortened arm.

"Ye're a tired man to be going back at this hour, sir, so oi'd counsel ye to stay here tonight an' set off early tomorrow".

"I'm indebted to you, Mr. Jolly, but I need to hurry back tonight in the hope that someone will be saved in time from this scourge. Thank you again, but time is running out for my mother, and probably my brother and others in our household."

"As ye wish, zur, but first ha' some vittles and mulled wine to sustain ye fer the ride whiles Jack an' me collect some cowpox matter. Then oi'll treat ye. Ye'll be sore fer a whiles after the pricking. Cover the sores with a length of clean linen, well secured. Now, if ye're fixed in yer mind t' brave dark and snow an' even footpads," he said meaningfully, then "have ye a pistol? Ye're most welcum t' bed down 'ere after some food and drink an' return in daylight. Then, when ye get back, remember to go over yer cow's teats and the cowman's hands fer the blisters."

Richard pulled out a bag and placed several sovereigns onto the kitchen table.

"Thank ye again, Mr. Jolly, but I must return home with all speed. Time is running out for my mother and those in our household and for the few workers we have. I'm indebted to you for your help in our time of great need, so will ye accept a token for your trouble? I refuse to take something for nothing from you, it's not my way to receive service without payment."

Ephraim pondered, shaking his head.

"I'll tek none o' yer money, zur, no hard feelin's, since ye've put yer trust in me to have an answer to yer problems. That's payment eno'. Finish yer drink an' rest up whiles Jack an' me collect some matter from our cow's blisters. And pray thet yer dear mother and the rest o' ye will survive this scourge afore it kills multitudes more."

Richard shook his head and staggered to his feet.

"Mr. Jolly, I need to see what cowpox looks like when I return to Wychcombe."

"As ye wish, zur. Jack! Come with us, oi'll need a hand t' hold the cows."

Father and son donned coats and helped Richard into his. Jack took the lantern, turned up the flame and opened the kitchen door, shielding the lantern top from the flurrying snow followed by the other two across the farmyard to a long-spanned barn. Jack opened the top and bottom doors and stepped inside, holding the lantern high. The lantern flame was reflected in dozens of eyes as recumbent cows turned towards them. The milkers were chained or roped to rings in the byre wall, chewing their cud and resting on clean straw, but, now disturbed, began to rise.

"Come behind us, zur, whiles Jack an' me pick out one or two from our herd."

Ephraim and Jack Jolly, followed by Richard, moved quietly along the cobblestoned channel, inching between two cows.

The snow had stopped, the snow clouds had lifted and Hal's hoofprints were visible by clear moonlight. The food and wine had warmed and sustained him and Richard felt refreshed and rested as he started the return journey. Nevertheless, Jack had passed a leather strap round Hal's girth and fastened it to Richard's breeches belt as a precaution. Richard's excoriated arm was sore but he held the reins firmly.

When Richard arrived at Wychcombe Farm early the following morning, Susannah Gomer was still fighting for her life. The smallpox was well established; her face suffused with angry blisters and pustules, her breath shallow and rasping, punctuated by a sharp but weak cough. Her sweat-bathed face marked a crisis well into its peak. Rachel applied a cloth immersed in chilled water then placed it next to a bottle of leeches. Richard, a witness to the weakening effects of blood loss on the battlefield and unconvinced of the benefits of removing the lifeblood of a sick person, had persuaded Dr. Needman that Susannah had been bled enough. Richard reasoned that sick patients needed all their strength to fight the disease ravaging their bodies.

Meanwhile, though sleep-deprived, Richard and herdsman Thomas had harvested pus from cows' washed teats and carried it in a bottle into the kitchen where Berkeley was heating in tongs two steel stocking needles to a red-hot glow over the hearth fire. Richard slipped out of his coat and sat at the kitchen table.

"Roll up your sleeves!" he commanded, and Asa and Giles complied.

"Now, Asa, sit opposite me and put an arm, palm up, on the table."

He signalled to the retainer, who removed the needles from the fire until their glow had disappeared. He turned to Berkeley, who handed him one of the cooling needles, one end wrapped in a cloth, then scraped open the shepherd's skin. Asa winced but made no sound. Handing the needle back to Berkeley, he took the second needle dripping in pus and spread it into the wounds. Berkeley then wound a linen strip around the wounds, cut a slit in the end and tied the dressing.

"Keep this dressing on as long as ye can, Asa," Richard advised.

"Aye, zur," replied Asa, "but what 'bout Thomas, zur?"

"He's already had the cowpox, Asa, he's got the blisters on his hands and he's safe from the pock."

Asa's simple mind struggled to grasp the significance of Richard's explanation but his trust in Richard overruled his confusion.

"Thankee, maister Richard. Shall oi check the ewes, zur?"

"You go home and rest up tonight. Thomas can look them over."

"Aye zur," Asa replied and left the room.

Richard eyed Berkeley.

"Your turn, Berkeley; I'll vaccinate and dress your wound."

"Yes, sir."

Berkeley rose after vaccination and Giles took his place. His face was flushed, a prelude to the appearance of pox blisters?

"Are you sure you're well enough to do this, brother? After all, it's only a few hours since you were vaccinated and you've had no sleep since?"

Richard refrained from speaking and signalled to Berkeley for the needles. Giles subjected himself to the procedure without a murmur. Richard rose from the chair, wearied by the sleepless night and vaccinating the others. His arm was painful.

"Yes, brother, I will retire for a rest. Do see that the

livestock are in fair condition and that mother is being looked after."

At this, an exhausted Richard retired to bed to recuperate.

CHAPTER SEVENTEEN

The Brave Pioneer

"Ma'am, I heard that the pock has spread in Wychcombe," Harriet informed her mistress as they sat in Katherine's bedroom at Home Farm.

"Harriet, you live there and you're extremely healthy. Why have you managed to keep clear of it?" Katherine responded.

Harriet's jaw dropped.

"I've been vacculated, ma'am."

"You mean vaccinated, my dear girl. Who did it? And how?"

Harriet hesitated.

"Beggin' yer pardon, Lady Katherine, but I can't tell anybody 'cause I swore I wouldn't, because of folks being afeared of scratching cow matter into human flesh."

Katherine looked sharply at her maid.

"Show me your arm, Harriet," she demanded.

"Bu ... but..."

"Show me!"

Tearful, Harriet undid her apron, unbuttoned her blouse, removed it and extended a bare right arm. Katherine gasped. Though the wounds had undergone healing, the skin was still angry and red-raw in appearance. Yet her thoughts and intentions overruled her shock at the sight of the reaction. As a mother-to-be, she needed protection on two counts from the Angel of Death.

"Who treated you?"

Harriet shook her head.

"But girl, why won't you tell me?"

Harriet remained silent.

"Would you be party to preventing me and my baby the protection we need against this sickness and death?"

Harriet sobbed.

"Please, Harriet!"

Harriet wiped her eyes and gazed into her mistress's tear-filled eyes.

"Ma'am, there be two local gentry who do this … thing with cow matter. I'll keep my oath but can tell you that one be a doctor an' the other be someone ye knows well who be a farmer."

Katherine's heart missed a beat. She presumed that the local doctor must be Dr. Needman, the only one in the district, but who could the farmer be? Hardly her father Sir Absalom; he would be against such a practice. She'd heard rumours of a farmer over at Mallowfields who'd been the first to try vaccinating to protect his family, but he wasn't local. Who could the farmer be? The only one she knew of was Richard Gomer.

Katherine retired early, securely locking her bedroom door and insisting that Harriet remained at hand in the room so that Hugo would hesitate to molest her in the presence of company even if he forced his way in. Katherine lay in bed musing. She must protect herself and the unborn child she carried. Somehow she must acquire the services of one of the two men to protect against the scourge. But how? If she tried to leave Home Farm under any pretence, Hugo would be suspicious and go after her. She would have to risk Hugo questioning an early call from Dr. Needman if she sent for him again since his recent visit. Who was the farmer?

Katherine winced as the needlepoint broke the skin of her forearm.

"We doctors consider this measure experimental with no clear guarantee that it will provide the protection you require, milady. Some of my medical colleagues suspect that vaccination with cowpox may be more dangerous than the pock. And who knows how it might affect your unborn child, Lady Katherine. However, it seems to have worked in some cases."

Katherine shivered, but she permitted Dr. Needman to smear the cowpox into the wound, then dress it with a linen bandage. He straightened up and looked closely at her.

"I gather that your husband is away. Is he aware of your desire to be vaccinated?"

Katherine shook her head.

"Keep warm, Lady Katherine, take plenty of gruel to keep your bowels moving and call me if you need help. However, I will call on you from time to time to make sure that your confinement is uneventful. Give my regards to your husband."

The impact of the cold formality of the doctor's last words were not lost on Katherine: "your husband".

Author's Addendum

Chapters 16 and 17 are dedicated to the discovery, work and courage of Benjamin Jesty (1736 – 1816), whom I have represented and characterised under the fictitious name of Ephraim Jolly.

During a visit to research authentic historical data for the Thresher trilogy regarding rural conditions in early nineteenth century Dorset, I was contacted by Mr. and Mrs. Jesty, residents at Waddock Cross, Dorchester; Mr. Jesty is a direct descendant of Benjamin's brother William. They had learned of my searches through the county NFU, and from meetings I had with Mr. and Mrs. Jesty, Benjamin Jesty's involvement in the history of smallpox emerged.

Smallpox has not been called 'The Angel of Death' without good reason; infection of an unprotected person with the virus caused disfigurement from the pustules and widespread death through a generalised systemic viral infection of the patient's body until the preventative effect of vaccination was discovered and applied. Although Benjamin Jesty, a dairy farmer and owner of Upbury Farm, Yetminster was little-known, he was an observant and intelligent man and had noted that during outbreaks of smallpox, certain people, particularly milkmaids who worked closely with dairy cows, showed no ill-effects nor clinical signs of smallpox. He deduced that the milkmaids' immunity was associated with cowpox, a related but much milder virus to smallpox characterised by blisters on cows' teats and udders and the appearance of lesions known as 'milkers' nodules' on the hands of the milkmaids.

Armed with his observations and strengthened by the courage of his convictions, during a local outbreak, Benjamin Jesty took his wife and two sons to a neighbouring farm and introduced cowpox material harvested from an affected cow into their arms with a stocking needle. His family remained unaffected and Benjamin's courage in pioneering a breakthrough in the prevention of smallpox potentially saved many lives. However, his actions aroused local opposition and ostracism based on the superstitious belief that it was evil and dangerous to introduce infected material from an animal into a human body. Benjamin Jesty's opponents expected vaccinated persons to sprout horns!

Nevertheless he stood firm, and his foresight and courage would ultimately be recognised, as the first known vaccinator twenty years before Dr. Jenner, whose work, connections with the medical profession and popular recognition overshadowed the recognition and acceptance of Benjamin Jesty's achievements. However, Benjamin's work was recognised by Dr. Pearson of the Pock Institute, a contemporary. His descendants have since strenuously campaigned that his pioneering efforts be recognised by the British Medical Association. Moreover, the use of cowpox material did not produce the uncomfortable side-effects that vaccinating with human smallpox material did.

CHAPTER EIGHTEEN

A Rescue Plan

"How's the herd, Thomas?"

"Well eno', zur. A stroke o' luck some o' them 'ad that cowpock, maister Richard."

Despite his concerns, Richard smiled. The recent smallpox outbreak had taken away their beloved mother, but the timely vaccination of himself, Giles and Asa had not just saved their lives; little sign of blisters on either Giles's or Asa's faces reassured Richard that his journey to Mallowfields had not been in vain. They walked into the cowshed; the familiar warm bovine smell met them, but an overpowering pungent smell of ammonia rose from the sodden straw and assaulted their nostrils. Richard sneezed then covered his nose with a handkerchief. Thomas edged his way along the wet channel, followed by Richard. The smell caused the latter to pinch his nose. The straw on which the cows and first-calved heifers were lying was soaked with cows' urine.

"Thomas, these cows need fresh, dry bedding and the drains unblocked of cow dung. Why hasn't it been changed?"

Thomas stood still, hanging his head.

"We been down to ower last quarter hundredweight,

which oi hoped t' save fer later, zur. After that, there be only hay, an' that be feed."

Richard, even with his limited farming experience, knew that the remaining straw would never last beyond January, let alone the end of the winter. Another headache!

"Maister Richard, what can we do?"

Richard needed time to think.

"In the meantime, Thomas, clear the drains, carry away the sodden straw outside, pile it in the field for fertiliser and replace it with a little fresh straw. Only a little, mind you; make it last as long as possible, there's a good man."

"Aye, zur, as ye say," Thomas replied as he took the pitchfork, shaking his head.

Richard stepped outside into the freezing air, his stump aching in response to the sudden drop in temperature. What were they to do? The severe winter showed no signs of abating and their straw and hay stocks would soon be gone, unless a benefactor loaned them a supply on the strength of a good harvest later in the year. The cows badly needed fodder to generate the milk the Gomers would need to use themselves and sell. He entered the farmhouse kitchen and, with difficulty, unbuttoned his greatcoat, letting it drop to the floor. He slumped into the fireside snug, holding his head in his hand. Not enough straw to last the winter and none of the precious hay could be spared for bedding. Where could they get fresh straw from? It was the wrong time of the year to buy any from the feed and fodder merchants. Only the landlords of extensive farmland might have some to spare.

He dismissed any help from the Joneses, and Sir Absalom was an unknown quantity even though he had seen off the rioters from their farm. Though they had plentiful corn to feed the sheep, the cows needed fodder for their stomachs, to chew the cud and produce milk. Without hay, the cows' udders would dry up and they would lose weight and be unmarketable. And the calves needed milk until they could be weaned; but weaned onto what, if there was no fodder for them? And there was little money to buy fresh stocks. Gargery had not pursued his offer to buy any of their corn. The use of their ample corn stocks was limited, because it was too rich for the sheep and could not replace the fodder the cows needed. So now they were strapped for money to buy hay and straw as well as to pay their labourers and have a living from the rest.

At this juncture Giles appeared. Richard shared his thoughts with him.

"Why don't we mix some of our straw with a little hay – it's all roughage to keep the cows cudding."

"But we need all the hay to feed the milkers and calves for the rest of the winter," Richard replied.

"Tell me, Richard, where are we going to get any fodder from? Don't tell me that Gargery will sell us any! And since he hasn't come back to make good his offer to buy some of our corn, where's the money coming from?"

"We could sell some of our older milch cows to reduce the demand on our stocks of fodder," Richard replied.

"It's a pity, Richard, that most of our land was planted with corn, with little acreage left for grass. I reckon that's why we're short of hay. And where's the corn straw? And who will buy our cattle now?"

"The straw was put in the grinder to make chaff for the horses. And what do you mean, Giles ... who will buy our cattle now?"

"Our neighbours bought what they required for the winter – milk and beef cattle at the September sales. Approaching Christmas, there's only the Fatstock Show and Sale at Dorchester for beef cattle, for which we've nothing to sell, since dairy cows don't qualify; dairy cow meat is no meat of quality for Christmas."

"If you're right, we'll have to slaughter some of our cows and use the meat to feed ourselves and the workers. But I believe that such a measure doesn't solve the problem of surviving the winter and building up our holding."

"But this is not the best or most opportune time to be slaughtering our cows, Richard. If we sell or slaughter some or all of our cows, with the little we get, we'll still be struggling to pay our way."

"Before we sell or slaughter, we need to plan for a longer-term future."

"This isn't Home Farm, brother, but a rump of land with acres of bog! We're small in acreage, livestock, and, of course, money. We have corn, but we need to sell much of it to survive, and Gargery hasn't made good his offer. And if we did sell any, what's left can't be fed to the sheep in any quantity. Asa would never forgive us if we interfered with him making the ewes forage for grass under the snow."

Richard pondered. Giles's thoughts endorsed his, but, to Richard, Giles's vision was limited. Giles interrupted his thoughts.

"So, what makes you think that we can transform what we have, landwise?"

"Brother, I'll try to answer your questions, but I'd be grateful if, first, you would answer a few questions from me," Richard replied.

"I honour your request, brother," said Giles, bowing mockingly.

"Apart from the gley, what is the soil structure of Wychcombe?"

"We both know that – it's chalk and limestone."

"And grass growth?"

"Well, it's pretty lush in spring and summer."

"Exactly. And the wheat crops?"

"Not bad."

"Exactly. Then would you agree that this land is fertile?"

"Yes, I suppose so, apart from the gley field."

"That's correct, though yields of corn and hay harvested from the other fields have fallen over recent years and why?"

"I don't know, though the land seems to keep up a level of fertility."

"But are we getting the best out of it? Or, to put it another way, how can we stop the downward trend in yields?"

"I suppose that every season we harvest a crop or make hay from cut grass, we're leaching goodness from the soil."

"Then what are we doing to replace that goodness?"

"Nothing."

"Not exactly, Giles. Is nothing given back to the land?"

"We don't give it anything. So, what else can replace what's taken away?"

"No, we don't, but other living beings do. How

long have the foxmoulds shown good grass growth and supported livestock?"

Giles smiled.

"As long as we've kept livestock on it." His face brightened. "I know what you're alluding to."

"Giles, we depended on Home Farm for the main crops. Our corn yields made our family prosperous. And the farm's livestock paid back what was removed from the major part of the foxmoulds by depositing their excrement as they grazed. But here at Wychcombe, we don't have the same acreage and stock. So how can we restore what's lost?"

Giles remained silent.

"Have you heard of 'Turnip Townsend'?"

"Wasn't he the farmer who used turnips as a crop to feed his sheep?"

"Yes, but the most important contribution he made to farming was his rotation of crops. You know that for over a hundred years we've never altered our system of growing corn in the same fields and grass in the foxmoulds. In the past, the ground became so stale that father and grandfather had to rest the land by making some fields fallow for a year."

"But they could afford to do that because they had Home Farm and could live on their prosperity without living frugally, Richard. Wychcombe was neglected and the presence of the gley swamp discouraged increased grazing or cultivation, because that whole field was barren and left uncultivated. We can't, because we're impoverished, and not by choice, either."

"Let's not broach that subject, it's unprofitable.

Townsend proved that by moving his crops around the fields in rotation, he could do away with resting fields for much longer."

"How did he do that?"

"He simply rotated four crops – clover grass, turnips, wheat and barley."

"But the foxmoulds have clover in them."

"He mixed the grasses with high-yielding strains and the clover grasses continued to provide nitrogen which fertilised the soil. And he folded his sheep on turnips as well as grass at special times. The sheep manure replenished the turnip fields. And by rotating those two crops with wheat and barley, he kept the ground from becoming sour and barren."

"But we need more than a quarter of our land under corn, Richard."

"Perhaps, brother, but now that the war has ended, the price of corn will fall, because importation will ultimately be allowed."

"*Ultimately*, but not while the vested interests in Parliament are insisting on keeping the price of corn high to prevent foreign imports glutting the country."

"True, but the repeal of the Corn Laws will come. And though we profited over our neighbouring producers from the storm last September, in a good year their yields will be much greater than ours, but there may be such a glut in a good summer that the price falls drastically. And a fall in price would affect us more than the larger enterprises if we rely too much on corn to keep us solvent. Gargery may have wanted our corn last autumn because of the storm catching our neighbours out, but their yields in a good year will persuade Gargery to decline doing business with us. That's why I believe that sheep and lambs will be a good cash crop."

"But Destro, Copley and Home will be rearing sheep too."

"But with selective breeding on fertile land, with breeds that make the best use of turnips and grass, we can still provide flocks for the market at almost twice the traditional lambs per annum by using our Dorset Horns, they're the most fertile of any breed. We can sell the cattle first, then till and crop the land, multiply the flock and include root crops. The sheep will also yield a wool crop for the market."

Giles could hardly take it in – radically change their traditional system of cultivation and breeding to adopt a system not proven in Dorset, even if it was claimed to be successful in more northern counties! And would turnips succeed as a crop on a different soil?

"But if we go ahead, how will our men adapt to the change? They've not known anything different in their lives from the accepted ways! And poor Thomas, what would happen to him, a herdsman all his working life and no cows?"

"We wouldn't get rid of all the cows, they'd just share the fields with the sheep and, remember, Thomas has helped Asa with the sheep, particularly at lambing time. He can put his hand to almost anything, as you know, so I have no misgivings about him working into a new system."

"But where is the market for our sheep and lambs?"

"There's always been a demand for mutton and lamb among the landed gentry and people like ourselves before we came to grief and I believe that with the opening up of mills in the big cities, there'll be a large and constant demand for meat by the middle class. And there's a good market for spring lambs and their meat."

"When do you hope to launch this ship of experimentation, brother?"

"Not just yet, Giles. Oh, and another thing, why can't we drain the gley, lime and reseed it and turn it into a water meadow?"

"How can we make that wasteland capable of producing anything, Richard? There's acres of gley which is barren and sour – worse, a dangerous bog to man and beast. It's well-nigh impossible to change something that's been there for generations!"

"I don't agree, Giles. What keeps the gley existing?"

"It's got to have water to keep it from drying up; what's that to do with removing the swamp?"

"We need to drain it *pro tem,* dig out the bad, sour soil and replace it with good soil from the foxmoulds to make it suitable for re-soiling, ploughing, hoeing, harrowing, liming and reseeding" Richard answered.

"But how are we going to drain that bog? I vouch it's deeper than we think."

"To drain it, we'd need to dig a ditch parallel, extend it south of the gley, then dig into the gley at the ditch's lowest point…"

"But the gley's lowest point could be deeper than the ditch," Giles interrupted.

"Then we'd have to keep making the ditch deeper. We could use those new clay pipes to drain the gleys. Once drained, we could then remove the bad soil and replace it with good."

"Pshaw! And if it all works, brother, how are we going to water the fresh soil?"

"Well, Giles, ye and I know that the gley always has a water supply from the fall of the meadow and surface water and that there's a common stream which runs through Home Farm on the west side of that farm's fields and continues through to the edge of the gley field and then goes underground. We could run a ditch from the stream, put in furze, bracken and stones, cover the channel with turfs and connect with the new soil replacing the gley."

In spite of Richard's answers, Giles continued his role as Devil's Advocate.

"That's sheer hard graft for the men, and replacing the gley with soil would require carting tons from the foxmoulds."

"There is an alternative, Giles. We could try to change the acidity of the existing gley soil by liming it. Ploughing in the lime repeatedly, watering and reseeding, should give us a fertile ley which as a water meadow will give us higher yields of grass."

"But supposing we get a drought and the brook dries up?"

"But it never has yet. The fall from north to south seems to maintain a fairly high water table and it could be that that's the source of the gley's supply. The field has never been without moisture, even in the hottest summer. And if the stream did dry up, then we could make a leat from the Bredey to irrigate the meadow and make it into a water meadow which would promote a quick growth of grass, provide prime grazing for the sheep and an extra hay crop. Think of it, Giles, at least two harvests of grass per annum!"

Giles was silent. Richard's ambitious scheme would require a prodigious feat of land cultivation.

"A water meadow? In place of the gley? And the whole field be made fertile?"

"Yes, Giles, I believe it's possible. A water meadow, so I'm informed, increases ground temperature to more than five degrees centigrade, which increases grass growth. It would solve our problem of too little grass for fodder and make us self-sufficient in winter. And before we sell the cattle and change our traditional systems, we need to ask ourselves: What's the best use of our land? Our land has to be the key!"

"Where's all the water coming from to irrigate the gley field if and when it's drained?"

"As I've said, we could run off water from the stream on our west side through a leat to that field and there's always been a spring on Home Farm which supplies water to the foxmoulds where we graze the sheep and cattle."

But a cold shiver passed through Richard's mind – what if the Joneses were malicious enough to choke the spring's source where it ran from Home to Wychcombe carrying their water supply to their farmland?

CHAPTER NINETEEN

Hugo plots, but...

"Have ye ever considered how Wychcombe gets its water, father? The Gomers must benefit from the spring that runs under our land at Home and flows southward below us to where Wychcombe Farm lies. Their foxmould fields benefit from the water that supplies Destro and Home – all three farms must be in the line of springs. What if that water supply didn't reach Wychcombe?"

Ezra Jones pondered. They now had Home Farm and Destro.

"Do they really need such a miserable parcel of land with acres of useless gley at Wychcombe Farm?" he queried.

He knew that Hugo's motives were personal rather than the benefits afforded by Wychcombe Farm. Hugo simply wanted to destroy the Gomers, whereas he, Ezra, was willing to overlook the loss of the money owed him by Ronald Gomer so long as they held the more valuable investment of Home Farm with its fertile soil and the rents coming in from their tenants. However, he would not confide this to his son, he'd rather use the loss of the money to make Hugo work the farm and make restitution for his carelessness in losing the money to the Irishmen.

Ezra inwardly sighed. His son was a disappointment and not in the same mould as his yeoman ancestry.

"We know that Home Farm, which is now in our possession, has a spring and a well where we draw water from in the yard. And water from the spring supplies the foxmoulds and has another well, and water from the spring, I guess, runs to Wychcombe land. On the west side of our land is a stream which flows from north-west of Destro, runs along our western border and supplies Wychcombe's gley field, I reckon," Hugo continued.

Ezra listened without responding.

"If the flow from Destro and Home Farm is blocked to Wychcombe and the stream diverted, that farm's land will dry up and the Gomers' crops and grass will fail."

"How? We can't block the spring without depriving ourselves and how do ye know that the spring and stream are the only source of Wychcombe's supply?"

"I don't, but a look at the deeds will tell us. They're held at the bank in Dorchester, as ye know."

"It rains, Hugo, and the land benefits first before the spring and stream are supplied. And rain isn't limited to Home Farm."

"But won't much of what drains into the soil go underground?"

January 20th 1816

Hugo was looking out of the south-facing window in Destro farmhouse to Wychcombe. The village was illuminated by fires. He sensed some satisfaction at the sight of Wychcombe Farm buildings silhouetted by the burning clothes and bedding of smallpox victims. Though inside Destro farmhouse, he could hear the thud of gravediggers' pickaxes and spades on frozen earth, the rattle of the wheels of carts carrying bodies to newly dug common graves where men, mouths and noses covered with neckerchiefs, shovelled lime onto the corpses. Poorer villagers who'd succumbed would not be interred in St. Cuthbert's cemetery; the common grave awaited them. The Gomers were too near the scourge for comfort; their mother Susannah had tragically died and there were rumours that Giles Gomer's face was spotted. Hugo smiled – by a clever ploy he'd stopped visitors from entering Home and Destro Farms by posting notices at the entrances warning that smallpox was already there! By hook or by crook, he'd keep the pock out.

Ironically, in spite of Hugo's warning notices, locked and barred house doors, burned clothes and bedding and quick burials in Wychcombe village's common grave, Hugo's precautions were powerless to keep infection out of Destro and prevent Ezra from contracting smallpox. Hugo gave his father a wide berth as Ezra's condition deteriorated. Her husband's state was causing Martha Jones much concern; she feared the worst. And the symptoms had appeared so suddenly. His face was sweat-beaded, his chest racked with explosive coughing. He raised a bare arm above the sheets, exposing leeches hanging from the skin. Martha replaced her husband's arm under the bed covers then sat down several feet from Ezra's bed. Hugo entered, keeping his distance from his father's bed. "How's father?"

"He's got the croup and a fever, but he still went out to help the milkers yesterday and later swooned. We got him to bed and called the doctor, who suspects the worst …"

"What, not …?"

Martha nodded.

"There looks to be the start of blisters on his face, he's also lost weight, and the way he's going, he'll soon be skin and bone."

"Perhaps it's a bad chill, mother. He forgets he's nigh on fifty and tries to work like a young labourer."

He left without another word. Two hours later, Ezra stirred.

"Where's Hugo?" he croaked, a relief to Martha that her husband was not too far gone to remember their son's name. But Martha did not know Hugo's whereabouts. Their son had disappeared, destination undisclosed. Probably back at Home Farm drinking himself unconscious and fleeing Destro like a rat from a sinking ship. Little did their son care for them, Martha guessed. All he was interested in was himself and acquiring the farms to line his own pockets.

"Martha," Ezra whispered.

Martha bent over her husband and cupped her ear.

"Yes, Ezra dear?"

"Call our ostler."

Martha did as her husband bidded without question, in spite of her curiosity. The ostler tapped on the door, entered on Ezra's command and crept in, cap in hand.

"What can oi do for ye sir?"

"Come closer," Ezra croaked. "Ride into Dorchester today, get the clergyman from St. Bartholomew's, our solicitor Mr. Hawkins, then go to Copley and ask Sir Absalom Goodboys to join us tomorrow. Then, call at Dr. Needman's and ask him to call in at his earliest convenience. When ye've done that, ye can return here to let me know. Is that understood?"

Hugo was sober for once in his life; he was riding the boundaries of Home Farm, contemplating his own future; his father being too sick to handle Destro's affairs and likely to be another smallpox victim; the stolen debt payment no closer to being found; and his poor relationship with Katherine. The cold air almost took his breath away, but sharpened his reasoning. Of first importance, then, was his control of the two farms. On the death of his father, he would then by inheritance be the owner of Destro and Home, not to mention a fair chance of acquiring Wychcombe and ousting the Gomers. No-one else knew of his recent stormy interview with his father. Then he could rule the roost and show Katherine who the master of the house was. He would make sure the men toiled to keep him in the finest of fashion and prosperity. He must concentrate on finding out where the money was that the Irishmen had stolen from him and make sure they were gaoled for many years.

Katherine retired early that night, locking her bedroom door. She insisted on having Rachel on hand to discourage Hugo from molesting her. Katherine lay awake musing. She must protect herself and the new life within her, but how? And where could she go? If she left the farm on any pretence, Hugo would be suspicious and go after her. He would question why Dr. Needman had recently visited more than once, exceeding his monthly calls, if she decided to send for him to help her. Katherine was relieved that she and her unborn child had been protected against smallpox. Who was the farmer whom Harriet had mentioned as someone who practised vaccination? Her heart missed a beat. Could it be one of the … she dismissed further speculation.

The next morning Hugo sat alone in the dining room. Katherine had chosen, as usual, to have breakfast in her bedroom. He cursed. If he hadn't been drunk! What a fool he'd been! He could have had his wife at any time, it was her duty to satisfy his natural desires in an age when no husband would be denied them. Now he couldn't get near her. At least she'd kept the bruises well covered when any company was around. And what was surprising was that she outwardly showed no signs of resentment, though she'd made it virtually impossible for him to be alone with her. She'd pointed out after his last assault on her that she must protect the health of her and their unborn offspring, so it would be sensible for them to sleep in separate rooms until after the child was born. Her meaningful look spoke volumes – hands off! Well, it wouldn't stop him getting drunk again and finding a wench to satisfy him. Once the urchin was born, dearest

Katherine wouldn't have an excuse to resist him! In the meantime, he'd ride to Destro to see how his father was. Happily, he might not recover and he'd inherit Destro and Home by right!

CHAPTER TWENTY

Ezra's Last Will and Testament

The hall clock at Destro Farm struck a quarter past ten in the morning. The day was overcast and the sitting room lit with lanterns in spite of the earliness of the day. The company were silent and gloom had descended over them. Sir Absalom Goodboys was seated next to his wife Eleanor, who sat next to their adoptive son Edmond, facing Ezra Jones's widow Martha, red-eyed from weeping, next to a vacant chair adjacent to where her daughter-in-law Katherine, now clearly pregnant, was seated. The chairs were set in a semi-circle facing an oak desk behind which sat a grey-haired, lined-faced middle-aged man dressed in a black suit offset only by a white shirt with winged collar above a black tie. He removed a gold watch and chain from his waistcoat pocket, opened the cover, consulted the timepiece, closed the cover and returned it to his pocket, perched a pair of horn-rimmed spectacles over the edge of his nose and peered unsmilingly at those present.

January 31st 1816

Ten more minutes elapsed without a word being exchanged between the occupants before Hugo Jones walked unsteadily into the room, gazed around with a blank expression, saw the seat next to his mother and slumped into it.

Edward Hawkins, the solicitor, gave Hugo a curt nod.

"Before I read Mr. Ezra Jones's Last Will and Testament, I must extend my sincere condolences to his widow, Mrs. Martha Jones, her son Hugo and Mrs. Jones's daughter-in-law Lady Katherine. I am aware of the will's contents, having been present and, at the late Mr. Jones's request, drew it up. Mr. Jones was at the critical stage of his illness and in order to testify that he was, in spite of his extremity, in full possession of his mental faculties and in case of any legal challenge …"

At this point, Hugo, who seemed to have dozed off, sat up with a start.

"… I was joined by Sir Absalom Goodboys as the other executor and signatory chosen by the deceased, who will testify to Mr. Jones's soundness of mind at the time. Mrs. Jones was also present. Without further ado, I will now read Mr. Jones's Last Will and Testament."

The solicitor opened a folder and took out several sheets of paper with punched holes tied with pink ribbon, and untied the ribbon, the rustle of paper the only sound in the room until he began to read:

"I, Ezra Charles Jones, being of sound mind, testify that this is my Last Will and Testament, dictated by me and drawn up in the presence of witnesses, including my beloved wife Martha, our family solicitor Mr. Edward Hawkins and my neighbour Sir Absalom Goodboys, owner of Copley Farm Estate, West Dorset. It is also a confession on my part of misappropriating money…"

Hugo Jones began to shift in his seat, wiped his sweating brow with a handkerchief and gazed fixedly at the floor.

"… in the seizure of land known as Home Farm owned by Ronald Gomer in lieu of non-payment of a debt of honour as his indebtedness to me resulting from losing thirty-five thousand guineas to me at cards."

At this stage, Edward Hawkins paused and took a sip of water from a glass tumbler. Every eye was riveted on him and the papers he held. He continued:

"And I confess as to my part in the above-mentioned deception, a sinful act that has belaboured my conscience and no doubt will leave a stain on the family name. It came to my knowledge that moneys withdrawn from the Dorchester branch of the Devon and Dorset Bank by Ronald Gomer intended to settle his gambling debt were misappropriated by his agent Bowen Dranley and at least one other party whose identity I am privy to but whose name I will not disclose. As Bowen Dranley died tragically, the other party must decide as to their responsibility in this matter. I colluded with that party in the covert confiscation of the money, knowing that it had been stolen from Ronald Gomer and with my full intention of seizing Home Farm by claiming non-payment of the debt. Some would call it 'having one's cake and eating it'…"

This drew a wry smile from Sir Absalom.

"… and it is to my shame that I was party to this deception and, in drawing up this will, I intend to make restitution for my complicity in this crime to the injured parties, namely, the dependants of the late Ronald and the Honourable Susannah Gomer.

"Ironically, I never received a penny of this money, which was alleged to have been stolen by a band of Irish rogues, money which in my folly I hoped to conceal as well as falsely claim Home Farm. Though I received not a groat of this money, that does not absolve me from my intention to steal it. My felony has led to the impoverishment of the Honourable Susannah Gomer and her sons Richard and Giles Gomer, forcing them to eke out a poor living from much unforgiving land and acres of poisonous swamp at Wychcombe Farm. Therefore I have instructed my executors that before willing the residue of my estate to my dependants, viz. my dear wife Martha and my only son Hugo and his wife and descendants through his marriage to Lady Katherine Goodboys, to expedite repayment to the sons of Ronald Gomer …"

Hugo, eyes blazing and fists clenched, rose to his feet and shouted:

"Home Farm is rightly ours! I will fight any attempt to give those brothers a groat of our money as recompense. There is no proof that we ever received any money from Ronald Gomer for his loss at cards!"

Although Hugo's words might have, to the casual observer, expressed fury, to an observant and discerning listener, there was a suspicion that he was blustering.

Edward Hawkins raised his hands.

"Mr. Jones, please sit down and let me finish."

Hugo sat down, shaking his head.

"Since I became the new and most recent owner of Home Farm as legitimate compensation for Ronald Gomer's non-payment of the gambling debt, my ownership of Home Farm cannot be challenged …"

Hugo gasped in relief and wiped his sweating brow.

"… however, since I became party to the theft of the moneys Ronald Gomer withdrew with the intention of repaying that debt, I have to accept some responsibility for this deception. That I never received the moneys does not absolve me from my intention to keep the money to myself and divide it with another party. I intended to keep and share the moneys as though I had never received it, truly an act of theft. When this will is read and the true facts revealed, I will have gone to meet my Maker and be beyond the law. Therefore, after taking legal advice, I have, in my will, made both adequate provision for my dependants and restitution to the offspring of Ronald and Susannah Gomer."

Hugo stood up, opened his mouth, uttered no words and rushed out, red-faced, shaking his head. Edward Hawkins looked up.

"I regret that Mr. Jones's son has seen fit to absent himself, but I must continue."

He bent down and continued to read the will.

"I have decided to offer on my death, to Richard and Giles Gomer, as descendants of their deceased parents and original owners of both Home and Wychcombe estates, Home Farm and its appurtenances or its equivalent value, which is, I am informed by land agents in terms of local land values, worth thirty thousand pounds, the equivalent value of almost all the moneys misappropriated from Ronald Gomer."

A united gasp rose from the company.

"I am offering this in spite of another person sharing the guilt for the theft and who should accept equal responsibility. The summation of the rest of my estate which will accrue from moneys deposited in the Dorchester branch of the Devon and Dorset Bank, plus the sale of my personal possessions listed in the codicil to this will, the proceeds of which will be put in trust, the capital and interest of which I bequeath to provide my dear wife Martha an adequate sum to live on comfortably and, following her death, the residual capital being held in trust for any dependants including the wife and any offspring of my son Hugo. I bequeath to my wife permanent residence on Destro Farm. Ownership of the farm will be shared between my wife and my son Hugo, *its future as a farming enterprise depending on his ability and commitment to make it profitable.* If my son fails to make the working of the farm profitable, then the livestock shall be sold and the land and outlying buildings shall be leased to another party on an agreed rental, the proceeds to go to my wife and son, then on my wife's decease to my son Hugo, his wife Katherine and on their decease to their descendants."

Signed: Ezra Charles Jones.

Witness and Signatory: Edward Hawkins, Solicitor and Executor with Power of Attorney.

Witness and Signatory: Sir Absalom Adoniram Goodboys, Executor.

Dated this day of our Lord January 25th 1816."

The solicitor secured the documents with the pink ribbon, placed the documents in the folder and closed it, placing the folder in his briefcase. The company remained transfixed and motionless as if paralysed by the disclosures, the silence broken only by gentle sobbing from Martha

Jones, comforted by Katherine, who had moved over to take the chair vacated by Hugo.

The solicitor rose.

"Mrs. Jones has informed me that refreshments are awaiting us in the dining room, so please join me there," he added. He approached Martha Jones, offering his arm, which she took and the pair left the room.

Sir Absalom joined Edward Hawkins over a glass of sherry.

"It seems clear to me that Ezra had no intention of bequeathing both Home and Destro Farms to Hugo, Mr. Hawkins. Ezra Jones's division of the ownership of Destro between his wife and son and his reference to the farm's future being dependent on Hugo's commitment to it reflects badly on his son following in his father's footsteps as a good farmer."

The solicitor nodded.

"Mr. Jones was aware of his son's unbalanced nature and uncontrollable temper, his drinking habits and lack of commitment to farming. Goodness knows how he'll react to the will, especially the part of it that I read in his absence. Ezra insisted that the statement should be included in the will that Destro would only continue as a farming enterprise depending on Hugo's commitment and ability to make it pay."

"I have a premonition that he will contest the will and fight tooth and nail to have it made null and void on the basis of his father's insanity."

"Then I fear, Sir Absalom, that he will lose if it goes to an appeal."

"Then if such an appeal fails, Hugo will do everything he can to prevent the Gomers receiving his father's bequest. On a different subject, have you any idea who could have been party to Ezra's felony?"

The solicitor made no answer but consulted his timepiece. He's not going to be drawn, Sir Absalom mused.

"My, my, how *tempus fugit*. Please excuse me, Sir Absalom, I have pressing business in Dorchester. Perhaps we can meet to discuss probate. Today is Tuesday; would Friday be convenient?"

Absalom Goodboys consulted a leather-bound diary.

"Yes, Mr. Hawkins, Friday will be most convenient. May I invite you to join me at Copley? The roads are fairly clear at the moment, but if the weather turns nasty, we can accommodate you beyond Friday. And our cook provides an excellent roast. Let's hope that the weather and roads will facilitate uneventful travelling."

"Excellent. Then shall I say that I will be with you on Friday at approximately twelve midday, weather permitting, of course?"

Sir Absalom nodded. They shook hands, the solicitor spoke briefly to Martha Jones, who instructed the butler to have the ostler arrange for the solicitor's horse and trap to be ready for Edward Hawkins to depart.

CHAPTER TWENTY-ONE

Hugh Contests the Will

"I'll contest my father's will!" Hugo raged at the solicitor, who was in the yard about to leave Destro after the reading of Ezra Jones's will. "He must have been out of his mind to offer the Gomers any of the land we rightly took in payment for Ronald Gomer's gambling debts!"

"But, Mr. Jones, your father was as clearheaded as you or I in spite of his illness and he insisted on admitting his complicity in defrauding Ronald Gomer's dependants," Edward Hawkins replied.

"Apart from the word of my dying father in this spurious will, was there any proof that we ever received the money, let alone took and secretly kept it then seized Home Farm as payment?"

"None to my knowledge, apart from your father's spoken and recorded testimony. Why should he lie when he knew that he had little time to live?"

"I believe that the pock 'ad addled his brain and ye won't persuade me otherwise. I've every right t' contest the will on grounds of my father's insanity!"

"Then I can offer you no further assistance in my office as an executor of your father's will. I would advise you, young Jones, to carefully consider the implications of such a step. The financial costs if you lose any case of litigation could be more than you can pay."

"Fiddlesticks! I have only your word of my father's state of mind…"

"And Sir Absalom's", the solicitor added gently.

"You both could be in league to tamper with his will!"

"I am extremely offended by your insinuation and no doubt Sir Absalom would be, should I disclose your slanderous accusation to him, but I will overlook what you've said on condition that you immediately withdraw those remarks."

"Oh, very well, I withdraw them," Hugo mumbled.

"For your mother's sake and yours, I urge you, look before you leap to contest your father's will. Now, I am a very busy man; please permit me to depart if you have nothing further to discuss with me."

At this, Edward Hawkins turned and walked towards his horse and trap without another word.

"But mother, it's as much in your interests as mine to resist surrendering any part of Home Farm for sale or to the Gomers for possession. And to sell Destro is unthinkable. They are our homes. To lose Home Farm on the claim that the Gomers were cheated out of their money is a fantasy. Mother, if the Gomers are allowed to reoccupy Home Farm, think of all the rents we'd lose from the tenants! And the corn contract with Gargery …"

Martha Jones raised her tear-stained face and looked her son squarely in the eye.

"Hugo, stop! Your father discussed with me what we should do after he admitted his dishonesty. We agreed that Destro should be leased if you failed to make it a successful farming enterprise so that I could continue to live comfortably and a trust fund be kept for you, Katherine and any offspring you both have. And if you succeeded, you would have Destro to provide a return on livestock and crops as well …"

"I won't think of surrendering Home Farm!" interrupted Hugo.

"Listen to me, Hugo," Martha Jones replied in a steely stone. "Your father and I knew for many years that you've never merited taking over Home, though you're our only offspring. All you've been interested in has been to spend whatever profit your father laboured for. You made no real effort to manage Home Farm, so your father changed his mind about giving you the ownership. Even the Gomers have harvested more corn on their small rump of Wychcombe Farm than you have on the bigger acreage at Home. And another thing – are you the other party in your father's admitted deception?"

Hugo avoided answering the question:

"Mother, you can't blame me for the weather spoiling the corn…"

"The weather didn't stop the Gomers from reaping well! What did you do, apart from spending your time drinking yourself helpless and scheming to destroy the Gomers? And you abandoned your dying father when he needed you most!"

Hugo was silent.

"Hugo, you couldn't farm a smallholding let alone two

large farms, so your father decided and I agreed that we would return Home Farm to the Gomers and you should prove yourself here at Destro and …"

"I'll resist any attempt to wrest a foot of Home Farm off us!"

Martha Jones held a hand up, weariness etched on her face.

"That's enough! I'm tired and grieving for your father and must retire."

She walked slowly but steadily from the room, muffling her sobs in a handkerchief.

Edward Hawkins and Absalom Goodboys sat drinking claret in the drawing room at Copley following a sumptuous meal of roast beef with all the trimmings followed by plum pie and custard.

"In spite of any challenge to Ezra Jones's Will, we must inform the Gomers that they're beneficiaries, Mr. Hawkins."

The solicitor gazed out of the window. The snow-covered meadows held an ethereal beauty and peace that contrasted with his thoughts.

"But if Hugo Jones decides to contest the will, he might appeal for a stay of execution with the objective of rendering the will void and preventing the Gomers from getting anything."

"I'll destroy Home Farm rather than surrender the sole

of my shoe's measure of ground to the Gomers," Hugo said to himself.

He had travelled on horseback to the Dorchester chambers of Sir Matthew Stanking K.C. Though he was determined to contest the will, he had misgivings about the cost even if he won the case. Home Farm had yielded a poor harvest following the disastrous autumn storm in September last year and Destro was struggling to make ends meet. Without proper management, the workers had been left to their own devices and their own native knowledge of the best they could do without proper supervision. Moreover, winter showed no signs of abating, when the land was not yielding a harvest and any fodder and the meagre corn stores harvested in 1815 were running low. And Sir Matthew's costs, like his reputation, would be high.

"Sir Matthew will see you now, Mr. Jones," an elderly retainer's announcement woke Hugo from his conflicting thoughts.

He followed the man through a door into a spacious room with a polished oak floor and furnished with Queen Anne chairs and a large settee, a large oak sappele table and matching chairs, probably used for meetings. In the room stood an enormous polished mahogany desk behind which sat a portly balding gentleman with flaming ginger hair descending down his cheeks as mutton chop whiskers on a rubicund face, with sharp eyes, a more rubicund nose below which sprouted a bushy moustache above generous lips. His double chin and ample neck were enclosed in a spotless white wing collar and cravat under an immaculate morning suit, giving a solid impression of prosperity.

Sir Matthew did not rise, and pointed Hugo to a seat facing him. He took out a gold snuffbox, poured a pinch of snuff onto an ample index finger, inhaled it, took out a handkerchief, trumpeted into it, then wiped his watering eyes with an unsullied section of the handkerchief.

"If you accept my services, Mr. Jones, they will not come cheap. They are based on an initial payment of fifty guineas and hourly costs of two guineas until you or I decide to terminate the contract. Do I make myself clear?"

Hugo hesitated, then nodded, which Sir Matthew took as confirmation.

"I require the original or a written copy of your father's will, to ascertain if there are grounds for an injunction to prevent its execution during probate and ultimately render the will void. That estate then reverts to your father's dependants, which includes yourself. Would you agree, Mr. Jones?"

Hugo preened himself.

"Of course, sir. I believe that my father was not of sound mind due t' him sufferin' the pock when the will was drafted and might have been duped into agreeing to sign the will."

"Any coercion or collusion by the executors will be difficult to prove, Mr. Jones, but I shall look into that. Who was the solicitor who drew up the will and who were the executors?"

"The solicitor, who was also one of the executors, was Mr. Edward Hawkins and the other executor was Sir Absalom Goodboys of Copley Farm."

"Were you present at the drafting and signing of your father's will?"

"No sir," Hugo replied.

"Why not, Mr. Jones?"

"I was attending to affairs at Home Farm, which my father had passed on ownership to me," Hugo lied.

Even so, Sir Matthew was mystified as to why Hugo had not been present, but did not comment.

"I will need to know the state of your father's holding at Destro and yours at Home and how that relates to your father's will."

It would be dangerous ground for this lawyer to get to know that Home Farm was not his, thought Hugo. Fortunately, his father's decision to remove Hugo from ownership of the farm was verbal and only privy to them both. Aware that time was money now that he'd hired the lawyer, Hugo quickly described the acquisition of Home Farm to add to the family holding of Destro.

"On settlement of probate, what was to be the outcome for you?"

"I was to be deprived of Home Farm, which, as I have explained, was recently seized by my father from Ronald Gomer for non-payment of a debt of thirty-five thousand guineas lost by Gomer at cards. My father, in an insane decision, appeared to have, for reasons known only to himself, decided to hand back Home Farm, lock, stock and barrel to Ronald Gomer's dependants."

"Have you any idea why, Mr. Jones?"

"I just can't believe that my father had pangs of conscience in 'is dying hours," Hugo replied.

"But if he truly had 'pangs of conscience', what motivated them?"

Hugo was beginning to understand why the K.C. was

so costly to engage, yet worth every penny he was hired for.

"Accordin' to what was written in the will, father had the notion that Ronald Gomer had withdrawn the money intending to pay off the debt, but it was stolen. So father never received it and felt responsible for seizing Home Farm," Hugo replied evasively.

"But I still don't understand why your father should have pangs of conscience if he had not received the money. What proof was there that the money had been withdrawn by Gomer for repayment and received without disclosure by your father and a second party?"

"None to my knowledge, Sir Matthew," Hugo lied.

"Mmm," the lawyer remarked, joining the tips of his fingers together. "And the rest of your father's estate – who are the beneficiaries?"

"My father's widow, that is, my mother, myself and, in the event of my death, my wife and any offspring from our union."

"Anyone else?"

"Not to my knowledge."

"Very well, then, that's all, Mr. Jones. Please ensure that I have the original or a copy of your father's will to hand as soon as possible. Goodday to ye, my clerk will see you out" Sir Matthew concluded, ringing a bell on his desk but remaining seated.

CHAPTER TWENTY-TWO

Jones versus Jones

By nine a.m. the courtroom at Dorchester was packed. The public gallery was crowded, with no spare seat available in the well of the court. In fact, the double doors into the courtroom could not be closed, being jammed to the walls on either side by the crush of people struggling to get inside the building spilling out onto the main street. The solitary soldier appointed to guard the courtroom entrance had given up his task of maintaining order and stood to one side of the milling mob, who by design or coincidence were in Dorchester on its weekly market day and livestock market. It was common knowledge that Hugo Jones, son of the deceased owner of Destro Farm near Wychcombe, was contesting his father's will on grounds of his father's insanity.

February 27th 1816

Below the bench and vacant judge's seat, the court clerk fussed over his papers, periodically adjusting his wig and straightening his black gown of office. To one side, level with the judge's seat but positioned at least twice a sword's length away to prevent any attempts by defendants to harm them, and connected to the underground cells with steps, was a dock, which afforded a place for courtroom witnesses to be called. Seated near the bench at two separate tables were Hugo, his counsel Sir Matthew Stanking and an assistant. Seated at the other table was Mr. Edward Hawkins and his assistant. Sitting on a row behind the lawyers were Martha, Ezra Jones's widow, and her daughter-in-law Lady Katherine Jones nee Goodboys, Katherine's adopted brother Edmond Goodboys, Sir Absalom and Lady Eleanor Goodboys. In the row behind them sat Richard and Giles Gomer. To their right, facing them, were three rows of raised benches reserved for the jury with more than adequate space, but due to the crush claiming seats today additional public seating was arranged on one of the rows.

"An' who be the legal gen'ilmen?" a workman, in muddy boots, woollen trousers and woollen jacket over a long brown smock, asked the soldier.

"Sir Matthew Stankin' fer Mr. Jones and Mr. Hawkins fer the others," the soldier replied.

The courtroom clock struck the half hour at nine thirty.

In perfect timing, Judge Sir Thomas Parsicker appeared through a door on a level with his seat.

"All rise!" cried the clerk and the assembly rose. Judge Sir Thomas Parsicker, a tall, bewigged man with birdlike eyes set in a pale aquiline face, hooked nose and bloodless lips, dressed in the gold and crimson robes of office gazed at length on the courtroom, brusquely nodded to the assembly and sat down, signalling their permission to follow. On cue, the clerk rose, bowed and handed a sheaf of documents to the judge.

"The quarter sessions of Dorchester assizes is now open, your Honour. Our case this morning, your Honour, is that of Jones versus Jones in which the plaintiff Mr. Hugo Jones of Destro and Home Farms in the parish of Wychcombe, West Dorset is applying for an injunction against the execution of the Last Will and Testament of his father Mr. Ezra Jones of Destro Farm on the grounds of his father's insanity due to a terminal illness."

Both the clerk and judge knew that the clerk's announcement was a mere formality to satisfy legal protocol, since the judge had already read the contents of the case in his chambers before returning the documents to the clerk before the proceedings.

"And who represents the plaintiff?" boomed the judge, his voice creating a shiver through a shabbily dressed section of attenders in the public gallery.

"Sir Matthew Stanking, K.C., your Honour," replied the clerk.

"And on behalf of the deceased?"

"Mr. Edward Hawkins, your Honour," the clerk replied.

The judge adjusted his spectacles, and opened and examined the papers supplied by the clerk. He looked up, stared severely at Sir Matthew and declared:

"As counsel to the plaintiff, Sir Matthew, do you wish to proceed first?" he demanded.

Sir Matthew rose.

"Thank you, your Honour. I consider it a great privilege

to represent my client Mr. Hugo Jones in your court. I will therefore briefly set forth my plaintiff's case for an injunction against the execution of his father's Last Will and Testament on the ground of his father's condition, dying as he was of the pock, raising suspicions that he was deprived of his sanity. Mr. Ezra Jones was, to quote the vernacular, your Honour, 'at death's door' and unfit to dictate and sign the aforementioned document. I will seek to provide circumstantial evidence that in Ezra Jones's condition, he was susceptible to coercion and unable to discern that he was influenced by unjust and prejudiced advice …"

"Objection!" Mr. Hawkins interrupted. "Counsel for the plaintiff has no evidence that Mr. Jones was susceptible to coercion and unable to discern that he was influenced by unjust and prejudiced advice."

"I will uphold Mr. Hawkins' objection unless you can convince me of a clear connection between your case and Mr. Ezra Jones's mental state, Sir Matthew," the judge declared.

"Your Honour, I will, if permitted, show without doubt that both the circumstances under which the will was drafted and signed, and the deceased's mental state as supported by expert testimony, justify this injunction and will pave the way to making the will referred to null and void."

"I will therefore overrule Mr. Hawkins' objection, Sir Matthew, but I will be watching for any deviation from your stated objective. Now get on with it," added the judge testily.

Sir Matthew called several witnesses to testify to the

character of his client These mainly included employees who worked on Destro Farm plus one or two of Hugo's drinking friends. Although the witnesses testified to the merits of Hugo as an employer or friend, Mr. Hawkins's questioning of them rendered their testimony unimpressive and unconvincing, raising the suspicion that they may have been coerced or persuaded against their better judgement. The lawyer's questioning dragged on for over two hours.

"Your Honour," declared Sir Matthew, "I now wish to call Sir Absalom Goodboys."

"Call Sir Absalom Goodboys," the clerk ordered a court officer and the peer's name was echoed throughout the courthouse.

To a buzz from the courtroom, Sir Absalom entered from the rear of the court and was led to the witness box and sworn in by a court officer.

"What is your full name and place of residence?" asked Sir Matthew.

"Absalom Adoniram Goodboys of Copley Estate, West Dorset."

"Sir Absalom, were you present at the drafting and signing of Mr. Ezra Jones's will?"

"I was."

"Who else was present at the time?"

"Mr. Edward Hawkins and Mrs. Martha Jones, Mr. Ezra Jones's wife."

"Was Mr. Hugo Jones, Ezra Jones's son not present?" exclaimed the lawyer, his tone expressing surprise at the omission.

"No, Sir Matthew."

"Why not?"

"Mr. Hugo Jones, I was informed, rarely visited Destro Farm during his father's last days."

"If this was so, why not?"

Sir Absalom was not being drawn. He knew from reliable local sources that Hugo spent most of his time drinking in Dorchester and riding around the countryside, apparently without concern for his dying father, but to say so would mark him of bias in trying to cast Hugo in an unfavourable light. Sir Matthew would then take full advantage to label Sir Absalom as an executor who was critical of Ezra's son, inferring that he might have been in favour of advising Ezra Jones to return Home Farm to the Gomers.

"I cannot say."

"Surely, as the father's next-of-kin and only son, he had every right to be present. And even if Mr. Hugo Jones was not present, efforts should have been made to locate and send for him, don't you think?"

"I cannot say whether Ezra, er … Mr. Jones had already sent for him," Sir Absalom replied.

"Doesn't it seem to you strange that Mr. Jones's father should not disclose his intentions to his only son?"

"If you've read Ezra's will, you would understand why, sir, though I was not privy to Ezra's intentions before the will was drafted," countered Sir Absalom.

"With all the executors and Mr. Jones's wife present, doesn't it strike you as tantamount to a conspiracy that the son was excluded from the drafting and signing of the will?"

"No, sir, there was no such thing as a conspiracy."

Sir Matthew changed his line of questioning.

"Are you a man of medicine, Sir Absalom?"

"No, Sir Matthew."

"Then how can you testify that Mr. Jones was of sound mind at the time that he signed the will?"

"Because I know when a man is of sound mind when I see one."

"Am I, in your opinion, a man of sound mind?"

"You probably are, though I would question your soundness in representing Mr. Hugo Jones," Sir Absalom calmly replied, to loud laughter from the court. Judge Parsicker frowned and Hugo glowered. Sir Absalom immediately regretted the faux pas which now exposed his feelings about Ezra's son.

"We shall see, Sir Absalom, we shall see. Thank you for your assessment of my soundness of mind, but you would admit that you're clearly not an expert in medical matters, to understate your lack of qualifications and experience. Sir Absalom, was a doctor present to certify Mr. Ezra Jones's soundness of mind?"

"No, not at the time."

"Sir Absalom, I gather that the Gomers are neighbouring land ... er, farmers to you. What is the state of your relationship with them?"

"We have always been on good terms with one another."

"Friendly, perhaps even very friendly?"

"We have been on friendly terms as neighbours."

"Then how did you feel when Ronald Gomer lost Home Farm in exchange for a gambling debt?"

"I felt very sorry for him, but concluded that he had brought it on himself."

"Sorry enough to influence Mr. Ezra Jones into bequeathing Home Farm back to Ronald Gomer's dependants?"

"Objection, your Honour! Questioning, nay, virtually accusing Sir Absalom in such a manner, Sir Matthew is subjecting Sir Absalom to unfair cross-examination!" Edward Hawkins cried.

"I will sustain Mr. Hawkins' objections and I must warn you, Sir Matthew, that I will be most severe with any further similar and unwarranted assumptions."

"Very well, your Honour," counsel for Hugo Jones replied.

"Sir Absalom, did you once confide that you hoped that Mr. Hugo Jones didn't take over Home Farm because he would let it go to rack and ruin?"

"I may have done," Sir Absalom replied.

"If you did voice such an opinion, and I do have it on good authority, wouldn't you agree that your opinion of Mr. Hugo Jones's so-called incapability would have prompted you to influence his father's disfavour of his son so that he deprived his son of Home Farm?"

Sir Absalom pondered. To claim that what he had voiced was untrue would brand him as an unreliable witness.

"It is common knowledge, and especially to his father, that Mr. Hugo Jones was not cut out for farming."

Sir Matthew turned to face the judge.

"No further questions, your Honour."

The judge looked across at Edward Hawkins.

"Do you wish to question Sir Absalom, Mr. Hawkins?"

"I have just one question to ask Sir Absalom at this

stage. Sir Absalom, to settle one matter – will you materially benefit from Mr. Ezra Jones's will?"

"In no way," was Sir Absalom's answer.

"You may step down, Sir Absalom. Please call your next witness, Sir Matthew"

"Aye, your Honour. Would the clerk summon Mr. Richard Gomer"

At the clerk's call, Richard rose from his seat next to Giles and walked to the witness box. Katherine's heart went out to him as he walked, white-faced and tight-lipped, his single arm swinging in time to his military gait. After swearing on oath over the bible handed to him by the clerk and stating his name and address, he waited, erect, for Sir Matthew to question him. The lawyer shuffled through the papers in front of him, delaying his cross-examination, but if he did it to discomfort Richard, the latter seemed undisturbed. At length, the lawyer walked over to the witness box.

"Mr. Gomer, what proof had ye that your father ever withdrew the thirty-five thousand guineas from his bank?"

"None at the time, sir," Richard replied.

A united gasp rose from the court.

"Then how can ye claim that the money ever left the family account?"

"At the time I was fighting under the Duke of Wellington against Napoleon at the Battle of Waterloo, but our late mother and my brother can testify that the money was withdrawn and given to our agent to repay Mr. Ezra Jones."

"But if your claims are true, and as my client alleges, no money passed hands to settle the debt, where is the proof that it was ever withdrawn?"

"The bank holds evidence that the money was withdrawn at our father's request."

"But, Mr. Gomer, it may have been withdrawn, but that does not prove that it was given to Mr. Ezra Jones. Isn't it a possibility that someone in your family, your brother or even your mother, may have withheld it?"

A horrified gasp and buzz of voices reacted to such a suggestion. The judge banged his gavel. Edward Hawkins rose to object but was halted by Richard's raised hand and sat down. Richard's pale face showed twin points of anger on his cheeks, but his words were measured:

"If what you suggested had been the case, our mother, a woman of the highest integrity, would never do such a thing to go against my father's wishes and dishonour him and the family name. Moreover, if she had held the money, she would willingly have surrendered it rather than forfeit Home Farm, the seat of generations of the Gomers, and land to our family of much greater value than the debt. And I have absolute trust that my brother Giles would never commit such a scurrilous act! Your inference is insulting to us and to the memory of our deceased mother and does you no credit, sir!"

A spontaneous burst of applause broke out from a section of the court.

"Order in court!" cried Judge Parsicker. "I'll clear this court at the next interruption! Sir Matthew, do you wish to withdraw your allusion that some member of the Gomer family could have withheld the money?"

"Your Honour, wouldn't *you* consider it a possibility? However, I'm happy to apologise and withdraw any

189

suggestion that the Honourable Susannah Gomer had anything to do with such an act."

The wily lawyer, in spite of his withdrawal, had planted the thought in the minds of the court.

"Then, Mr. Gomer, if the money was actually withdrawn, have you any idea where it now is?"

Richard paused before replying. If he claimed to have recovered incriminating notes on McAlerty's person, but had destroyed them, Sir Matthew would demolish such evidence on lack of proof. Richard was convinced that Hugo had stolen the money, which was stolen in turn from Hugo by the Irish tinkers, so should he disclose this? He was under oath to answer truthfully.

"I cannot provide any proof," Richard replied.

Sir Matthew smiled.

"Then we have only the word of a dying man of doubtful sanity that ..."

"Objection, your Honour! Learned counsel hasn't a scrap of knowledge or evidence that Mr. Jones was not of sound mind at the time of the drawing up and signing of the will. Sir Matthew was not present, nor *is he* a doctor of medicine."

"I will uphold Mr. Hawkins' objection on this occasion, Sir Matthew, unless you can give support to your claim," the judge replied.

In questioning Ezra Jones's sanity, Sir Matthew had again planted the thought in the minds of the court.

"I hope to pursue my claim later, your Honour, but I'm happy to withdraw my previous remarks since as yet I can only infer as to what I believe are the facts," Sir Matthew responded.

"Then I order your reference to withholding the

money to be struck from the court records and no more inferences, sir," Sir Thomas growled. "Now get on questioning Mr. Gomer with those instructions in mind."

"By all means, your Honour. Mr. Gomer, what I cannot understand from a previous statement you made is why you didn't fight to hold on to so precious an estate as Home Farm and come to some other arrangement to pay off the debt?"

"If you have any knowledge of farming as a livelihood, you would realise, sir, that the repayment of thirty-five thousand guineas by any other way than surrendering one of our two holdings would have been well-nigh impossible in our lifetime. To quickly pay off a debt of honour was more important to the family name and honour than resisting all attempts to hand over Home Farm."

"But let us suppose, and I will be circumspect, your Honour, it's only a supposition," Sir Matthew said, looking at the judge, "that someone in your family Mr. Gomer, had the means to recover the money, wouldn't it be possible to buy a very good property with that money, even on losing Home Farm?"

"How could we explain where such a large sum of money had appeared from if we had bought another property when we surrendered Home Farm and our family was reduced to our present state? It's obvious to people in West Dorset that we are little better than labourers on Wychcombe Farm."

"Perhaps, Mr. Gomer. No further questions for this witness, your Honour," Sir Matthew concluded.

"Do you wish to question the witness, Mr. Hawkins?" the judge asked.

191

"No, your Honour."

The judge pulled out his fob watch as the courthouse clock struck twelve.

"I think that this would be an appropriate time to adjourn this case until this afternoon," he said, closing the folder of papers in front of him.

Sir Thomas Parsicker turned to the members of the jury.

"In the meantime, I warn you not to discuss the proceedings of this case nor answer any questions relating to it to any other party. Court proceedings will resume at two p.m."

"All rise!"

On the departure of the judge, there was a steady exodus of those attending the case, though arranging for friends and relatives to guard their places until the return of the former. Some had had the foresight to bring in their own refreshments.

On the stroke of two, the jury filed in, followed seconds later by Sir Thomas Parsicker; the packed courtroom rose at the clerk's command and seated themselves.

"Sir Matthew, call your next witness, if you please!" boomed Sir Thomas.

"My next witness, your Honour, is Mrs. Martha Jones, widow of the deceased."

Martha Jones walked slowly across the courtroom and climbed into the witness box. She was sworn in and gave her name and address.

In questioning her, Sir Matthew adopted a gentle approach.

"Mrs. Jones, will you please accept my condolences at the tragic loss of your beloved husband from such a dreadful scourge? I'm truly sorry that I have to question you under such circumstances, but I hope that you appreciate that we all want justice not only to be done but to be seen to be done."

"Thank you, sir."

"Regarding your husband, what would you say, in your opinion, was his state of mind at the time he signed his Last Will and Testament?"

"He was as sane as you or I."

"But he was terminally ill, Mrs. Jones; surely he wasn't his normal self?"

"If you mean his bodily health, of course not, he was in the last throes of the pock. But his mind was as clear as a church bell and as sharp as a razor."

"But what made him treat his son so badly as to disinherit his ownership of Home Farm?"

"I had to agree with Ezra once he'd admitted to me of his deception, that he should make restitution for the benefit of the Gomers, however bizarre it might seem."

"Indeed, one has to admit that it was bizarre, in fact out of character, suggesting that his mind was in some way distorted by the disease. Wouldn't you agree, Mrs. Jones?"

"Ezra knew that Hugo could never make a go of farming, especially when he had the opportunity but failed to work the land well at Home Farm and produce good crops last year."

"But wasn't the weather which all the local farmers experienced to blame for Home Farm's poor corn crop?"

"Yes, but what impressed Ezra was the way in which the Gomers were able to harvest a first-grade corn crop and thresh it in spite of an impending storm a few days later, using a rusty old hand-thresher on limited acreage, when Hugo had more and better land to grow and harvest corn at Home Farm."

It was clear to Hugo's lawyer that he would find it difficult to make any headway with the witness on behalf of his client.

"No further questions, your Honour."

"Your witness, Mr. Hawkins?" the judge queried.

"No questions for the witness, your Honour," Edward Hawkins replied.

"However, at this point, I would be most grateful, your Honour, if you would permit me at short notice to call Dr. Prysumor, a medical specialist and consultant in infectious diseases, with a particular expertise in the study of smallpox, commonly known as the pock," Sir Matthew announced.

"You know that this would be a departure from normal court procedure, Sir Matthew, but if Mr. Hawkins has no objection on this occasion, I will consider permitting it," replied the judge, looking across at Edward Hawkins.

"No objections, your Honour," the solicitor responded.

"Then, Mrs. Jones, you may leave the witness box."

After the consultant was called and sworn in, he was asked to identify himself.

"Professor Granton Prysumor, Doctor of Medicine, Fellow of the Royal College of Surgeons, Fellow of the

Royal College of Physicians, International Specialist in Contagious and Infectious Diseases of the human species and in particular, as the learned friend has emphasised, the study of the diagnosis and epidemiology of smallpox and adviser to the British Medical Association."

Edward Hawkins' assistant whistled under his breath, but his principal remained poker-faced.

"Professor Prysumor, thank you for attending this court to give us the benefit of your comprehensive knowledge. I gather that you are a recognised international authority in the diagnosis and pathology of smallpox?"

"That is so, sir," Professor Prysumor boomed.

Edward Hawkins suspected that this man would be a formidable authority concerning smallpox, his particular specialist area. The doctor was, by Edward Hawkins' estimate, middle-aged, his head crowned with a high receding forehead encircled by auburn hair which flowed down his cheeks in generous sideburns, his face punctuated by small pupils under bushy eyebrows, a bulbous purple nose above a generous moustache and a rounded, clean-shaven chin. Physically stout, immaculately dressed in morning suit and exuding a confidence clearly fuelled by his expertise, his demeanour was authoritative and, to Edward Hawkins, possibly with a degree of arrogance which would brook no contradiction – could this be his Achilles heel?

"Professor Prysumor, as an eminent researcher in the study of smallpox, what is your opinion of the effects of its course in a patient in the advanced stages of the disease?"

"The patient would already be in a very parlous state of body and mind due to the toxic effects of large quantities of the pock in the blood, known to the physician as a viraemia."

"Professor, please explain to us what in effect is this parlous state?"

"The victi ... er, patient would by this time be covered with pustular foci of toxic exudate breaking out of the skin all over the body and be physically already weakened from the pyrexia ..."

"Your Honour, would the Professor please explain to the court in simple everyday language what 'pustular foci of toxic exudate' and 'pyrexia' mean?" interrupted Edward Hawkins.

"Professor?" queried the judge.

Momentarily halted in his stride, Professor Prysumor struggled for words.

"Er ... pustular foci of toxic exudate are multiple swellings like boils containing, er ... pus, and pyrexia is, er, a high temperature, your Honour," the physician explained.

"Thank you Professor, and could you explain, as Mr. Hawkins has requested, putting your vast learning into simple, everyday language?"

"I will try, your Honour," replied Granton Prysumor.

"Professor," Sir Matthew resumed, "a patient at the closing stages of their life would be extremely weak, but what about his or her mental state?"

"The patient would, because of his or her toxic state due to large amounts of the pox virus in the bloodstream, be delirious and have lost control of their faculties."

"Would that have been the case in Mr. Ezra Jones's condition?"

"Doubtless."

"Would such a person become insane, as has been suggested, Professor?"

"Without proper control of themselves, more than likely."

"What would such a condition lead to, Professor?"

"They would, in such a patient's confused state, be open to all kinds of suggestions, Sir Matthew."

"And would such a person be easily influenced to act contrary to their normal inclinations?"

"Of course."

"Even to signing a document that they would not sign under other circumstances, as in the case of Mr. Ezra Jones's will?"

"Regrettably, yes."

"No further questions, your Honour."

"Do you wish to question the witness for the plaintiff, Mr. Hawkins?"

"Yes, your Honour. Professor Prysumor, would that, in your opinion, be the helpless state on all occasions of someone critically ill with the pock?"

"Absolutely!" snapped the physician.

"Then how do you explain why Mr. Ezra Jones could dictate the writing of such a detailed and clear document as the will regarding his wishes?"

"In his state *in extremis,* he would have no understanding of what he was saying."

"Indeed? Then how could such a will so crystal-clear in its intentions be drafted?"

"Someone else must have drafted it and forced him to sign it!"

"Now, be very careful how you answer my next question, Professor. Who could be the 'someone else' you're referring to?"

"The persons present at the drawing-up of his will," declared the physician, unaware in his conceit that he was venturing where angels fear to tread.

"Are you impugning the integrity of three persons of unblemished character of such an act of felony?"

"As a highly qualified specialist with a knowledge of smallpox beyond contradiction, that is my opinion, and neither of the three persons who you refer to has a medical qualification or would have the temerity to challenge me," the physician declared.

"However comprehensive your knowledge, I would advise you not to find yourself subject to a writ for slander, so do be careful how you answer my next question: Would you then say that there are no exceptions to your claim that all critically ill sufferers from smallpox are unable to make independent decisions for themselves or even have the strength to sign such documents?"

"That is my conclusion, sir," the physician replied.

"Have you seen the will or a copy of it?"

"No, I have not, but…"

Edward Hawkins produced a document;

"I have the original of the will here. Now examine carefully Mr. Ezra Jones's signature. Is that the signature of a man who has lost control of all his faculties?"

The Professor examined the document.

"No, but that could be a forgery!"

"How can it be a forgery when Mr. Jones's own son admits that it is genuine? No further questions for this witness, your Honour."

"Any further questions for your witness, Sir Matthew?" queried the judge.

"None, Your Honour," replied Sir Matthew.

"Mr. Hawkins, are you ready to call your witnesses?"

"Yes, your Honour. I wish to call Mr. Hugo Jones."

Patent surprise appeared on scores of expressions. Hugo appeared through the door at the rear of the court and strode up to and into the witness box. He had had the good sense to quench his thirst during the lunch break, but avoid getting drunk. He was sworn in and, on request, gave his name and addresses:

"Hugo Jones of Destro and Home Farms, parish o' Wychcombe, West Dorset."

Edward Hawkins moved from behind his table, approached the witness box and fixed Ezra Jones's son with a steady gaze. Hugo stared back defiantly.

"Mr. Jones, why are you contesting your own father's will?"

"Ye know full well, Hawkins," spat Hugo, "it's been made very clear during this case."

"Aye, Mr. Jones, but I feel sure that the rest of the court would be desirous to hear why from your own lips," the lawyer calmly replied.

Hugo's expression darkened.

"You and old Goodboys knew that my father was unfit to dictate an' sign that pernicious document and conspired to force … er … influence him, that's why I'm contesting it," Hugo declared.

"Wasn't your mother present at the signing?"

"Yes."

"Then you must include her in your alleged conspiracy, Mr. Jones."

Hugo's forehead was beaded with sweat. He took a

handkerchief out of his coat pocket and wiped it off.

"I'd rather not comment."

"But surely, if your mother was present, you have to include her in your conspiracy theory?"

Hugo tugged on his shirt collar but refused to answer.

"Then, since you have nothing further to say concerning your mother's involvement, let's address the question of the missing money …"

"I know nothing …"

"Steady, Mr. Jones, you musn't pre-empt what you think I am going to ask you. Now, in his will, your father mentioned another accessory to his deceit in disclaiming receipt of the money Ronald Gomer withdrew to repay the gambling debt. Did your father disclose to you whom that other person might be?"

"I thinks it were a figment of his imagination, but, if it were true, why should he confide in me?" Hugo countered loudly.

"Why indeed? It's been rumoured that he didn't have much, if any, confidence in you anyway …"

"Objection! Hearsay evidence and blackening my client's character without proof!" cried Sir Matthew.

"I will uphold Sir Matthew's objection, so keep to the facts, Mr. Hawkins," growled the judge.

"Very well, your Honour. Mr. Jones, let us assume that your father was expressing the truth in his will …"

At this point Hugo was struggling to hide his discomfiture.

"Don't you think it strange that your father made no reference about this to you, especially when his wife was privy to the information and witnessed his and the executors' signatures without objection?"

In his mind Hugo clutched at straws. Sir Matthew observed his client's uneasiness.

"Your Honour, I cannot see where this hypothetical questioning is leading us!"

"Mr. Hawkins?" Sir Thomas queried.

"Your Honour, I suspect that Mr. Jones is withholding information which would help resolve this case and speed a decision one way or the other."

"Oh, very well, Mr. Hawkins, but keep to the facts!"

"Mr. Jones, please answer my question: Why would your father withhold from you the identity of the other person?"

"I don' know, unless it were a dead man whose name 'e didn't want to besmirch. It were common knowledge that Bowen Dranley, the Gomers' agent, were splashing money about that were not rightly his an' he was found dead at the foot of Golden Cap."

"But the agent's body was found months before your father's will was declared and signed. Surely your father was referring to someone else who was alive at the time the will was drafted, Mr. Jones?"

"I don't know."

"Would your mother have known?"

"Of course not! Father would never have …"

"Never have what, Mr. Jones?" interrupted Edward Hawkins, quick as a flash, sensing blood.

Hugo bit his tongue. He looked down; his hands were shaking.

"Wou … woul … would never have disclosed who it was to her …"

"Why not?"

"Because 'e never said so in the will …"

"But you claim that your father's will was written and signed when he was insane and now you're saying that he would never have disclosed it, as if he was in his right mind! But the question is, who's the person he's referring to? Could it have been someone close to him?"

"Who, since I was his only offspring an' he didn't tell me?"

"Who, indeed?"

Edward Hawkins smiled.

"No further questions, your Honour."

The judge looked directly at Sir Matthew.

"Do you wish to question your client whilst he's still in the witness box, Sir Matthew?"

"Yes, your Honour. Mr. Jones, what made you suspect that your father's Last Will and Testament was at odds with your knowledge of him before he became ill?"

"Well, sir, when he took possession of Home Farm for non-payment of Ronald Gomer's debt, he did not hesitate to grant me possession of the whole farm including its tenancies. If he 'adn't considered me able t' manage it, he would never have handed it over to me."

"Why not, indeed! Did he sign over possession to you in the form of a written document?"

"No sir, we trusted one another eno' to make a verbal agreement that when my dear father died, I would inherit Destro and Home farms auto … maticly as his one an' only heir."

"There have been rumours that you were never capable of making the farms profitable enterprises. How do you respond to that, Mr. Jones?"

"Malicious slander! My father would have made that clear when he took over Home Farm from the Gomers, because he would never 'ave passed it on to me!"

"But I'm informed that Home Farm's corn yield last year was below expectations, Mr. Jones. What say you?"

"The Gomers planted the corn afore we took over their fields, so a poor crop might have come from poor hoeing an' sowing and to top it all, we had a bad harvest due to the storm in September."

"But it has been reported that the Gomers, on poorer and fewer acres at Wychcombe Farm had a bumper crop."

"They was lucky t' get the sheaves in and threshed afore the rains came and our neighbours on bigger acreage suffered like us. You ask the Goodboys! My father knew that, but didn't take it out on me," Hugo protested.

"Then why should he bequeath that farm to the Gomers?"

"If 'e'd been in his right mind, 'e would never have done such a strange thing."

"What has been your relationship with your father?"

"We've always been close an' father and me ne'er had any secrets from one another, an' discussed the farm business together," Hugo replied.

"Thank you, Mr. Jones. I have no further questions for my client, your Honour."

"If both counsels have no further witnesses, we will adjourn the case and I will give my summing up when the court reconvenes at ten a.m. the day after tomorrow ..."

"I have no further witnesses, your Honour," Sir Matthew replied.

"I have one further witness your Honour, but he has not

yet appeared. It is essential to our case that his testimony is heard. I guarantee that he will appear if the proceedings are to be held the day after tomorrow," interrupted Edward Hawkins.

"This is highly irregular. Oh, very well, but your witness must be present in this courtroom the day after tomorrow at ten o' clock prompt in the morning," grumbled the judge.

"All rise!"

CHAPTER TWENTY-THREE

Judgement Day

"Though I wouldn't encourage you to break the law, possession is nine-tenths of the law, Mr. Jones, in spite of the possibility that you may lose this case," commented Sir Matthew.

Hugo and his legal adviser were seated in the lounge in Sir Matthew's chambers after the case had closed for the day. Sir Matthew's chambers accommodated his legal business and residence.

"Then I'll fight to hold on to Home Farm and keep the Gomers out," Hugo replied.

"And pray, sir, how will you do that?"

"I've got plans," grated Hugo.

"You must be aware that if our injunction fails, the Gomers have the law on their side."

"Then it's up to you to win the case, I'm paying you eno'!" Hugo blazed.

"Our chances of doing so might prove substantially better if you stopped concealing the truth and trying to pull the wool over my eyes," Sir Matthew remarked calmly.

Hugo's face turned pale. He had underestimated his counsel's perception in discerning his deceitfulness in not disclosing material facts about his own involvement.

"You have been more than economical with the truth in answering questions I've put to ye, Mr. Jones. For instance, there *is* evidence that after his loss at cards, Ronald Gomer himself withdrew thirty-five thousand guineas from the Dorchester branch of the Devon and Dorset Bank. The money was never recovered. If that money had been passed on to his descendants on his death, they would have repaid that debt of honour rather than meekly surrendering ownership of Home Farm, an estate so long prized through many generations of that family. So, what happened to the money? Up to now, the only explanation is in your father's Last Will and Testament. Perhaps you can provide further evidence? And did your father not confide in you?"

"No I can't, an' my father kept things close to his chest, tho' I heard a rumour that Dranley, the Gomers' land agent, had possession of it an' he disappeared at the same time as the money," Hugo replied, hoping that the lies and half-truths he'd expressed would convince the lawyer.

Sir Matthew remained silent for what seemed to Hugo too long for comfort. He looked into Hugo's eyes, the latter steeling himself not to look away.

"Such a large sum of money cannot disappear so easily, Mr. Jones. If what ye say about the land agent is true and if he had the money, what did he do with it?"

Oh, how Hugo could do with a drink to steady his nerves. He could feel the sweat beading on his forehead and his mouth felt full of gravel.

"Dranley were found dead in the sea at the foot of Golden Cap, having been unhorsed, so he couldn't tell any tales, sir," Hugo croaked.

"Oh, very well, it's all very unsatisfactory; I like things tied up, no loose ends, ye see. But if ye cannot offer further information, our case is found that much wanting. My butler will see you out, Mr. Jones, and here's my first bill," handing Hugo a sealed envelope, "and I'd be grateful for early payment, on or before the next court sitting".

Hugo was glad to exit Sir Matthew's chambers and make to the Prince William Arms to slake his burning thirst and sleep the night in town. He knew that he had to keep up the deception that he was not party to the theft of the debt money, otherwise he would lose Home Farm and possibly face charges of theft and perjury.

At ten a.m. the following morning, Dorchester's weekly Market Day, the courtroom, vestibule and steps to the main door were crowded with people all eager to hear the jury's verdict and Sir Thomas Parsicker's final judgement. Apart from the principals involved, the privileged and those fortunate to arrive early enough to be allowed a seat inside the courtroom, the less fortunate had spilled onto the pavement and street outside. It appeared from the crush that the town's population and visitors from outlying districts were in Dorchester to be present on the final day of the hearing. The cattle market was, as usual, punctuated by the lowing of cattle but no auctioneer's voice could be heard. Farmers were strangely absent from the market, having delegated the guarding of the cattle to their herdsmen.

"All rise!" resounded through the court as Judge Sir

Thomas Parsicker flowed in carrying a sheaf of papers. All eyes were riveted on his every movement and body language as he fussed over the papers, adjusted his spectacles and peered at his notes, then the court. His birdlike eyes fell on the benches of plaintiff's and defendant's counsellors.

"Where is Mr. Hawkins?" he demanded.

The lawyer's assistant shook his head.

"I don't know, your Honour."

"My time is precious, so I will make my summing up of the case for the benefit of the jury, who will presently reach their verdict in his absence. I will therefore not permit any further evidence on behalf of the estate of Mr. Ezra Jones. If learned counsel Mr. Hawkins wishes to have cause to appeal, then he must carry out due process."

At this Sir Matthew smiled and Hugo smirked, both aware that the judge's decision might well be in Hugo's favour. The judge summarised his findings in favour of an injunction to halt execution of the will on the grounds that Mr. Ezra Jones was not of sound mind nor reasoning at the time of the drafting and signing of it, which justified awarding the injunction to the plaintiff.

"I therefore recommend to the jury on the basis of witness evidence that the plaintiff's case is …"

"Your Honour! Your Honour!"

Edward Hawkins burst through the crowd and elbowed his way through at the open door of the courtroom followed by a second man and rushed to the judge's bench, equally breathless.

"What's this unseemly interruption about, Mr. Hawkins? You are late and I'm just delivering my summing-up to the jury, which is …"

"Your Honour, I indeed apologise for my lateness which I am happy to explain to your satisfaction later, and for interrupting your summing up, but I have been able to persuade a most important witness to testify …"

"Why was this witness of yours not present during the previous days of this case?" rasped the judge, highly irritated at this interruption.

"I apologise also for that and will, with your Honour's permission, explain why later, but it is in the interests of justice and your fair and just judgement that I have brought along this gentleman, your Honour."

The judge sat motionless and fixed the lawyer with a most forbidding look; the court remained silent.

"Your request is out of order and I've made my decision to …"

"With all respect, your Honour, I know you well enough to be certain that should an appeal against the granting of an injunction be made, you would be the first to regret such a decision if fresh evidence was revealed that overturned your original judgement."

The judge's eyes bored into Edward Hawkins, then focussed on his notes.

"There is no precedent in my experience on the bench to permit you to bring in fresh evidence so late …"

He paused. Sir Matthew's smile had not receded and Hugo Jones's expression was still euphoric, whilst the atmosphere in the court was electric, as the onlookers and those in earshot outside awaited the outcome.

"… however, though it's against my better judgement, I will give your witness a hearing, but if in my opinion you try to suborn my judgement, I will come down heavily on you, and have both you and your witness arrested for contempt of court."

Richard Gomer suppressed a cheer.

"Thank you, your Honour. I present as my witness, Dr. Abraham Needman, a local practitioner from these parts, and doctor to the Jones family for many years …"

"Yes, yes, get to the point, Mr. Hawkins, my patience is wearing thin!" Sir Thomas growled.

Dr. Needman was sworn in and gave his name and address. Though his flushed, sweat-beaded face was the result of a hasty rush to reach the courtroom, he was composed.

"Dr. Needman, are you not the Jones's family physician?" Edward Hawkins asked.

"I am, sir."

"And did you not minister to Mr. Ezra Jones's needs whilst he gradually worsened …"

"Your Honour, I object to a line of questioning which is going nowhere. Dr. Needman was not present at the signing of the will," Sir Matthew interjected.

"Your Honour, would you permit Dr. Needman to tell us his experience, which supersedes any conclusion to be made from his absence at the signing of the will?" pleaded Edward Hawkins.

The judge opened his mouth to speak, then nodded.

"Dr. Needman, please tell us in your own words what you witnessed," requested Mr. Hawkins.

"Mr. Ezra Jones sent Obadiah, his ostler, to summon me as he had realised that he would not be long for this world. Clearly, he was aware that there was little that could be done for him medically speaking, but he wanted some respite from his suffering. As I was busy tending to other smallpox patients, I was unable to go immediately. The next day, I rode to Destro Farm to hear from his wife that he had already signed his Last Will and Testament, still alive and lucid.

"I visited him on what was soon to be his deathbed and, after examining him, realised that he was terminally sick but his mind was clear and untainted by the pox. He informed me that he was going to his Maker with a clearer conscience and though he would not be arrested to be questioned whilst still alive, he would pass to a higher court to face the Judge of all the Earth for his felony. Though his pulse was weak and thready and his breathing rapid and superficial, I was convinced that here was a man who had never lost the strong fibre of his mind and spirit in spite of being stricken down by the pock. He spoke to me openly but within the confidentiality between physician and patient, with no evidence that his mind was impaired by the sickness and its irreversible progress. When I offered him laudanum to ease his pain during his dying moments, he was surprisingly slow to make up his mind. He said 'The pain's not so bad now I've made my peace with God'. As I was about to administer the preparation, he passed away. I only wish that some of my patients could have died so well."

"Dr. Needman, have you seen any of your patients die from this scourge?"

"Many, sir."

"Do you find your patients exhibiting the same clear-headedness that Ezra Jones showed?"

"Surprisingly, I have had a few other patients, though

close to death, who have been clearheaded in their last moments. He, like they, also was an exception to the rule that victims of the pox who are dying *in extremis* have lost their reason."

"But, Dr. Needman, Dr. Prysumor, the smallpox specialist, denies any exception to the fact that patients *in extremis* still possess their mental faculties."

"My experience as a practitioner contradicts such an opinion."

"No further questions, your Honour."

Edward Hawkins paused. The courtroom was silent as if digesting every word they'd heard. Sir Matthew sat with head bowed as if in contemplation. Hugo Jones shifted restlessly in his seat.

"Sir Matthew, do you wish to question the witness before I pronounce judgement?"

"I have one question for the doctor, your Honour. Dr. Needman, did Mr. Jones confide in you any information regarding his change of heart in returning Home Farm to the original owners whilst dictating his wishes in the Last Will and Testament?"

"He did."

The lawyer paused and looked across at his client, who was visibly shaken.

"Would you wish to tell the court what he disclosed?"

"That I cannot do, for I swore on Ezra Jones's firm request that I would not disclose what he had informed me, even to his dear wife. And as you well know, sir, a physician is bound to hold as confidential anything his patient informs him …"

"Dr. Needman, do you appreciate that if I so wished, I

could subpoena you as a witness, however hostile, on your refusal to disclose what Ezra Jones shared with you and you could risk serving a custodial sentence in one of His Majesty's prisons until you relent?" queried Sir Matthew.

"I fully appreciate your power to enact such a measure, sir, but to disclose what I was trusted to keep to myself I stand by my oath to Ezra Jones and my dedication to the vow I made as physician to the sick and dying."

Sir Matthew paused, then:

"No further questions, your Honour."

The ensuing silence, though short, seemed an eternity to the court. Sir Thomas, head bowed, made no effort to immediately follow the Counsel for the plaintiff's closing words. Then, addressing the jury:

"Though it may appear somewhat irregular for me to in any way influence you in deciding for or against Mr. Hugo Jones's claim, I believe that it would be in the interests of the parties involved and the wider public if I now guided you in reaching your verdict. In weighing the evidence of the witnesses and evidence given by the expert witness and the apparent change of mind Mr. Ezra Jones had during his final hours, I will now advise you to also consider Dr. Needman's testimony. I recommend that you take into account Dr. Needman's evidence in deciding whether the Last Will and Testament of Mr. Ezra Jones was, in the eyes of the law, fully valid and for its terms to be executed in accordance with that law. Otherwise, you must seriously consider that there are grounds for me to declare the will legally unacceptable. Having now heard the evidence on both sides of the case, I would recommend that you retire to come to a verdict."

"Your Honour, with your permission, we will adjourn at this moment to discuss all the evidence presented to us. When we've come to a decision, your Honour, we will return," the foreman of the jury stood and replied, bowing.

"Thank you, and we will wait for your verdict. In the meantime, the court will remain in session until you return. I myself will retire to the Judge's chambers until I've been informed of your readiness to return to this court," replied Sir Thomas.

"All rise!" bellowed the clerk as Sir Thomas Parsicker left the court, followed by the foreman of the jury leading out the other members.

Apart from judge and jury, no-one left the courtroom. Buzzes of conversation commenced and continued for what seemed to be hours. Some attenders succumbed to the warmth of the room and added their snores. "All rise!"

The judge and jury entered simultaneously. The judge sat down, signalling the jury and court to follow. The judge adjusted his spectacles.

"Foreman of the jury, have your members reached a verdict?"

"We have, your Honour."

"Kindly proceed."

"Your Honour, I speak on behalf of my fellow jurors that we unanimously recommend that having considered all the evidence presented, we conclude that Mr. Ezra Jones was of sound mind at the drafting and signing of his Last Will and Testament and that judgement should be made in favour of the executors of that will."

"Thank you, members of the jury, for your findings. Then I have no further course but to decide against the plaintiff in favour of the parties representing Mr. Ezra Jones in support of the validity of his will."

The outburst of cheering could not be stopped by repeated strikes of the judge's gavel until the people had exhausted their response in favour of the defendants. The judge recognised his futility to halt the popular reaction and leaned back in his chair as Edward Hawkins and his assistant shook hands, then shook hands with Richard and Giles. Sir Matthew Stanking sat motionless as Hugo Jones cupped his head in his hands and sobbed. His lawyer turned to him and whispered a few words, to which Hugo nodded. Sir Matthew stood up and addressed Sir Thomas:

"Your Honour, as my client does not wish to appeal, would you permit a stay of execution for an agreed period of time in the execution of Mr. Jones's Last Will and Testament concerning transfer of Home Farm to Richard and Giles Gomer? This will permit a reasonable period for the changeover and the transfer of livestock, farming equipment and feedstuffs to Destro Farm."

"I would have no objection with regard to the law, depending on the time required under probate, but I suggest that you discuss any terms with Mr. Hawkins and Sir Absalom Goodboys as well as the beneficiaries under Mr. Ezra Jones's will."

"Thank you, your Honour," Sir Matthew replied.

"All rise!"

CHAPTER TWENTY-FOUR

Aftermath

The reaction of three people – Martha, Katherine and Hugo Jones – contrasted sharply with that of others revelling in the crowded courtroom, but for different reasons. For Martha and her daughter-in-law, vast relief at the result but apprehensive of what the future held for them both, living with a frustrated, unbalanced son and husband. Deprived of Home Farm, the three would be under the same roof. On Hugo's part, losing his action hardened his resolve to plot some form of vengeance on the Gomers. But he had two hurdles, or rather, debts to clear – the costs of the case and Sir Matthew's likely bill 'For Services Rendered', which would precede execution of the will and expose how cash-strapped he was. He must hunt down the remaining Irishmen in order to pay off his counsel. Or else?

Hugo had never before experienced such a reversal in his fortunes since the Irish rogues had stolen and absconded with the debt money. Judge Sir Thomas Parsicker ruled that the Gomers had full rights to repossess the land and buildings at Home Farm, but ownership of the feedstuffs and livestock would remain in Hugo's possession, thus increasing the stocking of cattle and sheep on limited pasture acreage at Destro. The judge, after consulting both lawyers and Richard and Giles Gomer, had sanctioned a period of twenty-one days' grace for Hugo to exit Home Farm before the Gomers could occupy the farm. However, Hugo would waste more time hunting the Irish fugitives until there were only three days left before the takeover became law.

"They're not keeping the Home Farm stock, Hands!" Hugo had exulted to his chargehand days after the court order to surrender Home Farm to the Gomers. We'll get our men at Home to drive the sheep an' what's left of the cattle up to Destro afore the Gomers take over."

"Aye, zur," Abel Hands replied, doffing his cap, "and what about the fodder an' corn?"

"Leave the hay an' straw that's mouldy and bring the rest. As fer the corn, we'll move what's the best of a poor crop up to Destro. We have eno' there to feed the stock thro' the rest of the winter."

"When do ye suggest we start movin' the stock, sir?"

"Let them be on Home Farm land as long as possible … I'll let ye know," Hugo replied.

Abel Hands departed unhappy; he now had to depend on Hugo for further instructions.

March 19th

Hugo decided to move the stock only the day before the Gomers reoccupied Home Farm. Although Destro and

Home farms were contiguous, to move pregnant ewes and milking cattle was stressful enough but much more perilous over ice in a storm. Abel shuddered; casting cows and aborting sheep, broken limbs and missing stock would mean he'd soon be out of a job. Shielding his face from the sting from wind-blown snowflakes, Abel looked out of the yard at Home and saw nothing but drifts, but north towards Destro he perceived snow-blanketed fields, no drifts near the field-side hedges.

"Hold on, men!" Abel shouted over the howling storm to the men huddled together in Home's farmyard. We're goin' t' drive the stock up by the hedgerows an' through the fencing into Destro. We'll ne'er get them out o' the yards with drifts higher than a man's head."

"Derkins and Bliggers, go and pull open the fence by the track at the top of Home then wait for a whistle and we'll drive them onto the track then north round the edge of the copse and into Destro through the open gate and into the yard."

Muttering followed Abel's instructions.

"But wot about yon copse? We could lose stock there, or south into Wychcombe village," George Derkins queried as he and Joe Bliggers ran towards Destro.

"Ayes" accompanied Derkins's words from hardened labourers who viewed the drive in such dangerous conditions as a step too far.

"If we don't get them to Destro, the Gomers'll impound them an' we've only a day left afore they come, lads! Then it'll be the workhus fer us! An' the sooner this job's done, the sooner we get back to our warm cottages!" cried Abel.

Ten minutes passed. A blizzard had developed, sweeping the snow into vortices half obscuring the heaving mass of cattle and sheep. A shrill whistle penetrated the howling wind, lowing of cattle and bleating of the ewes.

"Get by, Whisker! Get on by!" shouted Ozzie Barker the shepherd to his dog, struggling with the men to contain mingling cattle and sheep.

"Harris, keep the sheep an' cattle moving with Ozzie through the gap in the fence and up the track an' through the open fence into Destro! Don't let them break south. Get yer mate to stop them breaking through any damaged hedges and down the track to Wychcombe!" Abel screamed above the din.

Abel's instructions came too late to prevent a maverick ewe dodging Harris's flaying arms and fleeing south, followed by two other ewes and a cow.

"Careful Harris, them ewes are heavy in lamb. Leave 'em be, they're marked with Destro's mark, we'll pick 'em up later."

With Whisker the dog's help, the labourers drove the rest of the flock and herd through Home Farm's open fence and onto the connecting track, then through a gap in Destro's southern field, slipping and sliding on ice polished by the swirling snow.

"Careful, men! Cows an' sheep wi' broken legs will only be fit for the knackers!" shouted Abel above the howling wind. The heaving, plunging mass of sheep, cattle and men moved up the snowdrift-margined track towards Destro.

Martha Jones and son Hugo were not on speaking terms. Katherine, despite the upheaval in moving to Destro, felt relieved and safer now living under the same roof as her mother-in-law, but she still took the precaution of choosing a separate bedroom with a lock and key from Hugo as she had at Home Farm. With Harriet as her maid and close companion, Hugo again realised that he would have to find his sexual satisfaction elsewhere.

At Home Farm, the workers and the tenant farmers were in turmoil. The sudden change of ownership from the Joneses to the Gomers now created confusion and uncertainty though conditions had been more uncertain when Hugo had taken charge. His instability, poor knowledge of farming, idleness and drinking habits had cast a shadow over Home Farm and resulted in the workforce struggling without a leader other than Abel Hands, who was equally limited, waiting for orders from Hugo that rarely materialised. However, it was common knowledge that the Gomers were struggling to make ends meet on Wychcombe and support the labourers already working on that farm, especially during the present winter and they were now hoping somehow to maintain good working relationships with those tenant farmers.

No crops were being harvested, and mutton and lamb to sell for the table was non-existent whilst the shepherds prepared for lambing in March. Milk production had been limited for the farmhouse as a result of Hugo selling off most of the dairy cows to generate cash for his own use. Summer and autumn productivity was confined to sheep breeding and barley and corn production, but grain and hay yields had been poor, decimated by the previous year's September storm. For the Gomers to return to their previous inheritance was a dim prospect.

Hugo Jones now realised that time was short to exact revenge on the brothers and fulfil his plan to reclaim Home and somehow seize Wychcombe Farm as well.

But the Gomers had another enemy plotting against them. This adversary laid out copies of land maps drawn up in 1804 for both farms and procured from the Land Agents' offices in Dorchester. To the west of and running alongside the boundary of Home Farm was a tributary which drained into the River Bredey.

"That must supply the western fields and perchance the gley meadow," he said to himself.

Eastwards, the two farms were supplied from a different source, he concluded, shown by the line of wells running from north to south. These were in the Home Farm yard, a Home Farm southlying foxmould field and in the yard at Wychcombe Farm.

"The source must be an underground spring which forces the water under pressure through the holes when the wells were dug. If the wells at Home Farm are choked to prevent the Gomers from drawing water from the ones at Home Farm, then the wells at Wychcombe Farm might dry up too if enough rubbish be put down the Home Farm wells," he reasoned.

That, he concluded, would take the life out of the pasture and cropfields and destroy any hope of yields for that year. All he needed to do was remove the hand pumps from the wells at Home once the farm had been vacated to await repossession by the Gomers and fill the shafts with stones and rubble. He wouldn't be able to go to Wychcombe Farm, the risk of discovery would be too great, but hopefully, the water running southward along the line of the underground water table would be obstructed by the rubble and stones. Any land above the well supplying Home Farm would be fed by water from the upper reaches to continue to supply Destro land, but he would be in a strong position to purchase Home Farm, since Hugo Jones would have little money after the court hearing to re-purchase the land himself.

With less than a day to go before takeover, and a day after Hugo Jones had cleared the farm of its meagre crops, moveable furnishings and livestock, he approached Home Farm at dusk, rode into the deserted yard and dismounted. He housed his mount in an empty stable and walked back to the well pump in the yard. He took hold of the rusty handle and pushed it down; in spite of the freezing conditions, crystal-clear water gushed from the nozzle onto the cobblestones. He tested the strength of the handle by pulling on it sideways. Satisfied with its firmness, he returned to the stable, released and mounted his gelding and rode out of the yard, then trotted him down a foxmould field to the well. This was a well-bricked hole topped above the ground by a brick surround holding a pulley system which operated through a strong rope from which hung a bucket. He dismounted and turned the handle of the pulley, then turned the handle operating the rope and lowered the bucket down the well until he heard the splash as it connected with water. He wound up the bucket, now brimming with spring water, placed it on the rim of the surround, cupped his hand, took a drink and threw the rest of the water on the ground. He mounted his gelding, rode through a break in the hedge onto the north-south track and headed north.

Chapter Twenty-five

Fire and Water

As Hugo's workmen had moved out one clear day before the final day of repossession of Home Farm, Richard and Giles decided to reconnoitre their recovered land. The snow had abated by mid-afternoon. Jamie saddled and led out Hal and Sally from the stable at Wychcombe. As Richard mounted Hal, he detected a distant flicker of light north of their position. He initially dismissed it as a lantern light; the light, now uneven and expanding upwards and outwards, accompanied by a distinctly heard crackle, urged him to take out his spyglass and focus on it – tongues of flame leapt into focus.

March 20th

"Giles! There's a fire at Home!"

The brothers wasted no time. Ignoring the hazardous snow-covered ice, the brothers exited Wychcombe and spurred Hal and Sally north into a canter between the snowdrifts on the north-south track until they reached the southern prong of the fork which wound towards the house at Home Farm. Now galloping their mounts along the track, they turned into the Home farmyard. Blinded by the inferno's flames and enveloped by smoke, they reined in and dismounted, coughing. Knuckling their streaming eyes, they gazed at a scene of destruction. The barns had disappeared under clouds of thick smoke and flames, though the farmhouse appeared undamaged.

"Quick, Giles, let's get buckets from the stables and fill them from the well in the yard!" Richard shouted through the roar.

Leaving their mounts loose in the yard, they ran to the stables, grabbed a bucket each and ran to the well. Horror momentarily paralysed them. The pump handle was bent and twisted and the well was choked to the top with stones and soil. They stood, transfixed at the damage, then:

"The foxmoulds!" they shouted in unison.

Giles took Richard's bucket until his brother had mounted Hal, handed it back to him and mounted Sally. They galloped their horses across the northern cornfield until they reached the first foxmould field and the second well – the remnants of the rope which had been used to lower the wooden bucket lay on its splintered remains amidst the wreckage of the brick surround, broken bricks which now covered the rubble-choked well.

"Curse Jones! He's getting his revenge in full for losing his case!" Giles cried, voicing Richard's suspicions, "What are we to do, Richard?"

A salient question, Richard mused, in spite of his shattered emotions as he watched helplessly. All hope of saving Home Farm's buildings and house had gone.

"The Bredey's brook's our only hope, if it's not frozen over, Giles," Richard commented, clutching at straws.

"But it's a half mile away Richard! That fire will have swallowed up everything before we can haul any water back to the house!"

The brothers stood in the field devastated – their reclaimed farm buildings destroyed by fire and their water supply cut off. Then they heard the sound of hoofbeats and bootfalls approaching, until Jamie reined in his mount, followed fifty yards away by Asa and Thomas, panting. All three carried buckets – Jamie on horseback holding one and Asa and Thomas two each, water splashing over the sides.

"We've come t' save the house, zurs. We saw the foxmould well broken, so went back to Wychcombe and used the well there. Too late t' save the barns, but we might 'ave enough water t' keep the house from catching fire."

In spite of his despair, Giles burst into laughter until he cried.

"But, Jamie, how, with five bucketfuls?" Giles laughed, wiping away tears.

"But look, zur! Outer wall of the farmhouse on the barn side be still dry. If we throws the water on that wall, it could quench any sparks a-flyin' over from them there barns. And we can fill our buckets with snow, and throw it on the wall, we might jus' keep the sparks off until the barns burn out."

About an hour later, the smoke-blackened firefighters surveyed the farmhouse overlooking the smoking ashes where once existed a cluster of barns.

"Thanks to the three of ye, we've saved the house. We can manage without the barns for a while, until we've harvested any crops we sow," croaked Richard.

"But we need barns to store the crops at harvesting. And how can we afford the wood to rebuild, Richard?" Giles queried despairingly.

"Building barns is not our immediate problem, my dear brother. Buildings aren't so important; it's the land that matters. We can replace buildings but not barren soil. And we know that the soil's good to grow crops and grass."

"But, the wells …"

"Though the Joneses acquired the deeds for Home, we have maps of the two farms down at Wychcombe which'll give us an idea where the water table is, but we're too tired and I'm unable to think straight just now. The light's drawing in fast and we have no lanterns to check inside the farmhouse. Let's turn in and get some sleep then return tomorrow."

The three workers nodded but Giles spoke up:

"But, if the firebug who started all this sees that the farmhouse is untouched, he could finish off the job before we return and leave us destitute of any buildings – no place for livestock, hay, crops nor human beings."

"What do you suggest we do, Giles – mount an overnight guard? In this weather? I say we take the risk that whoever started this fire isn't likely to come back tonight." Richard's tears striped his smoke-blackened cheeks.

The brothers stood over the ruined well in silent despair. Then:

"Curse Jones! I vow he'll not get away with this!"

Night was drawing in rapidly. The five men stood together silhouetted in the light of the dying embers of the barns as if hypnotised by the devastation and unable to break the spell. Giles spoke first:

"Let's go home, Richard!"

The workers grunted assent, but Giles's brother stood as if held in a trance and did not respond immediately. At length he spoke:

"No point in trying to unblock the wells, but we need to find the course of the water that feeds the springs and our wells and dig fresh ones."

"But the ground's frostbound and rock hard – it'll take weeks before the thaw! And how are *we* going to find the water table supplying the wells?"

"We'll need the services of a water diviner for that, Giles …"

"And if we do find it and dig fresh wells, how are we going to safeguard them from the destroyer of our hopes?" Giles interrupted.

"If you mean the one who blocked our wells and torched our barns, that's a timely question, but I doubt that he'll add to his crimes at present. He'll think he's achieved his plan, so we've probably nothing to fear from him."

"I wish I had your optimism, Richard."

"And if he comes here now, he will risk arrest for trespassing on our property…"

"I'll shoot him first and ask questions later!" interrupted Giles.

"In the meantime," Richard continued, "we must check our well at Wychcombe and use the water for both farms until we can dig wells at Home after the thaw. In the meantime, the ice and snow will keep the soil wet and feed the plants. Once the thaw sets in, we'll fill as many buckets as possible from Wychcombe and carry them using the drays and carts until we locate and dig to the spring when the ground is softer."

Faces and hands smoke-blackened, and exhausted, the three horsemen and two labourers on foot plodded their way back to Wychcombe Farm. The brothers dismounted and dismissed Jamie, Asa and Thomas after handing over the reins of their mounts to the ostler, then returned to the farmhouse.

"What next, Richard, now that Home Farm has no barns, no water and a derelict farmhouse?"

"Let's sleep on it, Giles," Richard replied, dropping his greatcoat on the floor. Then, addressing their retainer:

"That will be all, Berkeley. Lock up and turn off the lanterns after we've retired."

Nodding, Berkeley retrieved Richard's coat and left the kitchen.

At eight o'clock that same night, Katherine and Martha Jones were finishing their light supper when Hugo appeared. His boots were wet and a faint smell of woodsmoke now pervaded the kitchen.

"Just been cutting down and burning some rotten wood t' make a clearing near the copse," he volunteered, as if anticipating any questions as to his actions and whereabouts.

"What for, Hugo?" queried his mother.

"I want to extend our pastureland into the copse," Hugo replied.

"But why, Hugo? You must know that the soil near the copse is too rank to support anything but trees and bushes."

Katherine looked closely at Hugo. To her, Martha Jones's contradiction and a momentary hesitation on his part betrayed the weakness of his explanation.

"I'm going to have a go, even so, becos we need more land now that we've got the stock from Home Farm."

"Your father tilled all the ground here that would yield crops or grazing for most of his life. Do you think that you can improve on his husbandry?"

"My father didn't know everything!"

"Even less so do you, my son."

Katherine saw through Hugo's vain attempts to convince his mother. Where had he been and what had he been up to? They were questions she desired to voice, but on further reflection refrained. Without another word, Hugo stormed out.

At Destro, Hugo Jones peered out of his bedroom window. He opened his spyglass and focussed on the pile of dying embers that represented Home Farm's buildings. Well – all but one. His smile almost vanished; the plan was to leave nothing undestroyed. He'd given them a sporting chance to quench the flames, after all, they had two good wells, yet they didn't appear to have stopped the flames, as if they had no way of drawing sufficient water. He was astonished, if that was the case, because he knew that to deprive livestock of water was a crime of the worst sort among farmers. Now he would have to quench his thirst for revenge by finishing off the job and torch the house but not touch the wells.

He pondered; every scrap of furniture had been removed from the farmhouse and stored in one of the empty barns at Destro. The Gomers wouldn't be sleeping in an empty house for a while, so he must complete the job before they occupied it.

A loud knocking brought Hugo down to open the front door. Sir Matthew Stanking's retainer, dressed in a top hat, overcoat and muffler, faced him. Behind in the yard was a coach and pair and a coachman holding their reins. The retainer doffed his hat and extended a gloved hand holding a sealed envelope.

"Sir Matthew sends his compliments and his invoice for services rendered up to date. He would be grateful for an early settlement, Mr. Jones. Within seven days, perhaps?" he said, his words more an instruction than a query. He put his hat on his head, touched it, turned on his heel and climbed into the coach through the door held open by the coachman.

Hugo watched the coach disappear out of the farmyard and closed the door. He entered the empty kitchen, put his lantern on the table, sat down and with trembling fingers and thudding heartbeat tore open the envelope. He removed a single sheet and read its contents, then crushed the sheet, battered the table with both fists and buried his head into his hands. The sound of footsteps signalled someone's approach. Katherine entered.

"Who was at the door, Hugo?" she asked, entering the

kitchen a split second after Hugo had crushed the envelope and sheet in his fist.

"Oh, just a beggar wantin' money. I sent him packing," Hugo growled, not meeting her eyes.

"Did you give him what he wanted?"

"Why should I? I'm not throwing money away on useless vagrants who're too lazy to earn an honest penny."

"He might have been looking for gainful work like many ex-soldiers."

"He was begging fer money, weren't anybody I knew and we've no jobs for hire, so that settled it!"

"He might have been starving," persisted Katherine.

"We've no money nor food to waste on shiftless beggars, and that settles it!" he shouted.

He walked to the scullery, shoving the invoice into his trouser pocket, took a full flagon of claret from the shelf, removed a glass from the kitchen sideboard, uncorked the flagon, threw the cork into the kitchen fire and filled the glass with claret. At this point, Katherine retired, musing.

Her husband would not have shown such nervousness if the caller had been the vagrant he claimed to have seen off. And he was clutching something in his right hand which he didn't have when he came out of the scullery. Had she heard the snow-muffled sound of hooves as she had descended the stairs?

Hugo took the lawyer's bill out of his trouser pocket and smoothed it out on the kitchen table. He read its contents again, emptied his glass, refilled it from the flagon then with clenched fists again hammered on the table.

The old fake wants me to cough up two hundred guineas – where from? he said to himself. I've no ready

232

money unless I sell the rest of the cows. This is the worst time of year to sell any livestock. The next decent market and stock sale in Dorchester is a good month away and old Stanking'll be after his money long afore then! I'd have t' beg, borrow or steal to get two hundred guineas an' I'm not the beggin' type. Who's going to lend me anything now it's known all over the county that I've lost Home Farm? Neither have I any security apart from Destro, which I'm not giving up and nor would my mother. And steal? Where from? The only thing I've ever stolen has been stolen from me by them Irish scum!

John, the Guardsman, was seated in his second tied cottage, now at Destro, contemplating his situation with some foreboding. Certainly, he and his wife had a roof over their heads and he had a job in spite of the sacking of some of the Destro labourers and dismissal of all the workers from Home Farm who'd been employed under Hugo Jones. Goodness knows why men had been sacked when they would have been needed to look after the extra livestock from Home Farm. But word had it that Hugo Jones had lost a small fortune when his court action to stop his father's bequest to return Home Farm to the Gomers had failed. So, to cut his losses he got rid of workers to save money, and sold cattle to raise the payment to Sir Matthew.

"No more work and no more cottages for them I employed at Home Farm, now that it's gone to the Gomers, so ye'll have to tell them that they'll be looking fer work elsewhere or likely finish up in Wychcombe workhouse,"

Hugo had instructed Abel, the Destro chargehand, smiling to himself that Abel would bear the brunt of the workers' dissatisfaction. Now he could concentrate on finding the crippled Irishman and discover where *his* money was.

CHAPTER TWENTY-SIX

History Repeated

Giles rose early the following morning, following a sleep disturbed by Bruce and Sando's barking. At about five o'clock he dressed, and haltered and saddled Sally. The morning air was crisp with a cold bite to it, but his mare revelled in the early ride, treading the snow-sprinkled grass with a clear pull on the reins to encourage Giles's signal to urge a canter then a gallop. Acceding to Sally's desire to compete with the wind, Giles rode round the far circumference then galloped from south to north through each meadow from the gley swamp. He turned Sally northwards towards Home Farm and urged her into a steady trot.

March 24th

"Where are you going, Edmond?" Sir Absalom asked his stepson as Edmond appeared dressed in riding habit and carrying his whip.

"To Wychcombe Farm, father, to see if Richard needs any help; seemingly, some felon has blocked the wells at Home Farm."

He left Copley farmhouse, disappeared and reappeared a few minutes later riding one of the hunters.

Richard walked Hal around the edge of the gley swamp, carefully picking a path to avoid falling victim to its clutches. The swamp's level had not receded, even though he expected that the spring's waterline might have been interfered with by the blockage of Home Farm's wells. He turned Hal in the direction of Wychcombe farmhouse just as a horseman appeared at a canter from the west – it was Edmond. He bore down on Richard's horse without reining in, lifted his hand as if in salute and struck Richard's head forcibly with the stock of his whip. Richard slumped sideways in the saddle, then fell to the ground. Hal fled uphill towards the farmhouse. Groaning, Richard came to, fresh blood coursing down his face from the head wound. Edmond dismounted, holding his whip in one hand and a pistol in the other. He surveyed the countryside and, apparently satisfied, approached Richard.

"Wake up, Gomer," growled his assailant, "ye and me have a reckoning."

"Wh … wha … why, Edmond? Why did ye strike me?"

Edmond walked over to Richard, cocking his pistol and pointing it at Richard's head. For one moment Richard expected the lethal impact of the ball, but nothing happened.

"Get up, face me like the man you're supposed to be and be prepared to die like one! Unless you can give me one good reason for sparing your life!"

Richard raised himself up on his knees, pushing on the ground with his one arm, fell again, then rose shakily, trembling from the effects of the blow and in shock from the violent confrontation.

"Edmond! Why?" he cried.

Then he realised, and inwardly cursed himself for his carelessness. His mother had informed him that Edmond was the blood-brother of William Lesden, but he had never suspected that the surviving brother would seek to fulfil his brother William's plan to wreak a terrible revenge on himself and Giles.

Edmond's smile was far from pleasant.

"But you shot your brother to save my life."

"Not quite, Gomer. I killed him to keep you alive and unsuspecting 'til my plan was fulfilled and I could reclaim my father's land for myself."

"But how? Why? Your father destroyed himself through drink, and any hope of keeping ..."

Edmond Lesden again struck Richard across his head with the stock, felling him to the ground.

"Idiot! That wasn't why my true father fell by the wayside! Certain more powerful people like you Gomers robbed lesser mortals like father through enclosure. And father struggled to get enough water to raise grass and crops. Summer water from the wells were low at the worst time and made father suspect that you Gomers had sabotaged it!"

In spite of his throbbing, haemhorrhaging headwound, Richard spoke from the ground:

"Who told you all this? My parents would never do that! That's wicked slander..."

Edmond Lesden's riding boot drove the air from his lungs. This is history repeating itself, concluded Richard, just like his encounter with Edmond's brother. Then, there was a 'rescuer', but now that previous rescuer was his captor with no present hope of deliverance.

"When I learnt that I had a brother and discovered that he was alive, it didn't take me long to recognise the vicar's family resemblance. A careful watch on him confirmed his ambition to destroy you Gomers and take over your two farms. Now, I've inherited his plan to take your lives and land in repayment for destroying our father! My plan to block your wells coincided well with Hugo's plan to torch your Home Farm buildings! The time is ripe because Home Farm has no water to keep it fertile and you've no buildings left to store your crops. Who would want to buy a ruined holding, hardly better than Wychcombe Farm, a poor rump of land at best?"

With a superhuman effort, Richard gained strength to face this pitiless adversary.

"Even if you take my life, how can you lay claim to our farms? Giles is alive and he'll resist any attempt to seize our land."

Edmond's laughter chilled Richard's blood.

"Your dear brother doesn't realise that I with the help of my friend Hugo, will hunt him down. Hugo wants revenge for the loss of Home Farm and once your brother's out of the way, your land will be open to whoever has the strongest claim. You've no next of kin and with you and your brother dead, the land will go to the buyer who offers the most, which won't amount to much, a moderate sum if the livestock are included."

"And where will you get the money from?"

"My stepfather will provide it – he'll think that the land will be part of the Goodboys' estate but I've plans to transfer ownership to myself. And possession is nine-tenths of the law."

Richard, still reeling from physical and mental shock, remained silent. The bosom friend he'd trusted was the Judas who'd killed his own brother and blocked the Home Farm wells as part of his wicked plan. One enemy was bad enough, but to be the victim of two evil men was almost unbearable. But was Edmond Goodboys aka Lesden's plan foolproof? Did he think that killing him and Giles would be perfect murders and would Hugo Jones expect nothing in return from their wicked alliance? And would Sir Absalom Goodboys be taken in by Edmond's deceit? The whole wretched plot had the flawed seam of insanity which, to Richard's perception, had coursed through William and now Edmond Lesden's veins.

"Answer me, Gomer! Give me one reason why I should spare your life."

In spite of his scattered senses and pain, Richard gathered strength to confront this madman.

"Because you'll never get away with it. You already have your brother's blood on your hands and people will have their suspicions. Somebody may have witnessed you shooting your brother and you'll have no peace of mind as long as you're at large."

Richard wondered if he'd gone too far. He looked into the eyes of William Lesden's brother. How identical the embedded hatred which illumined the madness in Edmond Lesden's eyes and contorted his face. Richard felt detached from the reality of his peril and accepted that if help did not come in time, there would, he hoped, be a swift end to his suffering.

"Ah, Gomer, people around here believe that you killed my beloved brother and I'll make sure that a few well-placed rumours will stir up that belief."

"How will you cover up my death?"

Edmond pocketed his pistol.

"That'll be child's play, Gomer. I don't have to shoot you, just throw you in the gley. Your body will break what ice lies on top and, should your miserable corpse surface, they'll think you fell in or were thrown there by your horse."

Richard was rendered semi-conscious by another blow from the whip's stock.

Edmond walked towards the gley and touched its icy edge with his boot. The blue mucoid sludge flowed over the ice's surface. He looked at Richard, satisfied that he was rendered helpless to resist. He stopped, looked around and listened. His ears detected a faint sound of voices to the east. In order to gain a better vantage point, he walked about a hundred yards up the gley field's slope, still holding his crop.

John the ex-grenadier, Ozzie and Whisker moved south along the connecting road, searching for the three stray pregnant ewes and a pregnant cow. Ozzie held his dog on a piece of twine fastened through the sheepdog's collar, to prevent Whisker from chasing the Gomers' livestock.

They walked to the entrance to Home Farm and turned in, taking the northernmost fork to the farmhouse.

"We need to check if the Gomers 'ave put any stock 'ere sin' we moved maister Jones's to Destro afore we goes 'unting fer yon strays, John."

The pair and Whisker walked along the track between the snow-covered cornfields. Striving to be loosed, Whisker strained on the cord and pulled away from the shepherd.

"Heel, Whisker!" Ozzie shouted, yanking on the twine until Whisker's shoulder was brushing the shepherd's knee. "Now stay, dog!" Ozzie hissed, cuffing Whisker's ears.

Edmond heard the shepherd's command and moved up the slope to command a better view. He saw the sheepdog, whose markings distinguished him from the snow as the trio moved west across the fields to the farmhouse, disappeared behind the farmhouse then reappeared to walk south towards Wychcombe Farm. Edmond stood motionless, watching their movements. He questioned their boldness in travelling from Destro through the Home Farm fields, then traversing onto Wychcombe land. But he was more concerned that he and the unconscious Richard Gomer should not be seen, confounding his plan to get rid of Richard. Edmond pulled out a spyglass and focussed it on the two men as they moved in the direction of Wychcombe farmhouse and moved out of sight behind the buildings, he lowered his spyglass until they reappeared south of the farmhouse.

"If the Gomers see us, we needs tell them, that we're missing some strays," said the guardsman, "but we need to call at the farmhouse first lest we be accused of trespassing, Ozzie," he added.

Ozzie nodded as they stumbled over snow-covered corn stubble to the farmhouse. They rounded the dilapidated barns and approached the farmhouse door. The grenadier knocked on the door, which was shortly opened by Berkeley, the Gomer family retainer.

"Could we speak to master Richard Gomer, sir?" the grenadier asked, removing his hat.

"And who are you to be making such a request, pray?" Berkeley answered, viewing with disdain the ex-soldier in his faded red greatcoat and, with some alarm, John's musket.

"Zur, we be from Destro an' we be beggin' permission t' search fer three stray ewes and a cow which escaped when we were driving the stock from Home to Destro," Ozzie interjected before John could reply, "an' we be askin' fer help from maister Richard's men if they be around, zur."

"Such requests are not in my power to grant, but if you proceed south to the gley field, you may find him there. The fields are clear since our ewes are bedded down in the barns and the cows are inside too. But you must keep that dog on a lead and refrain at all costs from firing off that musket to avoid disturbing the stock, even though they're inside."

Berkeley closed the door on them.

"You know, Eleanor, I have an uncomfortable feeling that Edmond knows more than he's disclosing about the

242

vicar's death," Sir Absalom remarked to his wife as they reclined in the lounge at Copley.

"Why do you say that, dear?" Lady Goodboys replied.

"For more than one reason. I thought that he would have expressed some sign of shock or sorrow at the death of the vicar, but not one iota, even during the vicar's funeral service. Secondly, he seems to be spending a great deal of time in the company of both Hugo Jones and Richard Gomer, separately of course because they're hardly bosom friends of one another. How can he be friends of both, when the Joneses and the Gomers have been at loggerheads and Hugo lost his case to hold onto Home Farm?"

"But there could be a simple explanation, dear."

Sir Absalom refrained from replying, then after several minutes:

"What worries me is the possibility that Edmond and Richard Gomer have a connection with the vicar's death; his body was found at Wychcombe Farm, remember."

"Why don't you have a word with Edmond, dear?"

"Hmmm, I doubt that he would disclose anything to me, especially if he was implicated. He's been so tetchy and ill-tempered lately. What's going on in that head of his and why?"

There was a knock on the sitting room door.

"Enter!" boomed Sir Absalom.

The door opened. The ostler's head appeared.

"Beggin' yer pardon, zur."

"Well, Smith, what is it? And don't stand there, come right in."

The ostler stepped gingerly into the room, cap in hand, and touched his forelock.

"'Ave ye heard, zur? Somebody blocked they wells at Home Farm an' set fire to the farm buildings. The butler thought that I should tell ye, zur," he added apologetically.

"When?"

"Day afore yisterday, zur. Asa, maister Richard Gomer's shepherd told me. He said that the wells were blocked at least a day afore the fire. It be round the villages yesterday that all the barns 'ad gone up in flames."

Sir Absalom, shocked, composed himself.

"That'll be all, and close the door behind you."

Strange, thought Sir Absalom, he could have sworn that Edmond told him about the blocking of the wells two days ago, and his adopted son had claimed that he'd remained in the house for three days previous to that. How could he have known?

Whilst Ozzie, John and Whisker had proceeded south of the Wychcombe farmhouse, Giles rode north through the broken hedgerow fence into the southernmost field of Home Farm, galloped Sally up to the farmhouse, circled the burnt-out ruins of the barns and entered the farmyard. Giles dismounted, tied Sally's reins to the bent wellhead handle, walked to the farmhouse door and turned the handle – the door was unlocked. He walked into the hall – its emptiness gave a ghostly impression, coupled with a strong smell of woodsmoke. The walls and floors appeared intact. He tested the first step, then, satisfied that it was undamaged, mounted the stairs and peered into each room until he reached the furthest room by the landing. He entered this room and approached the window. Unlike the smoke-blackened windows downstairs, this window gave a clear view of the southern fields of Home Farm and the more distant southern aspect of Wychcombe Farm. The view also took in the gley meadow and swamp. He stared – a recumbent figure lay near the edge of the swamp, two horses stood nearby and some distance away another figure – someone standing on the meadow's brow holding what he guessed was a whip. The latter's stance seemed familiar, but minus his spyglass, could not identify the man. Giles was puzzled; who were the two people, one lying and the other standing further away looking this way and that? His attention was drawn to two figures, one leading a dog, treading through snow beyond the farm buildings. Instead of proceeding into the gley meadow and swamp, the two men turned east towards St. Stephen's church ruins. Giles focussed on the figure at the brow of the meadow; the man was holding a spyglass to his eye and was pointing it in the direction of the two men and the dog. The man closed and pocketed the spyglass and moved towards the swamp. Giles was equally curious and indignant. Who were these people on Gomer property, the man at the gley bog and the two men with a dog? Then he heard gunshot.

John and Ozzie trod slowly through the foot-deep snow, conversing in low voices.

"No sign of the cow or the ewes, Ozzie," John

remarked, "perchance they were taken inside by the Gomers' herdsmen."

"Ye may 'ave somethin' there," Ozzie replied, "but let's go on to Wychcombe t' see if the stock went that far. We kin ask down there an' if we get no satisfaction, go back t' Destro."

Whisker could bear his captivity no longer; his neck was sore from tugging at the twine, which seemed to tighten with every tug, then being yanked back against the shepherd's knee. He was accustomed to the freedom of rounding up the sheep without a rope's restraint. Barking, he lunged forward, pulling the cord from Ozzie's grip and sped west towards the gley meadow.

"Come back 'ere, Whisker!" Ozzie screamed, then whistled, but the dog quickened his pace west. He began circling and sniffing at the eastern edge of the gley meadow, as if something had claimed his attention. John, fearing that Whisker might scare away the strays, loaded his musket and took aim over the dog's head.

"No, no, don' shoot 'im, John!" cried Ozzie, but John had already pulled the trigger.

The ball whistled over Whisker's head and hit the gley swamp with a crack of ice and a splash.

On hearing the shot, Giles rushed from the room, ran downstairs out of the house without shutting the door, ran to the wellhead, took the reins, mounted Sally, dug his heels into her flanks and sped towards Wychcombe Farm.

CHAPTER TWENTY-SEVEN

Conclusion?

Edmond heard the musket report and trembled when the ball whistled over his head and hit the ice covering the swamp. Preoccupied with his plans to get rid of Richard, he was taken completely unawares. That musket ball was meant for him, he guessed. Was someone onto him? Giles Gomer, perhaps?

Shaking with fear, he looked around – he was alone. His horse had bolted. Without hesitation, he dragged Richard to the edge of the swamp, broke the ice and pushed him in, then fled west towards Copley, leaving his victim to drown. He stumbled through the snow, and slipped and fell through a break in the thorn hedge separating Wychcombe and Copley farms. He staggered north into the field, avoided the farmhouse and made a detour to the stables.

"Smith!" he shouted, whereupon the ostler appeared.

"Get me a fresh horse and hurry, man!" Edmond shouted, as the ostler gaped at Edmond in muddied riding gear but horseless, knowing that Edmond had departed earlier on another mount.

Smith scuttled away and a few minutes later led out a saddled gelding.

"Shall I tell Sir Absalom where you're off to, maister Edmond?"

Edmond snatched the reins off him, mounted and, in spite of the icy conditions, galloped off without a word, leaving the ostler scratching his head.

Whisker, likewise, shaken by the musket report, turned tail and ran back to Ozzie and John. Once Ozzie had restrained the sheepdog, the company moved east to continue to search for the strays.

Giles carefully guided Sally through the snow and negotiated the mare through a breached hedge into Wychcombe Farm, then spurred her into a canter. He rode through the northernmost field then west and galloped Sally, who jumped a fence into the gley meadow. He walked Sally down the hill and reined the mare up by the swamp. Richard's body lay face-down, partly supported by a layer of broken ice, his legs already below the exposed bog's mucous. Dismounting, he ran to the edge of the gley, walked Sally within feet of the swamp, made Sally kneel, sat down between her and the swamp and tied the reins to his own legs. He turned face down, stretched his hands out and grabbed a fold of his brother's coat.

"Up, Sally!" he commanded the mare. Sally rose. Then, tightening his hold on Richard:

"Back up, Sally!"

The mare backed, tightening the reins to draw Giles back. At first the swamp refused to surrender Richard.

"BACK UP!" Giles shouted.

Giles held onto Richard's coat with all his might as Sally continued the tug-o'-war. Giles's arm muscles shrieked with pain but with the help of the broken ice, which acted as a slide, and assisted by Sally's pull, Richard was dragged onto solid ground.

"Well done, Sally!"

Giles untied the reins, rose and patted Sally's neck. Taking out a neckerchief, he cradled Richard's head and shoulders in his other arm and wiped away the blood and foetid mud from Richard's face. Richard opened his eyes, to Giles's heartfelt relief, then his mouth, but no sound emitted.

"Who did this to you, Richard?" Giles asked, but Richard's lips moved soundlessly.

"Can you stand, Richard? Then, I'll help you," Giles offered and supported his brother to rise and half-carried him to Sally. He lowered Richard to the ground, took hold of Sally's foreleg and, holding the mare's halter, turned her head sideways and forced her to sit. He assisted Richard to climb on Sally's back, then, taking hold of the reins, pulled on them. Sally immediately rose and Giles led the mare up the hill towards the farmhouse.

Edmond Goodboys slowed his horse into a steady canter through the packed ice and snow in Copley's north-eastern fields. He avoided riding directly east in the direction of

Home Farm. Cutting north, he passed through a break in the hedge between Copley and Destro and entered the Jones's property. Keeping the copse to his right, he rode east until he saw a gap in the trees which offered a clear view south to Home Farm and Destro. He reined in, took out his spyglass and focussed it on the house at Home Farm; there were no signs of life, just the solitary farmhouse amidst the burnt-out ruins of what had been the barns. He focussed on Wychcombe Farm buildings but detected no life nor movement there. He swung the spyglass to take in the gley meadow, then the swamp – Richard Gomer's body was no longer visible. He swept his glass to the east and observed two men and a dog moving towards St. Stephen's ruins. He focussed more sharply on the trio – one man was carrying a musket. If that was the weapon that had discharged the ball which nearly hit him, then why hadn't the men followed it up by pursuing him? If there was another reason for the gunshot, then he was not being shot at. But Edmond dismissed that reasoning, suspecting that someone had tried to shoot him. He would take no chances. Pocketing the spyglass, he stood in the saddle and looked for any signs of pursuit; apparently satisfied that there was none, he spurred his horse towards Destro farmhouse. But he had been seen.

Giles and Berkeley carried Richard into the kitchen, laid him on the floor and undressed him. Berkeley went out of the room and returned several minutes later with a bucket and a tin bath. He went out into the yard and returned with a bucketful of snow and ice, which he poured into the bath. This procedure was repeated several times, then Berkeley added water from a large kettle suspended over the hearth fire. Berkeley and Giles gently immersed Richard in the bath until they were satisfied that Richard was clear of all the filth from the swamp. They lifted him onto towels placed by Berkeley on the floor, rubbed him dry then dressed him in a nightshirt and carried him upstairs to Richard's bedroom, laid him in the bed, and covered him with the bedclothes. Giles left Berkeley to start a fire in the bedroom hearth, descended and entered the kitchen. He poured himself a measure of whisky into a glass, downed it in one swallow and sat down at the kitchen table. Who had attacked Richard? And why? Would his brother ever be able to give them the answers? Surely Hugo Jones was their sole enemy – it couldn't have been anyone else? How could Richard communicate without a voice? Would he be able to write the name of his assailant? In the meantime, he would get Berkeley to remove the bath, empty its contents down the open drain, then secure the farmhouse doors and windows for the night.

Edmond rode into the farmyard at Destro and reined back his mount into a sliding, slipping halt which nearly hurled its rider onto the ice-covered cobbles. He dismounted and left the horse standing in the yard without waiting for the ostler to take the reins, and walked to the farmhouse door. He banged on its oak surface with the bloodstained stock of his whip and waited. The door was opened by a young woman, probably the parlourmaid, he thought.

"Is your master in?" he asked.

"Mr. Hugo is in the house, sir. Who shall oi say wishes to speak t' him, sir?"

"Tell him that Mr. Edmond Goodboys wishes to speak to him."

The maid disappeared into the house and returned almost immediately.

"Please come this way, Mr. Goodboys," she said.

Edmond Lesden nodded and followed her into the hall, and was led into the sitting room where Martha Jones and Katherine were seated conversing. He entered on introduction. Mrs. Jones and Katherine turned to face him.

Martha Jones found her voice:

"Goodday, Mr. Goodboys."

"Goodday Mrs. Jones," Edmond replied, bowing and "Katherine," he said, nodding to her. "May I speak to Hugo, Mrs. Jones?"

Katherine, detached, regarded Edmond perceptively. Despite his politeness, she detected a hard edge to his voice; his eyes were cold and expressionless and the knuckles of his right hand were white, gripping his horsewhip.

"Mary, will you please inform my son that I would be most pleased for him to join us," Mrs. Jones ordered the maid.

Mary curtsied and left the room, leaving Edmond being eyed by the two women.

Moments later Hugo appeared, his eyes devouring the scene, clearly shocked at seeing Edmond. Before he could compose himself, his mother spoke:

"Hugo, Edmond Goodboys wishes to speak to you. No doubt you'll wish to accompany him to another room."

Hugo and Edmond departed after the latter had excused himself; the two men left without closing the door fully, their footsteps fading whilst addressing one another with raised voices. Words which drifted to the three women's ears:

"Wychcombe ... the swamp ... shot at ..."

Katherine's heart missed a beat; Edmond's appearance and Hugo's patent shock at seeing him ... Hugo was no friend of the Goodboys' family since Hugo's father and Sir Absalom Goodboys had drafted Ezra Jones's Last Will and Testament, yet for some mysterious reason Edmond had demanded a meeting with Hugo ... why?

Hugo confronted Edmond Lesden in Hugo's bedroom.

"What d'ye mean coming here, 'specially when the world thinks we're enemies?" Hugo demanded.

"I believe that I've removed the biggest obstacle to our repossession of Home Farm," Edmond replied, ignoring Hugo's question.

Hugo's eyes opened wide; Edmond's reference to a shared ownership was not lost on him.

"Ye don't mean ..."

"Yes Hugo, Gomer senior has gone ..."

"Gone where?" Hugo interrupted.

"To the bottom of Wychcombe Farm bog," said Edmond Lesden, emotionless.

An indefinable look flitted over Hugo's face which did not escape his companion's notice.

"Are you still with me in our enterprise, Hugo?"

"If it's to drive the Gomers out of their land, I'm as committed as you."

"Are you? I don't think you're as committed as me," Edmond Lesden replied.

This man will stop at nothing, thought Hugo. He's just admitted killing Richard Gomer as if he was swatting a fly. Did he kill the vicar?

Edmond continued:

"I shot dead my Reverend brother William Lessop-Dene to save Gomer's life and threw William's body into the gley swamp so that I alone could avenge my father's memory and reclaim our family's land."

"But …"

"It's a pity that William's body was discovered. Only you and me share the secret that I was the one who killed him. And I'm trusting you to keep silent as long as you live. Now it's up to you to deal with Giles Gomer. I'm sure you'll find a way."

Villain though he was, Hugo wanted to destroy the Gomers' livelihood and take over Wychcombe Farm, he drew the line at deliberate murder.

"You're still with me in our venture, Jones?"

"Er … if it means getting Home and Wychcombe farms, I'm with you."

Edmond Lesden's face creased into a smile, eyes stone-like. He knew that Hugo Jones hadn't really the stomach to go through with his plans, but he'd deal with him later.

"Then our next step is …"

"Edmond's staying for two nights afore he rides to Bridport on business, mother."

"Just for the night, then, and where will he sleep?"

"He can sleep in my bed, mother and I'll bed down on a sofa downstairs."

Katherine mused, alarmed, her suspicions roused. Why was Edmond staying here, before riding west to Bridport when Destro lies further east than Copley? And why is he meeting Hugo here as if they were bosom friends? Something was seriously wrong. And what was wrong with Edmond? It was as if his normal affable attitude and nature had disappeared, revealing a cruel and arrogant mien. He had looked through them as if they were part of the landscape. She could no longer trust this man who was her brother. She felt helpless to do anything in her state, now almost six months into her pregnancy.

Next morning Berkeley tapped on Richard's bedroom door, although the elderly retainer did not expect his master to voice a response. Berkeley opened the door; Richard had managed to raise himself against the bank of pillows.

"Good morning, master Richard. Are you feeling better?"

With an effort, Richard nodded, lifted a shaking finger to his lips and slowly shook his head. Berkeley placed a glass of warm milk on the bedside locker. At that moment, Giles entered with a pen and small open bottle of ink. He handed them to Berkeley and supported Richard's shoulders.

"We know that ye cannot speak just now, but we want you to write down the name of the villain who attacked you. Berkeley will hand the pen to ye to write on the pad he's holding. Do you understand, brother?"

Richard looked at Giles and nodded. Berkeley, now at Giles's side and by Richard's sound arm, dipped the pen in the ink bottle, put the bottle on the locker and passed the pen to Richard's hand. With a great effort, he put pen to paper, but the pen fell from his fingers onto the floor.

"Try again, brother, we'll help you," encouraged Giles, lifting Richard's slumped form.

Richard tried twice more, resulting in illegible scrawls before Richard dropped the pen.

"Rest well, Richard, we'll try again after Berkeley has fed you some hot victuals." Giles lowered his brother onto the flattened pillows, drew up the bedclothes and, with a sign to Berkeley, left the room. Tears ran down Richard's cheeks; his memory had not failed him though his voice and strength had. How could he expose their betrayer?

March 30th

At Copley the next morning, Smith the ostler was worried that two days had elapsed since Edmond Goodboys had left in such a hurry. It was really none of his business, he consoled himself, but …

"Smith wishes to speak to you, Sir Absalom," the retainer announced to the peer and his wife who were in the sitting room.

"Oh, very well, show him in," commanded Sir Absalom.

The ostler stood gingerly on the threshold, cap in hand. He touched his forelock.

"Well, Smith, what is it? And come in, man, don't stand half in and half out of the room."

"Beggin' yer pardon, zur, an' sorry t' trouble ye, oi felt ye ought t' know, that master Edmond came horseless t' the stable. He took one o' the geldings after oi saddled it and took off in a terrible 'urry. He didn't say where 'e were goin', but 'e went north-east."

"How long ago, Smith?"

The ostler hesitated, screwing up his cap.

"Two … days an' a half, mebbe three days, zur," Smith quavered.

"Why didn't you report his absence to me until so many days after he left?"

"Sorry, zur, but oi didn't want to disturb ye fer nuthin'…"

"For nothing! My son might have been thrown and injured, or waylaid and left for dead!"

Eleanor Goodboys' hand touched Sir Absalom's arm.

"There may be a simple explanation for Edmond's absence, dear; he may have spent some nights with the Gomers at Wychcombe," she said.

"Oh, very well! Smith, saddle up one of the hunters for me, I'm going to visit Wychcombe first."

"Be careful, dear, there may be footpads or unemployed soldiers roaming the countryside for prey," added Lady Goodboys. "Take one of the men with you."

A few minutes later, Sir Absalom rode unaccompanied

out of Copley onto the southern Dorchester–Bridport road, turned east, then north onto the intersecting north-south track then west into Wychcombe Farm. He followed the farm track into the farmyard, reined the hunter in, dismounted, and handed his reins to Jamie. Sir Absalom walked up to the farmhouse door and knocked, which Berkeley opened seconds later.

"Good morning Berkeley. May I speak to the Master?"

"Master Richard is indisposed, Sir Absalom, but master Giles is here. Shall I call him?"

Sir Absalom nodded.

"Do come into the lounge, sir."

Berkeley led the way into the lounge and, after offering Sir Absalom a seat, left the room. Giles appeared minutes later.

"Goodday to you, Giles," spoke Sir Absalom, extending a hand.

"I am well, Sir Absalom. May I ask what brings you here?"

"Lady Eleanor and I are concerned for our son Edmond. He departed from Copley two to three days ago and has not returned. It's unlike him to stay away for so long. He reported that he was to visit this farm to call on Richard."

The peer's last words startled Giles: there had been no sign of Edmond at Wychcombe Farm. Perhaps he changed his mind and went elsewhere, or had been waylaid by footpads in transit? Or, was Edmond involved in the brutal attack on Richard and left him for dead in the gley bog? Would Edmond, Richard's friend, be the one who attempted to murder him? He dismissed the thought. The only person whom he suspected of having the motive to harm his brother was Hugo Jones, especially following the results of the court case. He would wait for Sir Absalom to leave then he would arm himself, confront Hugo Jones and get the truth out of him.

"No-one has seen Edmond here, Sir Absalom. Richard was attacked and left for dead in the gley swamp some days ago. He was so badly injured that he cannot tell us who the villain was."

Sir Absalom absorbed the news with shock. Was there any connection between Edmond's disappearance and this attack on Richard? He dismissed the thought. Where could Edmond be? Was he safe or in danger? Had his horse thrown him or had he been waylaid and robbed, even killed?

"Giles, I must leave to seek further information about Edmond's movements. I do hope that Richard recovers and can disclose who attacked him."

Giles rang for Berkeley.

"Berkeley, will you please instruct Jamie to saddle and bring Sir Absalom's horse to the yard."

Sir Absalom rode out of Wychcombe, turned left and rode north along the connecting track between the north and south Dorchester to Bridport roads, then turned left through an open gate into Home Farm, derelict and unoccupied, looking for signs of Edmond's horse or his son or both. He avoided entering Destro land but rode towards the copse north of Home.

Giles waited until Sir Absalom had departed then ordered Jamie to saddle Sally. Giles rode due south-east, though he had no idea who had attacked Richard at the gley swamp or where the attacker had gone. Giles trotted Sally into Wychcombe village. Suddenly Sally stopped and neighed, followed by, to Giles's surprise, an answering whinny, then, hoofbeats. A horse appeared at a gallop and at the last moment skidded to a halt by Sally and rubbed up against her. Giles grabbed the horse's reins and, on examination, recognised it as the stallion that Edmond had ridden on the night of the riot. Where was Edmond? He slapped the horse on the rump; the stallion leapt forward and galloped west. True to form it sped along the icy south road and turned through an open gate into Copley. Giles spurred Sally on, following the stallion to the stables, where Smith was restraining the stallion.

"Maister Edmond'll be pleased his stallion's come back, maister Giles," said Smith, "'e 'ad to remount after he'd been unhorsed. Thankee, zur, for finding him."

Giles pondered. So Edmond was unhorsed and returned to Copley for a fresh mount. And Sir Absalom had heard Edmond announce earlier that he was riding to Wychcombe Farm to visit Richard. Was Edmond there at the time and scene of the crime?

"Where was master Edmond going to on the fresh horse?"

"He never said, 'e seemed in such a hurry, but 'e went north-east, zur, towards ..."

"Destro?" Giles completed Smith's sentence.

"Aye, zur."

Why Destro? Giles thought. There's no love lost

between Hugo Jones and the Goodboys, especially after he'd lost the court case. Giles retraced his route south then east towards Wychcombe then turned north along the interconnecting track and turned through an open gate into Home Farm. He passed into the copse along a rough track to approach the southern aspect of Destro and was halfway through when:

"Maister Giles Gomer!" a high-pitched voice screeched, causing Sally to rear up in fright.

Giles turned Sally to face the denizen of the copse, barefooted and clad in a filthy, ragged black dress, her shoulders covered by a tattered sheep's fleece. Her matted black hair almost covered the small black eyes, toothless mouth and crinkled face.

"Curse ye, Crazy Mary! Ye could have had me thrown!"

"But oi may ha' saved ye from bein' killed, if ye wants ter know who's at Destro."

"Then tell me," Giles demanded.

"Not so quick, zur! What oi knows is worth crossing me palm."

"I've no time nor money to barter with ye, crone!" Giles replied, turning Sally towards Destro.

"But ye will, if ye wants to save yer life, maister Giles."

The urgency of Crazy Mary's tone cautioned Giles to wait. He felt in his pocket, found two florins and threw them to Mary, who examined the coins with affected disdain.

"Ye Gomers 'ave fallen on 'ard times, it seems, so oi'll sell wot oi knows cheaply. Edmond Goodboys went to Destro yesterday an' asn't come out yet. Oi reckons 'e be friens wi' yon Hugo …"

Her words faded in Giles's ears as he rode towards the edge of the copse and passed onto Destro land.

Edmond Goodboys and Hugo Jones were at the head of the stairs, and through an oriel window spotted Giles entering the yard.

"Now's your chance to get rid of Gomer, Hugo," Edmond hissed.

"Not here!" Hugo hissed in return.

"If I act as a decoy, you could follow us into the copse where we can deal with him."

"Bu … but we haven't time to get t' the stables and saddle our horses."

"Not if we're quick eno' and go round the back of the house. Come on!"

Edmond ran down the stairs and disappeared in the direction of the rear door, Hugo trailing on behind.

Giles rode into the yard at Destro, dismounted, left Sally in the yard, strode up to the farmhouse door and hammered on it; a young maid opened the door.

"I'm master Giles Gomer and I wish to speak to your mistress."

Giles followed the maid down the passage; she opened a door into the sitting room and announced:

"Master Giles t' see you, ma'am."

Both Martha Jones and Katherine started in surprise.

"Show him in, Mary," commanded Mrs. Jones.

Giles entered, nodded to Katherine and bowed to Martha.

"Goodday, ma'am, Katherine. I wish to see Edmond

262

Goodboys, whom I have on good authority is staying in your home."

"Yes, though he was due to depart early today, so I would imagine that he's gone."

"Could you be certain of that, ma'am?"

"More or less, sir," responded Martha.

"Would you know then, ma'am where he intended to go?"

"I have no idea, sir."

Martha's being evasive, mused Katherine; Edmond could still be here. She looked at Giles – the same Giles, transparent, without a shadow of deceit or malice, rather different to …

"Then I'll take my leave, ma'am," said Giles, turning to leave.

Katherine spoke for the first time:

"I'll come with you to the door, Mr. Gomer," she said, rising and accompanying Giles.

Giles and Katherine walked slowly into the hall, their hands brushing,

"Be careful Giles dear. Edmond is not the friend you think he is and I suspect that he's plotting some evil with Hugo," she whispered, her hand gripping his.

"I know, Katherine," Giles replied.

He squeezed her hand, took a last look at her, opened the farmhouse door and closed it behind him.

Sir Absalom Goodboys approached Destro through a track on the eastern edge of the copse. Clearing the trees into

Destro he saw Edmond galloping his horse further west into the copse, followed some distance behind by Giles Gomer on Sally. Sir Absalom pursued the two horsemen into the bowels of the forest, then heard the sound of a single gunshot and hoofbeats growing fainter. He spurred his mount on and overtook a riderless horse, narrowly avoiding the body of a man lying face down. He reined in and dismounted, leading his horse to the body.

He dismounted, bent down and turned the body over ...